# THE
# JAMESON
# GIRLS

BY

JAN

HILLIARD

ABELARD-SCHUMAN

*LONDON AND NEW YORK*

c. 3

H R

PRINTED IN GREAT BRITAIN BY WILLIAM CLOWES AND SONS, LIMITED,
LONDON AND BECCLES, FOR THE PUBLISHERS, ABELARD-SCHUMAN
LIMITED, 404 FOURTH AVENUE, NEW YORK 16, N.Y., 38 RUSSELL
SQUARE, LONDON, W.C.I, ENGLAND

Fanny, Lily, Isabelle, and Mildred await the death of their tyrannical father and at the same time ruminate on their past.

ON MONDAY MORNINGS MRS. PRINGLE ALWAYS FELT LIKE A RAG. "Oh, Lordy!" she groaned at the beginning of each week. "Never again, girls! I'm on the wagon." This morning, to add to her general indisposition, she had overheard the substitute night nurse, who was leaving as she came in the front door, refer to her as "the maid." "I've left some instructions for the maid," the fool was saying to Fanny, "about sterilizing those bottles." What does she think I *am*? Mrs. Pringle asked herself indignantly. For your information, Miss Rabbitface, she said silently, watching the nurse's back down the driveway, it just so happens I'm a family friend who happens to be helping out. I'm not a servant to be ordered about by anyone. Nobody's ever called me a *maid*, and I've been here over thirty years.

When she went into the kitchen, she found two quart bottles on the drainboard, one with a note stuck in the top. She screwed the note into a ball and threw it into the garbage.

The house was a large white clapboard structure with green shutters—the kind described in real-estate advertisements as a "Colonial mansion"—set on a high wooded precipice overlooking the Niagara River. The kitchen, a pleasant modern room added some years after the original house was built, had a Dutch door leading to the back garden, and from its windows a magnificent view of the gorge. A faint odor of spice and vinegar from last week's pickling hung over the immaculate pale-blue counters and the table beside the window, where Lily, the youngest of old King Jameson's four daughters, was eating breakfast.

Mrs. Pringle, having changed into her workaday clothes and consumed three cups of coffee, lit a cigarette and rested a bit, gathering strength for the daily grind. Yesterday's make-up clung patchily to her sagging jowls, and a row of mahogany-colored spit curls decorated her forehead. Those damned

5

nurses, she thought, eying the dishes in the sink. Always eating. Coming into the kitchen as if they owned the place, helping themselves, ordering hot water, heating broth. It was no wonder the old man was dying, the way they shoveled slop into him.

Lily sat on a kitchen stool beside the window, balancing a plate of scrambled eggs on one knee. She picked daintily at her food and held a piece of toast with the tips of her small fingers while she gazed at some indefinite spot on the far side of the room. Pale-yellow hair like corn silk hung down to her shoulders. The depthless stare of Lily's china-blue eyes, her porcelain prettiness and childish figure, often gave people the impression that she was not quite real. Across her right cheek, going back into the hairline, was a long oblique scar, where the skin, whiter than the rest of her face, was stretched tight and shone as if polished; but even this scar looked unreal, a flaw that had no connection with violence. She looked so fragile and innocent, so untouched by the world, that Mrs. Pringle, as always, felt a clutch at her heart.

Lily had been shopping again, by the look of things—which of course was nothing new. The outfit she had on this morning was one Mrs. Pringle had never seen before: black velvet toreador pants trimmed with rhinestones, a white satin blouse, a red cummerbund wrapped several times round her narrow waist, the ends hanging down in a fringe, and red sandals on her bare feet. The pants were real silk velvet, too. Nothing but the best for Lily, Mrs. Pringle thought fondly. She considered the costume a trifle extreme for morning wear, but would never dream of upsetting Lily by saying so. If Lily showed up for breakfast wearing cloth of gold and the crown jewels, nobody would raise an eyebrow, for, after all, what was more important than keeping her happy?

"My, don't we look pretty today!" Mrs. Pringle said in the tone of playful indulgence she used when addressing Lily. "All our new clothes!"

6

A hint of complacency touched Lily's mouth, but she did not smile or turn her head.

Mrs. Pringle ground her cigarette out in a saucer and turned to the window. "Cooler this morning," she remarked with satisfaction, as if she herself had been instrumental in dispelling the heat of the past week. "And about time, too. I thought I'd never get through the night. Hiccups, my God! I told Ernie this morning I'm off gin for life." She pulled back the curtain and, after a cursory examination of the sky for flying saucers, looked down the garden toward the river.

Beyond the protective stone wall that formed the limit of the back garden, the embankment dropped away sharply to the river, fifty feet below. This morning a blue haze filled the gorge. The cliffs of the American shore were still in shadow, though the white houses perched on top of the bluff caught the sun. From her position Mrs. Pringle could not see the river itself, only a section of the opposite bank, where clumps of goldenrod and purple asters spilled from every cranny in the rock wall. It was the second week in September.

Mrs. Pringle was afraid of heights, but she could never go into the back garden without being drawn as by a magnet to the stone wall, where, gazing with dread fascination into the gorge, she pictured what would happen if she fell over. Down the bank, trees had somehow found root and grown along the granite ledges, their exposed roots thrusting into crevices; and stunted bushes of sumac and wild cherry pushed upward through a tangle of vines. Viewed from the safety of the garden, the river was deceptively placid; only the foam patterns showed how swift and treacherous the current really was. As far as Mrs. Pringle knew, only one boat had ever crossed the Niagara this far up, and that was the *Lilybell*, now rotting in the boathouse at the foot of the cliff.

On the lawn, half a dozen canvas chairs were grouped about a rustic table under a clump of white birches. Flowers massed along the borders had a disheveled late-summer look. Spikes of gladiolus held up ragged petals; petunias, bruised by last night's rain, lifted torn scraps of purple velvet to the sun. At the end of the stone wall, near the strip of beechwood that separated Hawkrest from its neighbor, a neglected summerhouse perched on the edge of the embankment. It was built around the bole of a half-dead butternut tree. From the branches of this tree a cardinal whistled, and down the bank another answered.

"Summer's just about over," Mrs. Pringle observed sadly. She was suddenly aware that her new corsets were killing her. I should never have put them on, the way I feel this morning, she thought. I'll be dead by noon.

"Well, no rest for the weary." She dropped the curtain and heaved her stout figure all the way round. She expected no reply and received none, for conversing with Lily was sometimes much the same as talking to one's self. But she gave Lily a long look, gauging her frame of mind, then hugged her and kissed the top of her head with a murmuring smack. "Eat your breakfast, honeybun," she admonished.

Lily's halfsister Fanny came in, walking heavily and tugging at her girdle through her skirt. She placed her square hands on the table and lowered herself into a chair. The clothes she had put on fresh that morning already looked rumpled. Her cotton blouse was coming untucked at the waist.

Mrs. Pringle took one look at her and jumped to conclusions. "There now, dear!" she soothed, one arm round the drooping shoulders. "Is it the old gentleman?" In the girls' presence she referred to their father in this manner; at other times she called him "the old bastard" or "the old B.," or sometimes, with great sarcasm, "His Majesty." "Is he dead?"

Fanny shook her head. "He's sleeping."

"Sleeping?" Mrs. Pringle tried to suppress a look of disappointment. She dropped her hand from Fanny's shoulder.

"I thought it wouldn't hurt to leave him alone for half an hour."

"Of course not," Mrs. Pringle agreed. Serve the old B. right

8

if we left him alone all day, she was thinking. "You're worn out, and no wonder," she said. Her voice was rich with sympathy, but of a different kind now. "I don't suppose you got a wink of sleep all night. I know those nurses. They spend half their time in the kitchen making snacks for themselves, boiling water to sterilize their spoons, while somebody else stays with their patients. Here's a nice hot cup of coffee, dear. Just what you need."

Upstairs, in the big bedroom overlooking the river, King Jameson was dying. He had been unwell for months with what the family physician—pottering old Dr. Randolph, one foot in the grave himself—had described as the natural consequences of extravagant living. He was so overweight that during the past summer, when he had walked upstairs, he had found it necessary to pause on every tread, panting and wheezing. But still he had continued to eat and drink too much, blaming everybody but himself for his indispositions. He had been confined to his bed for two weeks now, growing steadily weaker, and yesterday Dr. Randolph had suggested sending for Mildred and Isobel, the two married girls. "Well, that looks like the end of him," Mrs. Pringle had said thankfully. "If you ask me, it'll be a miracle if he lasts the night." But here he was alive this morning. He just wouldn't die, it seemed. The night nurse had gone off duty at eight; another was due at four that afternoon. In the meantime, Fanny and Lily would take turns at their father's bedside. They could do little for him except spoon medicine and broth into his mouth and listen to his complaints while they waited for him to die.

Fanny stirred her coffee round and round and heaved a long sigh.

"God moves in a mysterious way," Mrs. Pringle quoted piously, echoing the sigh. Mighty mysterious, if you ask me, she grumbled to herself. What good does it do anybody, him hanging on like that? Seventy-nine, and so crotchety there's no reasoning with him. In a burst of optimism on Saturday she

9

had bought a black hat for the funeral. I hope I haven't gone and wasted my good money, she thought as she ran water into the sink.

"The train's due in half an hour," she reminded. "Isn't somebody going to meet Mildred?"

Fanny looked up. "You're going to the station, aren't you, Lily dear?"

After a moment Lily turned her head. "Not *me*!" she said in a tone of gentle reproach, denying any such intention.

"Oh, honey! You promised to meet Mildred."

Lily shook back her yellow hair. "She can take a taxi."

"We thought you'd *want* to go," Fanny said with exaggerated disappointment, as if she had offered a special gift.

"I wish *I* could," Mrs. Pringle remarked enticingly. "I just wish I didn't have all these old dishes to do, that's all. There's nothing I'd like better than a drive down to the station in a nice car."

"I don't feel like going to the station this morning." Lily rested her chin on her hand. She swung one dainty foot in a circle.

"Tell you what," Mrs. Pringle suggested. "Why don't you both go down? I'll keep an eye on the old gentleman while I'm doing the beds. Kill two birds with one stone—" She looked horrified and clapped one hand over her mouth. "What I meant," she continued after a moment, "Mildred will *expect* . . . ! And you know how she carries on." She looked from one to the other, sharply. I can't say that I blame them for not wanting to meet the train, she told herself. But somebody's got to go down. They needn't think they can palm this job off on me.

"I was only thinking of your poor sister," she said, throwing some cups into the sink with such force that water splashed up over her pendulous breasts, "coming home to her father's deathbed and nobody there to meet her."

"We'll both go," Fanny decided, rising. "You'll come with

me, won't you, honey?" She brushed Lily's hair back with her fingers, smiling down at her.

"Oh, well . . ." Lily agreed grudgingly.

Mrs. Pringle brightened immediately. "There now, dear!"

Lily slid off her stool. "I *hate* Mildred!" she said, pausing in the doorway as if she had just remembered this.

Mrs. Pringle and Fanny ignored the remark, though they exchanged a quick look. Getting Lily to meet the train was a bit of strategy they had planned. If she thought it was a special privilege, she might be lured into forgetting that Mildred always rubbed her the wrong way.

"You know what I'd do if I was going down to the station to meet somebody?" Mrs. Pringle asked in a wheedling tone. "I'd put on a nice summer dress."

Lily tilted her head stubbornly.

"Especially if I had a lovely white linen only been worn once hanging in the closet. Didn't I say to you yesterday, Fanny, I said 'I never in my life saw anything as pretty as Lily looks in her new dress.' Weren't those my very words?"

"It does look sweet on you, dear," Fanny said with a persuasive smile.

Lily regarded her suspiciously, then shrugged her shoulders in resignation.

"There now, honeybun, you run along and change like a good girl, while Fanny's bringing the car round." Mrs. Pringle sent Lily off with an indulgent smile.

Mrs. Pringle's feelings with regard to the four Jameson girls were sharply defined. Mildred she detested. Fanny—well, Fanny was kind and generous, never interfering. Mrs. Pringle was fond of her, and respected her. But Lily and Isobel had always occupied a special place in her heart because they were the daughters of Hazel, the old man's second wife.

The house, Hawkrest, had been so named by Hazel years ago during a period of preoccupation with the English novel.

Hazel read for educational purposes only, studying the manners and speech of upper-class (preferably titled) British characters who were forever drinking tea in the drawing rooms of ancestral country houses; and occasionally she jotted down on a pad some principle of lady-like conduct. She felt that the name Hawkrest aptly described the location of her home—high on its wooded crag above the river—if not the house itself. Hazel had been dead for years, but the name, in black wrought iron, still formed an arch over the gate, the size of the letters sometimes leading motorists to mistake the house for a summer hotel.

Often when she felt down in the dumps, Mrs. Pringle grew sadly sentimental, remembering the old days when the house had echoed with laughter, when there had been something doing every minute. All our troubles began after Hazel died, she would think. Before that, everything was lovely, everybody was happy.

To comfort herself, she would pour a drink from the bottle she kept behind the dusters in the broom closet. Though it was her job to keep the decanters on the dining-room sideboard replenished, she was rather particular about helping herself from them. For one thing, she filled the decanters with the cheapest brands she could find in the cellar, while her own private bottle was the best the house had to offer. *He* never knew the difference, the silly old fool; he'd drunk so much he'd ruined his palate. And after all, wasn't it common justice for her to have the best, after putting up with so much all these years?

"We must get out more," Fanny was always telling Lily. "We must have *interests*." By this she did not mean associating with other people, for she had never encouraged Lily to do that, and in any case they were rarely invited anywhere nowadays. "Getting out" to Fanny meant observing the world from a safe vantage point, motoring to nearby cities to visit art galleries, fashion shows, and plays—any place where they could mingle with crowds yet keep to themselves. She had few friends, but did not mind this, for she liked being at home, found great satisfaction in running the house, having someone to care for; and she loved routine domestic tasks like polishing furniture and sorting linens, planning meals and watering her ferns.

She had never been pretty, had always been big-boned, with large square hands and thick ankles; but whereas at twenty she had been considered ungainly, now the salesgirls in the corset shop complimented her on the youthfulness of her figure. "So many women run to fat around the middle, and sag *here*," they said, zipping Fanny into a size eighteen junior model. Fanny had not aged perceptibly in fifteen years. Nothing infuriated her more than being asked her age, which she always gave facetiously as twenty-five. She read a great many books on how to live, how to develop character, how to make friends. From these she had learned that busy people are happy people, so she tried to fill up every hour of her day. This year she had a great collection of homespun skirts—the cloth woven on a loom in the attic—and a still greater collection of cablestitch sweaters. She carried her knitting bag everywhere. On winter evenings she made tooled-leather handbags and designed hideously unbecoming hats for herself. Fanny's quilted spread covered the spare-room bed, her hooked rug lay on the floor. She also did the gardening, with the part-time help of a handyman. In early spring she could always be found in the potting shed, her canvas gloves thrown aside, digging her square white nails into a pile of leaf mold.

When she went shopping in the little town, she exchanged greetings with everyone she met, and called each person by name; but she could not be at ease with people who remembered that her father had spent six months in the county jail, or who, when entertaining out-of-town visitors, pointed out the house she lived in as a curiosity and told tales of strange goings on there.

Awareness of her civic responsibilities sometimes drove her

to attend a club meeting or a church bazaar; but she had lost, or had never possessed, the knack of mingling with people. Escaping at last, she would hurry home, and after making sure that Lily and Mrs. Pringle were there, that everything was the same as when she left, would wander through the house moving ornaments an inch to the right or left, straightening rugs, flicking specks of dust off the polished tables, absorbing the peaceful atmosphere of the familiar rooms until she felt safe again.

She often thought longingly of helping the needy families of the town, of going into their poor homes with great baskets of food and warm sensible clothing, of being welcomed as a friend and benefactor. But an unfortunate experience earlier in her life had made her afraid to play the good Samaritan. The father of six children, a ne'er-do-well who had never provided more than the bare necessities of life for his family, deserted them altogether. Fanny went immediately to see the mother, to offer help. The basket she carried was filled to the brim with nourishing food, and her heart was overflowing with kindness and love as she thought of the *good* she could do for the unfortunate woman and her little ones. She was totally unprepared for the woman's animosity, the pure hatred in her eyes as she refused what she called "charity." "I'm not a charity case," she said, drawing herself up proudly.

"But it's not charity," Fanny protested. "I only want to help."

"When we need help, we'll ask for it," the woman said. "We don't need people like you snooping around, meddling in our affairs, thinking you're better than we are just because you happen to have money to throw away." The children, following their mother's example, regarded Fanny with hostility.

This encounter—and particularly the hostility of the children —discouraged Fanny terribly. She felt bruised for weeks afterwards. If she could only understand *why* her kindness had been resented! Since then she had not dared to offer help to any poor family. But once a week she visited the Orphans' Home, with baskets of fruit in summer, with hand-knit mittens, socks, and mufflers in winter, with cash contributions at all seasons. The orphanage children had acquired no false pride, and were grateful for her gifts.

Periodically, to keep up with the world of fashion, she visited the hairdresser's, and emerged looking exactly the same as before. She was secretly rather proud of her hair, which was a beautiful dark brown with a natural wave. Cut short, it framed her face becomingly, though the effect was lost the minute she put on one of her hats.

She had learned long ago to put up with her father's theatrical tantrums, to endure his fits of temper with her mind half on something else. She had never really considered marriage, or going out into the world to make a career. The only thing she wanted was to stay at home with Lily and watch over her, for ever since the accident that killed her mother and almost killed her, Lily had been considered too delicate to face life by herself. It was for Lily's sake that Mrs. Pringle had stayed on at Hawkrest all these years, too. Neither she nor Fanny spoke much of their feelings in the matter, but each knew how the other felt. It was a thing they understood without words, that had sustained them both through a number of crises.

Both Fanny and Mrs. Pringle spent hours each day thinking up little schemes to keep Lily happy. They encouraged her, tactfully—"just so long as she doesn't get the idea we're *pushing* her into anything," they cautioned one another—to develop various interests. So, when Lily found the old butterfly net in the potting shed, and caught a yellow swallowtail, an illustrated book on butterflies was ordered immediately. Her watercolor sketches of wildflowers were highly praised. Thus encouraged, she took to scrambling up and down the river bank beyond the beechwood to gather ferns and plants for sketching —risking her life at every step, Fanny thought anxiously as she hovered near an upstairs window keeping watch; for though the part of the bank where Lily went exploring sloped off gradually, dropping away in uneven terraces guarded by shrubby growths and vine-hung trees, and narrow paths had been worn by animals and adventurous boys, it was nevertheless a dangerous place. Lily collected things in a bored way, as if she could think of no other means of occupying her time, and rarely preserved for long the specimens she gathered. She drove the family car, and went shopping by herself, buying more clothes than she could ever wear. No attempt was made to curb this extravagance. If it made Lily happy to spend money, then let her spend as much as she would. She filled out her days with other trivial pursuits—fixed her hair, painted her nails, admired her clothes—and had seemed content until recently with her uneventful life. Watching her, Fanny and Mrs. Pringle had exchanged congratulatory smiles over her head.

Lulled into a state of optimism, Fanny had looked forward to the years ahead, seeing herself and Lily living quietly and happily together, going on little trips, shopping for clothes, never leaving one another's side, with Lily safely bound in a web of devotion. When their father died, they might even go to Europe. Fanny pictured the two of them exploring old cathedral towns, motoring through the French countryside. She had a pile of travel folders hidden under a stack of handkerchiefs in her bureau. She had made no plans for the trip as yet, had scarcely glanced at the folders. During the summer she could not do so without wondering guiltily what people would say if they saw her—they might think she was waiting for her father to die, and now, since Theodore Fairfield had arrived in St. Charles and threatened her dream, she felt that to plan anything would only be inviting disappointment.

Theodore—his full name was Theodore Bellingham Fairfield—was a guest at Mrs. Kinch's small hotel, the Willows, which was situated just beyond the strip of beechwood bordering the Jamesons' garden. Described by Mrs. Kinch, who was fussy about whom she took in, as "a Boston socialite"— extremely wealthy, she understood, though of course he was too much of a gentleman to talk about money—Theodore was handsome and charming, and indeed appeared to be such a true gentleman that it was difficult to think of him as a menace. But for the past month he had been courting Lily so assiduously that there could be no doubt as to his intentions. He called on Lily every night, took her for long drives about the country during the daytime—in a rented car, for he had left his own limousine at home, he said. Fanny and Mrs. Pringle grew more and more apprehensive. He could destroy their happiness in a minute if he decided to marry Lily and take her back to his home in Boston; for with Lily gone, their lives would be meaningless. Watchful as they were, it was impossible to tell how the affair was progressing. For all they knew, Theodore might have proposed already, and been accepted. Lily admitted nothing, and they knew it was useless, even risky, to question her. It was useless to offer advice, too, for in the end, as always, Lily would do as she pleased. Lately, however, they had been heartened to note that Lily seemed to be losing interest, even to the point of appearing bored by Theodore's attentions. Not that this really meant anything. Experience had taught them not to rely on appearances where Lily was concerned.

They had said nothing to Mildred and Isobel. "Best to wait and see what happens," Mrs. Pringle had cautioned Fanny during one of their talks. "You know Mildred. She'd be home like a shot to give him his walking papers; and how would Lily take that? *He's* got it bad," she had said reflectively after a minute. "Lily's acting pretty indifferent right now, but if we started raising a fuss, giving her the idea we're all against him, it would be another story, no doubt." If anyone else had so much as hinted to her that Lily had a stubborn streak, she would have denied it instantly and reiterated that nobody, *nobody*, possessed a sweeter disposition.

"We can only hope that she is growing tired of him," Fanny had said.

"If she does, there's plenty of others who'd be only too happy to console him."

Fanny had looked away. Mrs. Pringle had come closer to the truth than she guessed. Evenings, when she sat knitting and thinking about him, seeing his wistful smile, Fanny could not even make herself wish that he had never come to St. Charles and disrupted her peace of mind.

Already, though the past week had been the hottest one of the season, and the breeze that stirred the poplar trees was still warm, still scented with late summer, there was an indefinable foreboding of autumn in the air. Fanny backed the car into the driveway that curved past the front door and sat waiting for Lily. The swallows were gathering in flocks, making trial flights, sweeping in a patchwork pattern across the sky, then all changing direction suddenly, as if blown by the wind. The fir tree was hung with bunches of tiny yellow cones. A bronze oak leaf fluttered down and rested for a moment on the windshield, like a butterfly, then drifted to the ground.

Fanny propped her elbows on the steering wheel and frowned at herself in the rear-view mirror. Her lipstick had rubbed off already, and her eyes looked tired. Her nerves were in shreds, and no wonder, after sitting up half the night with her father. She looked impatiently at her watch and was about to sound the horn when she remembered that he was now sleeping. If he were wakened, he would be furious to find himself left alone with Mrs. Pringle.

It was only during the past week, since he had been really ill, that Fanny had felt any affection at all for her father. During all the years he had shouted and stomped about the house, becoming more and more infatuated with the legend of himself as a tyrant, she had ignored him as best she could, and kept out of his way. He had not needed her then. Now he did, and to Fanny being needed meant a great deal. Instead of sounding the horn, she pressed the accelerator to the floor. The car heaved and coughed.

Lily came through the front door at last, leisurely, pausing to snip off a spray of mint, which she crushed in her hand. She wore the white linen dress.

"Hurry, darling!" Fanny called patiently. At the gate where black-eyed Susans grew, Lily leaned out and snatched off a blossom, which she stuck into her hair over one ear.

Two elderly ladies sat knitting under a red umbrella on the lawn of Mrs. Kinch's guest house. When the car passed, they raised their heads, then turned to one another, hitching their chairs together. Theodore was in the summerhouse, his handsome head bent over a newspaper. Though he did not raise his eyes, Fanny's hand made a flurried movement toward her face as she remembered her faded make-up.

If Lily noticed him, she gave no sign. But Fanny, when she turned her head, received a quick impression that Lily had been watching *her*, had just that moment averted her eyes and erased the remnants of a smile from her lips. She could not be sure, however, for Lily's expression was as preoccupied as ever; her slender transparent face, with the blue eyes that so often seemed to be staring at nothing, looked as if no emotion had ever disturbed it.

Out of the corner of her eye Fanny gave Theodore another fleeting inspection, then concentrated her attention on passing a boy on a bicycle who had appeared, it seemed, from nowhere. She hoped that nobody noticed how inexpertly she did this. Fanny felt, at times, that an automobile was a completely unmanageable piece of machinery. Driving, she assumed an air of confidence she did not feel, and gave elaborate signals, hoping to deceive other motorists.

The train had not arrived when they reached the sooty red station. Only the locals stopped here. As Fanny parked the car, an express thundered by on the outer track, and a bag of mail came sailing through the air to land in the middle of a laurel hedge. Mr. Romano, the stationmaster, picked it up, looking curiously over his shoulder at Fanny and Lily. He knew why they were meeting the train, for he had sent the telegrams summoning Mildred and Isobel.

Though they both lived in New York, Mildred and Isobel rarely visited one another. Mildred gave the excuse that they lived at opposite ends of the city, but the truth was that they had never got along—or, rather, that Mildred had never got along, for Isobel had her mother's maddening habit of not noticing when people tried to quarrel with her. Mildred had been married to one man, Harry McKinley, for nineteen years; Isobel's present husband, Eliot Whitmore, was her third. He was older than Isobel, a quiet, middle-aged man from a good family. Isobel simply didn't seem to realize, Mildred reiterated in long letters home to Fanny, how *lucky* she was to find a good respectable husband like Eliot after the scandal of two divorces.

Nobody could deny that Isobel had contributed her share to the general fund of gossip about the Jamesons. Her first two marriages had been stormy affairs. "It's not her fault," was Mrs. Pringle's excuse when the stories drifted back to St. Charles. "She can't look a man in the face without him making a fool of himself." Isobel had given the whole town something to talk about when she fled from her second husband's home in Albany and drove all night through rain and thunder until her car broke down just outside St. Charles and she had to be rescued by a police cruiser and driven home—all this in nothing but a pink crepe de Chine nightgown that grew more and more diaphanous as the story was repeated. "I got sick and tired of listening to the same damned jokes over and over," was the airy explanation Isobel had given for this shocking performance. "They weren't even funny the first time."

The trouble with Isobel, Mildred always said, was that she was too much like her mother, going through life like a spoiled darling, all gaiety and laughter, thinking only of herself. She had no sense of duty whatsoever. Mildred wrote home faithfully once a week, long letters filled with advice, with assurances that she was *thinking* of them all, sharing their burdens from afar. Isobel, though she sent home extravagant impractical gifts, wrote only when the spirit moved her, and that was seldom. Her letters, written in a careless scrawling hand, were gay epistles filled with exclamation points, no advice, and no assurance that she intended to burden herself with family cares. But Fanny read these letters over and over, and tucked them away in a tarnished gilt box already crammed with ancient keepsakes.

Immediately upon receipt of Fanny's telegram, Mildred had telephoned home in great agitation to confirm the gravity of her father's illness, then caught the next train out of New York. She had arrived in Buffalo in the early morning, where she waited for the local to St. Charles. Isobel was taking the morning plane to Buffalo and would arrive home on the afternoon local.

Half a dozen people were waiting for the train. Mrs. Kinch was down meeting her last batch of guests. Her season closed officially in mid-September, but sometimes special guests were allowed to stay longer. All summer the garden at the Willows was dotted with red umbrellas and little tables, where retired elderly couples and aging spinsters sipped tea. People with children were encouraged to vacation elsewhere, for once a child had fallen over the garden wall into the gorge and had been saved only by some bushes. In November of each year Mrs. Kinch closed up her house and went to Florida.

"And how's your poor father this morning, dear?" she asked Fanny.

"He seems to have improved slightly since last night; but Dr. Randolph thought we should send for the girls."

"It's always such a shock, even when one is prepared." Mrs.

21

Kinch spoke as if Mr. Jameson were already dead. "I remember when Mother passed on . . ."

Fanny murmured appropriately. Lily sat on a bench and gazed at the tracks curving into the distance. Smoke from the express still hung in the cutting.

Mrs. Kinch, having offered sympathy, now felt free to speak of her own affairs. "We'll soon be putting the clocks backwards, or forward, whichever it is. Well, I'm not sorry to see the end of summer. Such a worry, catering to all sorts and conditions. The Spencers have gone; you knew that, of course. And Miss Abbott, and those people from Detroit. That leaves only the two Miss Baxters and the Lewises coming in this morning. And Mr. Fairfield, of course," she added, looking archly at Lily, who tilted her head with a show of indifference but smiled faintly, secretly.

Fanny scowled and turned her head with a listening expression.

"She's coming," the stationmaster said, pulling out his watch; and a moment later the old-fashioned wooden local, with smoke billowing sideways, appeared round the bend. Mrs. Kinch rose and straightened her hat, stooping to peer into the clouded mirror of the gum machine.

The train stopped, blowing out a puff of steam as if to express contempt for the small station with its cindery flowerbeds and faded red paint. Bored faces looked from the window as Mildred and three other passengers descended. Mildred was all in black: a black silk suit, wrinkled in the front from sitting down, a velvet hat with a veil, even black gloves. She's come prepared, Mrs. Kinch thought without malice, and turned to greet her own guests.

Mildred looked like a spinster dressed up for the role of a harlot in a play. She wore dark-red lipstick and heavy powder which did not quite conceal the grayness of her skin. The look of strain about her eyes came, not from loose living, but from worrying about her husband, and from poor eyesight. Worry also preserved her figure. She possessed a great knack for achieving a too-considered effect in her clothes. One got the impression that she had spent hours tacking extra pockets, buttons, bits of trimming to her originally well-cut suit. Three worn mink skins were draped about her shoulders. Her hair was a curious shade of tarnished orange, curled too carefully about her ears.

She descended from the train with a handkerchief in her hand, her face contorted. A porter followed with two bags. Fanny braced herself.

By turning her face half away, Lily managed to receive Mildred's wet kiss on the cheek. Fanny was kissed on the mouth.

"I came the minute I got your wire," Mildred said, closing her eyes and leaning her forehead on Fanny's shoulder. "I'm not too late?" She lifted her tear-stained face and pressed the handkerchief to her mouth.

"No." Fanny backed away.

"Thank God!" Mildred raised the sodden handkerchief from her mouth to her eyes and began to weep in earnest. "I kept thinking all night: what if I arrived too late?"

"Are these your bags?" Fanny asked briskly, fumbling in her purse for a coin to give the porter. "The car's over here." She picked up the suitcases.

"I kept thinking of Papa dying, with only you and Lily there . . ."

Lily stood a little apart, watching with a cool blank stare.

"Here's the car." Fanny herded Mildred past the curious bystanders, feeling exposed, awkward, as she lumbered across the platform with the two bags. She looked straight ahead, for she felt that every eye in the still-waiting train was on her.

"Where is Isobel?" Mildred turned round so suddenly that Fanny bumped into her.

"She's coming by plane. She'll be on the four o'clock."

"The four o'clock? Why the four o'clock? Why couldn't

23

she get here sooner? If she's coming by plane, that means she hasn't even left New York yet. Why couldn't she leave last night?"

"I don't know. There must have been a reason."

"Reason? I don't know what could be more important than being with Papa at a time like this."

"I'll put your things here," Fanny said. "Lily, do you want to get in back with the bags? And you in front, Mildred, so we can talk?" Mildred smiled wanly.

"Now!" She arranged her furs and stripped off her gloves as Fanny laboriously maneuvered the car out of the narrow parking space. "Tell me about Papa." She lit a cigarette and inhaled deeply.

"He seems to have rallied a bit this morning."

Mildred looked up quickly. "How do you mean, rallied?"

"He seems a little better this morning. He was sleeping when we left."

Mildred put out her tongue and removed a shred of tobacco. She tapped ashes from her cigarette to the floor. After a moment she said, "From your telegram, I assumed . . ."

"Dr. Randolph thought you and Isobel should be at home. He was quite worried yesterday. We all were."

"I had to leave a note for Harry. He was visiting somebody at the hospital when your wire came—one of the staff—and I couldn't reach him before the train left. If I had known . . ." Mildred threw away her cigarette. "Who is with him now?"

"Pringle's keeping an eye on him. He has a night nurse, and one from four o'clock until midnight. Jessie Hutchins—you remember her."

"Why *her*?"

"We didn't have much choice. There aren't many nurses in town, you know, and she seems competent. Lily and I have been taking turns sitting with him during the day."

"Today was our nineteenth wedding anniversary," Mildred remarked reproachfully.

24

"How is Harry?" Fanny asked. "His mother called yesterday," she added quickly, fearing a recital of domestic martyrdom. Harry had been a local boy. His mother still lived in St. Charles.

Mildred was a born worrier. She had lain awake all night in her uncomfortable berth while anxious thoughts about her father, about Harry, even about trivial happenings of the day, chased each other around in her mind. The smell of the Pullman car was depressing, reminding her of other times she had hurried home to the gloomy atmosphere of calamity. Time and again, as she lay against the pillows taking aspirins and drinking black coffee from a thermos she had brought from home— for she felt it would be altogether wrong to allow herself the luxury of sleep on such a distressing journey—she pictured her arrival at her father's bedside, just at the moment he lost his grip on life. She saw his hands falling away, palms up, on the white sheet, and herself kneeling beside the bed. Then she saw herself running downstairs to telephone Harry, receiving his assurance that he would catch the next plane up to comfort her. But sometimes, going over scenes such as this, a nightmare quality crept in. Her father, instead of lying back still and pale, hands falling away on the white sheet, was sitting up when she entered his room, haranguing, as usual, about this and that. Or, when she tried to telephone Harry, she could not reach him. She heard, quite realistically in her waking dream, the futile ring, ring, ring of the telephone on the Duncan Phyfe stand in their apartment, with Harry God knew where, but not in the place he should be if he had any regard at all for her feelings, not waiting anxiously to hear from her.

It had not occurred to her to eat anything during the tedious two hours in Buffalo waiting for the local; and by now she had taken so many aspirins on an empty stomach that she felt lightheaded. Talking buoyed her up and kept her alert, but as soon as they turned into the River Road and Fanny became silent, she felt herself sinking back into a dreamy, bodiless state. The drooping elm trees along the road seemed to crouch over the car, reaching down with menacing arms. She watched, as if hypnotized, the black ribbon of asphalt flowing toward her.

As they topped a slight rise and the house came into view, Fanny began to slow down, for she always had difficulty making the turn at the gate. A man was walking toward them along the edge of the highway, slapping the dusty goldenrod with his gloves, which he carried in his hand; a slender handsome man in a dark business suit. His face was narrow and pointed, with a small mustache and a trim Vandyke beard which looked navy-blue in the sunlight. As the car approached, he removed his Panama hat and held it against his breast in a courtly old-fashioned gesture. For a moment his eyes looked straight into Mildred's, curiously and—she thought—boldly. She stared back at him, reminded of a dream that sometimes haunted her. The man belonged to night time and city streets, seemed out of place walking along a country road on a summer's day. He looked pale, as if he had not been out in the sun for a long time. In the moment before the car passed, he inclined his head and smiled.

"Who was that?" Mildred sat upright, blinking. "Do you know that man?"

Fanny looked fixedly at the road ahead. "Mr. Fairfield," she volunteered in a vague voice, as if she were not quite sure.

"Who is he?"

"One of the guests at the Willows."

"He seems to know you."

"Yes . . . well, he's been staying there for more than a month."

The change in her voice made Mildred curious, dispelled her lethargy. She studied Fanny with her head on one side. "You're not blushing, are you? From your actions, I'd almost think you were interested in him and pretending not to be."

"My actions? I don't know what you mean!"

26

"The way you didn't look at him, and your voice."

"Oh, for heaven's sake!"

Mildred twisted round for another look at the wayfarer. He stood on the brow of the hill, looking back, and she fancied that he was still smiling. Lily, in the back seat, glanced over her shoulder at him, too, then indifferently aside.

"He looks like a gambler," Mildred observed, facing front again. "Gloves—on a day like this! Where does he come from? Is he a foreigner? He *looks* foreign enough."

"No, he comes from Boston, I think."

Fanny's answers were too offhand, Mildred thought. "What does he *do*?" she persisted.

"How should I know?" Fanny demanded impatiently as she turned into the driveway under the arching letters. The rear bumper scraped against the gatepost with a tinny sound.

"You've had the house painted!" Mildred exclaimed. "You didn't *tell* me!"

The house was set far back from the street, half hidden by laurel bushes and low shrubs. Two towering white pines guarded the driveway. The grass under them was brown, covered with fallen needles. Great masses of autumn flowers grew along the borders. For the painting, the clematis had been pulled away from the tall white columns beside the front door, and it now lay over the lilac bushes in smothering confusion.

King Jameson had bought the house when the family moved to St. Charles in 1921. The site—the high embankment overlooking the river like a fortress—had attracted him for other than romantic reasons. His wife fell in love with the house, which she said reminded her of southern plantation houses, though, as King pointed out, she had never seen a plantation and wouldn't know one if she fell over it. The owner, a widow whose only son had been killed in the war, was persuaded to

27

sell not only her home but the furnishings she had spent a lifetime collecting.

King had a flair for bargaining. With great sympathy and tact he convinced the poor bewildered widow that she would be better off in completely new surroundings, that reminders of her past happy life—such as damask tablecloths, antique chairs, brocade hangings—would only add to her grief. He really preferred new furnishings, he said, but because he was kindhearted and she was alone in the world, he would take the whole lot off her hands. What she called heirlooms he referred to as "second hand." He helped her with the job of cataloguing the contents of the house, with the result that the Adam chairs in the dining room were listed as "eight second-hand chairs," the tapestry loveseat in the hall as "one second-hand settee," and so on throughout the house.

He was immensely proud of Hawkrest. Though alterations were made from time to time, modern plumbing installed, and fussy details eliminated, he was careful to preserve the original lines both inside and out. After a time he began to speak of it, in an offhand way, as "the old family mansion," as if he had always lived there, and to invent little stories about his childhood and his parents. "My father picked this up in London," he would say, running his hand over a piece of fine carving. His father had left London in an immigrant ship at the age of three, to live and die in a Chicago slum, and King himself had spent the first twenty years of his life there, in a dark tenement under the el, but these facts were easily forgotten under the spell of the white house on the river bank.

# CHAPTER TWO

MILDRED'S OLD ROOM WAS JUST AS SHE HAD LEFT IT NINETEEN years before: the same striped wallpaper, flowered carpet, and chintz flounces. An old pair of curling tongs still dangled from a hook above the dresser; faded copies of *Pinkie* and *Blue Boy* hung side by side on the opposite wall. Mildred and Harry slept in the pink enameled bed when—which had not been often lately—they came home for a visit. Neither was entirely comfortable in the room. The virginal school-girl look of it depressed Harry and made Mildred feel, when he made love to her, as if she were committing adultery, with the photograph of her mother looking down in disapproval from the mahogany highboy. Coming into the room alone, however, she was only reminded of how nature had tripped her up; for after all her frantic fears lest Harry might not ask her to live with him forever—how many nights she had lain awake in that bed with the shadow of spinsterhood hanging over her!—she had found that marriage was not at all what she had expected.

She had expected marriage to change both herself and Harry in some magical way; their lives would become rich and full of meaning because of the *understanding* that would develop suddenly, burst into bloom the minute the vows were uttered. But it was not long before she discovered that Harry not only didn't understand her one whit better than before, he didn't know what she was talking about when she complained about this lack of understanding. It was a great disappointment, but Mildred felt there must be a cure. Perusal of countless articles on the art of making marriage work convinced her of this, and set her probing like a surgeon with a scalpel, trying to uncover the root of the trouble. This involved a great many candid talks with Harry, a thorough dredging into causes and effects, which of course had come to nothing, since Harry was uncooperative.

This morning she paused only long enough to throw her hat and furs on the bed, then crossed the hall to her father's room.

"He may be asleep," Fanny, on her way up with the bags, cautioned.

Mildred paid no attention. She opened the door of her father's room.

He was propped up in an old-fashioned brass bed with pillows at his back. His eyes were closed. A large colored photograph of his second wife—a pretty, dark-haired woman with breasts like two plump grapefruit in a nest of tulle—hung over the mantel. Mildred could never look at this picture without feeling that the bold smile was directed at her, the eyes following her about the room. In a minute the mouth would open to offer advice, gaily, but with a hidden barb. "You'll never catch a husband that way, honey! Men don't like mopey women. You'll be an old maid if you don't watch out." On the mantel under this picture were other photographs of Hazel, in the coy poses and unflattering styles of the twenties. The window curtains were partly drawn, and a depressing smell of stale air and medicine hung about the room. The huge brass knobs on the bedposts gleamed. A clean white cloth was spread over the night table, on which were laid bottles and spoons.

Mildred believed that her father was not really asleep. She went to him and placed her hands on his shoulders, peering into his face. "Papa . . . ?"

"Perhaps later . . ." Fanny, having deposited the suitcases, came up behind her and made the suggestion anxiously. "I don't think we should waken him."

"Papa, dear." Mildred touched his forehead.

"Eh?" He woke with a start. His eyes glared blankly into hers. "Who's that? What—?"

"It's me, Papa. Mildred."

He made champing motions with his mouth. A string of saliva ran down his chin. His forehead was mottled with brown spots, like huge freckles, and a few wisps of white hair stuck up from his bald head. His stomach made a mountain under his hands.

"I've come home," Mildred said. Tears started from her eyes and fell on his hands.

The old man stared vacantly at her. Then his eyes focused and his face purpled with anger. "What in God's name are you sniveling at?" he demanded in a wheezing, petulant voice.

"I've come home to be with you," Mildred faltered.

He hitched himself sideways, his eyes filled with hatred. "The first decent sleep I've had in two days, and you wake me up to tell me you've come home! Who for God's sake asked you to come?" He began to stutter, his breath coming in gasps. "Get away from me!"

Mildred laid her head on the counterpane and wept.

"Get away from me!" he wheezed again, throwing himself as far from her as he could. "I don't want *you* blubbering over me."

"Now, Papa!" Fanny said severely. She took his shoulders and made him lie back among the pillows, then poured medicine into a spoon and held it to his mouth. When he pushed it aside, spilling the brown liquid over the bedclothes, she measured out another dose.

"He never liked me," Mildred told Fanny, back in her own room. "He never liked us. It was always Isobel and Lily. He never liked our mother."

"You know he's always been unreasonable. I warned you not to waken him. Dr. Randolph said the least disturbance—"

"He wasn't asleep." Mildred wiped her eyes with finality. "Is he still around—Dr. Randolph? He's a thousand years old."

"Papa likes him."

"I thought he died long ago; drank himself to death."

"He does drink a lot, but he's rather a nice old man. Besides, Papa won't have anyone else."

Mildred took off her skirt and hung it over a chair. In her

slip, she examined her drawn features in the mirror, holding her hair behind her ears with both hands, pulling the skin tight across her cheekbones. When she dropped her hands, the slack lines of her chin dropped, too. "Naturally I didn't sleep a wink last night," she said to excuse her appearance. "Lying awake worrying, thinking about Papa . . . And then to be treated like this!"

"Why don't you have a good sleep now?" Fanny suggested. "We'll call you when lunch is ready. I forgot to ask if you'd had breakfast."

"Breakfast? How could I eat at a time like this?"

"I'll bring you up something."

"No, I couldn't . . ." Mildred closed her eyes. "I have such a headache," she went on pathetically. "The worry all night, and then to have Papa shout at me like that. As if I'd ever done anything to deserve such treatment. And having to leave a note for Harry when he expected me to be there . . ." She blew her nose.

"And Isobel not being here," she continued. "What could be more important than coming home at a time like this? And when she does come, I suppose Papa will welcome her with open arms . . ."

It was true that King Jameson was less critical of Lily and Isobel, the children of his second marriage, than of his two older daughters. Whenever Fanny and Mildred thought of their mother, they called to mind a darkened room and the smell of camphor. They could not really remember what she looked like before her illness. Mildred had a vague recollection of an upright woman in a white apron, her hair drawn back and skewered with steel hairpins into a braided bun. During the last three years of her life, the first Mrs. Jameson was confined to her bed, or to a chair beside the window in her room, where she watched the people in the street below. She was white-faced, hollow-eyed, and rather frightening, with her hair in two thin pigtails over her shoulders. In later years Mildred rejected the true picture of her mother for one she had made up herself, patterned after the photograph in her room, which showed a prim young woman in a boned shirtwaist, hugging a bunch of artificial roses.

Mildred also remembered the third-floor flat, on a street of narrow red-brick houses in Chicago, where they lived at the time of her mother's illness. The high front steps of the houses were all alike, and sometimes Mildred was afraid that when she came home from school she might go up the wrong steps and find herself in unfamiliar surroundings. At that time her father ran a small cigar store. He had not yet learned that there are easier—though less respectable—ways of making a living.

Hazel, when she first came to keep house for them, was a jolly, careless girl of eighteen, very pretty, who played games with the children and laughed a good deal, throwing back her head and showing all her white teeth. For a short while Mildred was happy. Then she made a discovery. Her father, who was supposed to be sleeping on the living-room couch, was spending every night in Hazel's room. Mildred, eleven at the time, had picked up enough information at school to understand why he went there. She was, in fact, rather taken up with the sexual act at that time, having observed it in animals and been severely criticized by her mother for asking questions. The act, which she had regarded as frenzied and rather silly, but no doubt necessary and therefore to be accepted as normal, then assumed quite a different aspect in her mind. In relation to her father and Hazel, it became morbidly fascinating. She became adept at spying, at creeping out of bed into the dark hallway, listening at the keyhole. Sometimes she heard whispers and smothered giggles, or the slap of a hand against bare flesh. She saw nothing. But the giggles told her that her father and Hazel were enjoying something that should not be enjoyed. Fear of further criticism prevented her from telling what she knew, so the secret lay in her mind and fed upon itself.

Mrs. Jameson died at last; and the funeral was hardly over before Hazel and King were married. Later on, Mildred understood why there had been such an indecently short interval between her father's bereavement and his second marriage. Isobel was on the way. Her parents had been married less than two months when she was born.

During the war, which to Mildred meant the First World War, the Jamesons moved often, each time to a better neighborhood, for King had abandoned his cigar store and was prospering as a petty racketeer. Mildred never asked what business, exactly, he was engaged in during those years. It was humiliation enough to know that Hazel had dragged him down to her own level. When he left Chicago and moved to New York, it was because of some trouble, some failure to conform to certain rules laid down by people who had more influence than he. In New York he must have placated the right people, for he was more successful than ever. He bought a fine house; Hazel had charge accounts at the better shops. It was then that he began to encourage the nickname of "the King." Three years after the end of the war, however, he found it expedient to move again, this time out of the country. He bundled his family and as much money as could be immediately converted into cash—a considerable amount, for he had apparently foreseen that such an emergency might arise—into the first north-bound train and crossed the border into Canada.

He could not have arrived at a better time, for prohibition was turning every border town into a potential gold mine. He bought the white house on the river bank and set up business as a rum-runner. His office was a two-by-four cubbyhole under the stairs. He also established a real-estate office on Main Street as a blind—and to please Hazel, who yearned for the outward aspects of respectability—but this venture was never a profitable one.

Hazel, who had acquired polish during the prosperous years, became very much the lady of the manor once the family settled in St. Charles. She served tea to the wives of local businessmen with fine haughty grace. She thought this custom of afternoon tea quite British, quite in keeping with the English-novel character she had adopted. For twelve years Hazel enlivened the drab little town with her presence, though after the first six months the leading matrons ignored her invitations to tea. "As if I cared about those old bitches!" she said, thumbing her nose in the direction of the town. "There's plenty of other people in the world." She swept in and out of shops, wearing the most extravagant styles, dispensing smiles and good cheer in all directions. Everybody talked about her. She drank, they said, she gave wild parties, she flirted with every man she met, carrying on under her husband's very nose; she was shallow and frivolous, and she would kill herself one of these days, the way she tore around the country in her blue roadster.

And one day when she was out driving with Lily, who was eight at the time, Hazel did just that. She ran the car into a tree and killed herself. Lily was badly injured.

In later years, though this accident was rarely mentioned in the Jameson household, it was much thought about, for it changed all their lives. It ruined Lily's. And from the day of his wife's death onward, King Jameson became increasingly eccentric, his language and actions grew more unbridled. He had always blustered and strutted, but after Hazel died the house rang with his shouts, the chandeliers in the dining room tinkled as he stomped about imagining himself a sort of modern Henry the Eighth, drinking, roistering, chasing women, giving not a damn for anything or anybody.

He grew so reckless in the transaction of his business that the law finally caught up with him. He spent six months in the county jail. He did not feel that this was any disgrace, nor did many of the townspeople, who depended upon him for employment. He looked upon himself as a martyr whose sacrifice merely revealed the corruption of the government. "The bastards are trying to break me," he told friends and employees who went to see him on visitors' day. But his business did not suffer. He was able to direct operations quite successfully from his temporary asylum.

Mildred, almost prostrated by the disgrace, nevertheless hurried home to stay with Fanny and bear the brunt, as she put it. They drew the blinds and sat like people in mourning, waiting for the tide of gossip to recede. No one could understand why they minded so much. "It's not as if you'd done anything to be ashamed of," Mrs. Pringle pointed out sensibly. "Nobody's blaming you—or him either, for that matter. Everybody knows it's nothing but politics."

Isobel, who had come home, too—not through any sense of duty, but because she was divorcing one of her husbands—simply refused to be concerned about the family's reputation. "We never had any reputation to begin with," she told Mildred. "People know what we are. Papa's a posturing old roué, and a crook into the bargain. All the tears in the world won't change him. And as for you, trying so hard to pretend we're not *common*, as you put it, you're simply wasting your time. We are common. How could we be anything else? I *like* being common," Isobel said, as usual goaded by Mildred's outraged expression into saying more than she really meant.

"That's easily seen from your actions," Mildred remarked acidly.

It was during this period that Mrs. Pringle's natural antipathy toward Mildred crystallized into open hostility.

"I simply can't understand her," she complained to Isobel. "Carrying on like that over a little bit of scandal. As if anybody in the world cared! And when your poor mother died—the sweetest woman who ever drew breath—she never shed a tear."

For Mrs. Pringle the bottom had dropped out of the world when Hazel died. On Saturday nights, over beer at the local tavern, she had given her friends so many detailed accounts of Hazel's doings and sayings that they had grown tired of listen-

36

ing. Lately she had found a new audience in Mrs. Kinch, whom she invited over from the Willows for afternoon coffee and a good chat about the old days. Mrs. Kinch listened with gratifying attention, for it was all new to her.

Mrs. Pringle, having for politeness' sake touched—but briefly—on the weather and other topics of local interest, would steer the conversation around to Hazel. "Oh, she was a perfect devil! Always teasing and carrying on. And pretty as a picture. Isobel takes after her, though she'll never be the beauty her mother was. When she flashed those dark eyes of hers and smiled, the men noticed, believe you me! She had only to nod her head, and they'd come running. Lord, the way the old B. carried on when she died; even threatened to throw himself in the river. A pity he didn't. No airs about Hazel, though she could be high and mighty when she wanted to be. Like a duchess when she had tea parties, inviting the mayor's wife and all that stuck-up crowd—that was when they first came to St. Charles, before those bitches started looking down their noses. Sitting there drinking tea as if butter wouldn't melt in her mouth, though she couldn't stand the stuff, making them all look like bumpkins with her stylish clothes and lady-like manners. Then, as soon as she'd seen them out the door, she'd come running to the kitchen. 'Daisy, for God's sake, where's my gin?' And while she washed away the taste of tea, she'd tell me about the party. Mimic! You never heard anything so funny in your life. The way she'd imitate Mrs.—I forget her name, the mayor's wife. Many a time we laughed ourselves sick."

Mrs. Pringle remembered the name of that long-ago mayor's wife perfectly well. She had good reason to, for the lady's son, Eliot Whitmore, now a successful New York importer of wines, was nobody else but Isobel's third husband.

"Everybody loved Hazel. Everybody, that is, except a few old hens like Mrs. Whatsername, and it was nothing more nor less than jealousy on their part, because she knew how to wear

37

clothes, and because their husbands couldn't take their eyes off her. She knew they didn't like her, but she never let on—to them, that is. You couldn't *make* her quarrel, she was that good-natured—sweet as honey to everybody. This house hasn't been the same since she died. Parties! Any occasion was an excuse for a party. 'Daisy,' she'd say to me, 'we've got to get these girls married off or we'll have a couple of old maids on our hands.' She meant Mildred and Fanny. 'We'll have a party,' she'd say. 'Invite all the young men.' But when the young men came, it was *her* they wanted to dance with. She'd say to them, 'Why don't you dance with poor Mildred or poor Fanny, sitting there in the corner by herself?' And they'd go off and dance with the girls, but the minute the music stopped they'd crowd around her again. We haven't had a party in this house since Hazel was killed."

Mrs. Pringle would dab at her eyes with a paper napkin, and Mrs. Kinch would nod sympathetically and observe that the good always die young.

When Fanny had gone, Mildred lay down on the bed. With her eyes closed, she began to half think, half dream, about the man they had met on the way home from the station, about the way he had looked at her. But he's a perfect stranger, she told herself impatiently as she plumped up the pillows. Why am I thinking about him when I have so many real worries— when I need rest? She made a great effort to occupy her mind with these real worries, but in a little while her thoughts strayed back to the stranger.

He reminded her of a magician she had met some months before at a party given by Harry's lodge. Harry had been unkind to her that evening—she had forgotten now what he had done—and though they had sat together during the magician's performance, Mildred had remained reproachfully silent, blinking back tears, building up little revenges in her mind. To avoid looking at Harry, she had kept her eyes steadfastly on the magician. Her seat was so close to the stage that he could not help noticing her unwavering interest, and after a time he seemed to be addressing all his remarks to her, his smile was for her alone. When refreshments were served later on, he had deliberately placed himself beside her, and they had talked about his art. For her benefit he repeated one or two simple tricks with a handkerchief. He looked at her the way she had always imagined Frenchmen looked at women, with the merest hint of something in his eyes—a suggestion of intimacy—which she pretended not to see.

That night Mildred dreamed that he came to her with soft comforting words, telling her that he cared, if nobody else did. She returned his embraces with wanton eagerness, and when she woke up she lay in the dark, deliberately reconstructing the dream, trying to go beyond the point where it had ended. She had dreamed about the magician a number of times since then. She had never seen him again. Sometimes she fancied that she caught a glimpse of his face in a crowd, but when she looked a second time he had either disappeared or resolved into someone with quite ordinary features.

Mildred dreamed a good deal. Often, when she woke up, a disturbing remnant of nightmare clung to her, in which people she loved and trusted betrayed her in various ways. These dreams faded from her consciousness with morning, but the one about the magician did not. Sometimes, when she was alone during the day, she thought about him. Seeing the dark-haired man on the road that morning, she had thought for a minute that he was the magician. She realized now that they were not really much alike, but the meeting had disturbed her just the same. To steady herself, she decided to telephone Harry. She threw a dressing gown over her shoulders, thrust her feet into a pair of pink satin mules, and slapped downstairs to the telephone. She had lied when she told Fanny that Harry was visiting a sick friend the previous night. He had really stamped out of the apartment in a huff because Mildred insisted upon questioning him about a new girl in his office. She could never quite believe that he was satisfied with his married life, and was always trying to trip him into admitting that he preferred some other woman to her.

After much delay, the call was put through to the New York bank where Harry worked. He was trapped into admitting he had forgotten their anniversary, then spent some minutes assuring Mildred that he had not really forgotten. Years of practice had not made him proficient in the art of vindicating himself. When he got nowhere, he abandoned the attempt and became heartily solicitous about his father-in-law, urging Mildred on no account to consider leaving her father's side until she was no longer needed there. "Don't worry about me," he repeated. "I can manage. Your place is with him."

"You sound as if you wanted to be rid of me."

"You know I'll miss you. But if your father needs you . . ."

"He's better this morning."

"Well . . . but don't you think you should stay for a day or so, in case anything happens?"

"If you're sure you want me to."

"It's not what I *want* . . . !"

"And if you think you can manage by yourself."

"Don't worry about me," Harry said.

I expect he can manage, Mildred told herself, going up the stairs, her head throbbing worse than ever. She began to invent situations, reasons why Harry would want her to stay in St. Charles. She recalled what she had heard about office parties, then remembered that they usually took place around Christmas time. But perhaps, in her absence, Harry meant to give parties in their apartment, or, worse, take a girl up. She saw Harry and the girl in her frilly bedroom: a girl with big breasts and hips. Creating this fantasy, she forgot that Harry hated parties, that he was bald and paunchy with bags under his eyes, that he never looked at another woman for the simple reason that he was too lazy. He spent his evenings slopping around

40

the apartment in a white sweatshirt and a pair of khaki trousers worn at the seat and knees, drinking beer and watching television. It was next to impossible to induce him to take his wife out, even to a neighborhood movie, though twice each month he sailed off cheerfully by himself, to his lodge meeting.

"Because I'm getting old and losing my looks," Mildred, back in her room, said to her unhappy reflection in the mirror. To console herself, she finished unpacking her bags and set a photograph of her son, who was dead, on the table beside the bed. Then she took two aspirins and lay down with a handkerchief soaked in witch hazel over her eyes. At noon Fanny came up with a tray.

"I couldn't eat a thing," Mildred said. "But leave it there," she added. "I might manage a little of the soup."

"Try the cold chicken, too," Fanny urged. "We saved it especially for you. It will do you good." She pulled a shopping list from her pocket. "I'm going to the market to pick up a few things. Is there anything you'd like? I've remembered your favorite whole-wheat bread, and mustard pickles . . ."

It was comforting to be at home again, to be *considered*. Mildred sat up, and as soon as Fanny had gone, she pulled the tray toward her and drank the soup. By the time she had finished the chicken she felt quite refreshed. She washed her face and applied make-up.

When she entered her father's room half an hour later, he was struggling to get out of bed, while Lily sat in the leather chair beside the window, doing her nails.

Swearing in a vehement undertone, the old man clawed at the bed until he had heaved his enormous body into a sitting position. His face grew purple as he tried vainly to reach the stick propped against the night table.

"Why don't you *help* him?" Mildred ran forward.

"He's not supposed to get up." Lily spread her fingers fanwise on the arm of her chair and drew a sweep of red polish across each nail.

41

"To be so heartless . . . !" Mildred cried. "Don't you see he needs help? What is it, Papa?" she asked, bending over him. "Do you want something?"

He leaned against her for a moment, catching his breath, then with a triumphant lunge thrust his feet over the edge of the bed and grasped his heavy maple cane. Leaning on it, his hairy legs spread wide apart, his nightshirt twisted up around his stomach, he wheezed and panted, gathering strength for the next move.

Mildred tried to pull down his nightshirt. "Do you want to go to the bathroom?" she asked.

"Get away from me," he said savagely, making a threatening motion with his stick. She stepped back hastily. He sagged over the cane, his malevolent glance darting about the room. "My God, are you still here?" he demanded, realizing suddenly who Mildred was. "I told you once, I won't have you sniveling over me. Go back where you came from. I'm not going to die, if that's what you're waiting for."

"Don't pay any attention to him," Lily said, blowing on her nails.

He tried to stand, pushing himself up with his cane, grunting, straining, gasping for breath, and swearing in a passionate whisper.

"Please, Papa, get back into bed," Mildred pleaded.

He sat back, glaring at her from under his bushy white eyebrows, then raised the cane in both hands and struck out furiously. It missed her, but crashed against the bottles on the night table. A brown stain spread over the rug. Bits of glass glinted up.

When Fanny arrived a few minutes later, he was again sprawled grotesquely on the bed. She drew the sheet over him and began to sponge up the carpet.

Mildred went downstairs. She had intended to carry her share of the burden by sitting with her father all afternoon,

42

but now she could not bear the thought of entering his room again. Mrs. Pringle sat in the kitchen reading, with her shoes off and her feet propped on a chair. "Well, you got here, I see," she said without a smile.

"How are you, Pringle?" Mildred glanced significantly at the lunch dishes in the sink. "Resting?" she inquired.

Mrs. Pringle smiled back just as frostily and said, Yes, as a matter of fact she *was* resting. As any fool can see, her eyes added.

In the garden, Mildred leaned on the stone wall and looked down the gorge. Far below, the river was blue-green, with swirling foam patterns. Gulls coasted down the air currents, starkly white and angular in the sunlight. She stared, fascinated, at the rocky cliff that dropped away from the summer-house, and grasped the wall with both hands to steady herself.

After a time she turned her back on the gorge and wandered around the garden, examining the flowers, pinching off a bloom here and there. Her eye was caught by a figure moving in the strip of beechwood beyond the low hedge. It was the man they had met on the road that morning. He strolled along one of the interlacing paths, going away from her, and was soon lost from sight. Faint sounds of conversation and genteel laughter drifted across the wood from the garden of the Willows next door, where Mrs. Kinch's other guests were gathered.

As if she were being watched, Mildred continued her inspection of the garden. She moved casually along the border, pausing to sniff a late rose. When she came to a break in the hedge, she stepped through it and sauntered into the wood.

As curiosity drew her along the path, blackberry vines reached out maliciously and caught at her stockings. The beechwood was warm and secret, filled with ripe autumn smells of berries and turning leaves. When the man rounded a thicket suddenly and came face to face with her, she was unprepared.

"Oh!" She tried to step aside, but the path was too narrow. "I didn't know anyone was here."

43

He smiled and raised his hat, unsurprised. Mildred wondered if he had been watching her from the thicket. His eyes were a queer yellowish green, very bright, and she thought they did not match his hair, or his dark pointed beard. "I must apologize for trespassing," he said with an engaging, sad smile. He seemed to take it for granted that Mildred knew who he was, even to give the impression that they had arranged to meet there.

"It's so beautiful here in the woods," he added wistfully, almost apologetically.

"Yes." Mildred looked away at last. "Yes, very nice . . ." she said faintly.

He waited a moment before he stepped aside to let her pass. As she hurried away, she felt that he was watching her through the screening vines. At the river bank, which sloped away more gradually here, the path dipping down sharply among the trees, she was forced to stop.

She sat on a boulder, listening, hearing nothing but the faint rustle of leaves and the beating of her own heart. At the end of ten minutes she made her way slowly back to the garden.


## CHAPTER THREE


THE HABIT OF AFTERNOON TEA, BEGUN BY THE SECOND MRS. Jameson, had persisted through the years. At four o'clock Mildred and Fanny sat in the living room waiting for Mrs. Pringle to bring in the tray. Jessie Hutchins, the four-to-midnight nurse, had arrived, and was now bustling around upstairs. Lily, without being prompted, had driven down to the station to meet Isobel.

Mildred put on her glasses and laid out a hand of solitaire. "I wonder if Lily should be encouraged to take the car out by herself."

"Yes, of course. Why shouldn't she?" Fanny said without looking up from her knitting.

Mildred pressed her lips together. "You won't look facts in the face, will you? You persist in pretending that Lily is capable—"

"You remember Dr. Brenner told us we should encourage her to do things by herself," Fanny reminded, "not treat her as if she were different from other people."

"Well . . ." Mildred shuffled the cards and dealt them out again with a slapping sound. "How *is* Lily? I never can tell, from your letters."

Before Fanny could answer, Jessie Hutchins ran downstairs. Having given her patient a sedative, she took time off to exchange schoolgirl reminiscences.

"We're none of us getting any younger," she summed up. "Sometimes I feel ninety. This working for a living—believe me, girls, you don't know how lucky you are!" She glanced enviously around the room. "For me, it's been nothing but drudge, drudge, drudge, ever since Albert died. How is Harry?"

"He's well," Mildred said stiffly.

Jessie's eyes narrowed. "That Harry! He used to be so cute." She settled her untidy figure more comfortably. Her starched uniform strained across her knees, the buttons gaping to show a pink slip and a bulge of dimpled flesh above rolled-down stockings. "Harry used to be an old beau of mine," she said, turning to Fanny, who knew this already. "Such a card! I haven't seen him in—let me see—fifteen years. He'd never know me now." She sighed, glancing ruefully down at herself. "Remember how slim I used to me, Mildred? Then I had all that trouble with my tubes, and that operation . . . I suppose I

45

ought to get back to my patient." She rose reluctantly, glancing at the cups on the table.

"When the tea's ready, I'll bring you up some," Fanny offered.

"She was *never* slim!" Mildred said resentfully when Jessie had gone upstairs. "Even at school she had a backside like a hippopotamus. And as for Harry being an old beau of hers, as she calls it—"

"Mildred, you remember that man we met on the way home this morning?" Fanny asked abruptly, laying aside her knitting.

Mildred looked down at the cards, and lifted a queen to see what was under it before she spoke. "What man?"

"The one we met on the road. You said he looked like a gambler."

"Oh, that one." Mildred moved another card, frowning. "Well, perhaps not a gambler, exactly—but foxy. Like the fox that came into the garden that time we had the pigeons." As she spoke, she saw the fox's pointed face, the way he seemed to be smiling over his shoulder at her the night she caught him killing a pigeon in the garden. "What about him?"

"His name is Theodore Fairfield," Fanny said reluctantly, as if she hated to come to the point.

"Yes . . . ?"

"Was that the car?" Fanny lifted her head, listening. She rose and went to the window. "Yes, here they are," she said with relief.

"What about this man—this Theodore Fairfield? Surely that's not his real name? It sounds like a Victorian novel."

"I'll tell you everything later. Don't ask me about him when Lily's here."

"Lily?" Mildred's voice sharpened.

"Hush!" Fanny warned as the front door opened.

Isobel was like the picture in her father's bedroom. Beside Lily's frosty paleness she looked full-blown, vivid. She was thirty-eight. Her one child, a daughter by her first husband, was married and the mother of a month-old boy.

"So it was a false alarm," she said, throwing off her hat and kissing Mildred and Fanny lightly on the cheek. "Lily tells me that Papa is out of danger for the time being."

"It's hardly a joking matter," Mildred said. She didn't know why it was that Isobel's overripe beauty infuriated her so. It seemed an affront for any woman to be so much like those rosy nudes in old paintings. Mildred's own figure seemed suddenly too angular, lacking in grace. "Papa was very low last night," she said severely, "and he may have a relapse at any moment. Why didn't you come sooner?"

"I couldn't get away."

"*Couldn't?*"

Isobel looked at Fanny. "Do you think I should go up now?"

"He's asleep. But if you want to just peek in . . ."

"I'll wait." Isobel seemed relieved. "I'll go up later." She looked around. "Where's Pringle?"

"Here I am, honey!" Mrs. Pringle came bouncing in from the kitchen, flung her arms around Isobel, and kissed her, while tears ran down her cheeks. "Such a long time!" She held Isobel at arm's length and beamed damply at her. "You haven't changed a bit. And a grandmother now, aren't you, dear? My Lord, you don't look a day over twenty yourself."

"You look wonderful, Pringle. You're losing weight, aren't you?"

They fell into each other's arms again, chattering and laughing. After a time Mrs. Pringle tore herself away and went off to the kitchen with Fanny to bring in the tea tray.

As they passed through the hall, the telephone rang. "Hello!" Fanny shouted into it. "Oh . . ." Her voice flattened, became formal. "Yes, thank you, he's resting now . . . yes . . . it's very kind of you to offer, but I don't believe . . ." A long pause, then, reluctantly, "Yes, she is here."

"Lily," she called.

47

"Whoever can that be?" Mildred wondered, straining her ears toward the hall, where Lily's thin childish voice was saying something about a spangled fritillary. "Spangled fritillary?" Mildred raised her eyes to Isobel's as if she had heard something obscene. Isobel shrugged and spread her hands in a helpless gesture, then began to hum a tune. "Hush!" Mildred said impatiently, but she had missed half of Lily's conversation.

"Of course, come if you like," Lily was now saying.

"Who on earth is she talking to?" Mildred asked as Fanny returned from the kitchen.

Fanny looked appealingly over her shoulder at Mrs. Pringle, who followed with the tea tray.

"Here we are!" Mrs. Pringle sang out gaily. She placed the tray on a low table and lifted a corner of the cloth triumphantly. "Scones, dear!" she said to Isobel. "The minute I heard you were coming, I whipped up a batch."

"Pringle, you're an angel!"

"Don't spoil your dinner, now," Mrs. Pringle warned with a playful shake of her tinted curls.

"Did you bring my toast, Pringle?" Mildred asked.

"There! You did ask for toast, didn't you? We don't generally have time for special orders, with the dinner to be got and all the other work piling up, but I'll pop the toaster on."

"Never mind, if you've forgotten."

"Sure? I can have the toaster going in two shakes. Generally, though," Mrs. Pringle continued with maddening cheerfulness, "when people want something special like that, they go out and make it themselves. However . . . what kind do you want, white or whole-wheat?"

"Never *mind*!" Mildred said. She watched Mrs. Pringle's stout figure disappear into the hall. "Well, Lily?"

Lily, who was no better than other people at interpreting such questions, chose to ignore it. She turned to the window

48

and pulled up the blind, which Fanny had lowered against the afternoon sun.

The sudden light hurt Mildred's eyes, but she decided not to complain. "Aren't you the secretive one! Getting telephone calls from mysterious people. Who was that?" she asked, curiosity forcing her to abandon subterfuge.

Lily, who had pulled back the curtain to scan the garden, glanced over her shoulder, considering Mildred's motive. "It was only Theodore," she said after a moment.

"Theodore?" Mildred looked up quickly, and raised her cup to hide her face.

"Theodore Fairfield," Lily said patiently, as if well aware that she was giving known information. "He's stopping at the Willows. He wants to come over tonight."

"Your tea, Lily," Fanny said in a cross voice, holding out the cup.

Lily accepted it and sat down beside Isobel.

They drank in silence. Mildred stared at Fanny, who avoided her eyes. "Why is he coming here?" she asked at last.

Lily reached for a scone, then, seeing that Isobel's plate was empty, handed her one, too. "To see me," she said with a hint of complacency.

"I don't think I understand." Mildred set her cup down carefully. "Is he coming on business? Who—*what* is he? I heard you mention a—what was it?—a spangled something or other over the telephone."

"A spangled fritillary. It's a kind of butterfly. He has found the chrysalis."

"Is he a naturalist, then?"

"Oh, no." Lily brushed her fingers together fastidiously. "He thinks I'm interested in butterflies, that's all."

"Is this a new beau?" Isobel asked, smiling.

Mildred glared at her, scandalized. Trust Isobel to put ideas into Lily's head.

Fanny now laid aside her ruffled attempt at indifference.

Careful, careful! her eyes warned Mildred. This will take handling. We must not scoff or show disapproval, for that will simply drive her into his arms. They knew all the rules, having —with what they believed to be great subtlety—discouraged Lily's first suitors years ago, following the advice found in women's magazines. Lately, however, Mildred had read only the articles devoted to straying husbands and how to deal with them. She picked up her cup with determined nonchalance, but could not help asking questions.

"What does he do? For a living, I mean."

"I don't believe he does anything." Lily flicked a crumb off her skirt, looking down with a hint of secret amusement.

"Most people do something," Mildred persisted.

"*I* don't." Lily grew tired of the game. She looked away, and her face took on the vacant expression which meant that she would listen to no more questions.

Fanny, her tea forgotten, picked up her knitting and attacked it, then, having thought of an excuse to remove herself from the scene, rolled up the wool and thrust the needles through it again. "I must take a tray up to Jessie." She sent Mildred a pleading glance.

Mildred ignored it. "Because you have a father to support you," she explained patiently. "Not all people are so fortunate. And men, even if they have money, usually do some sort of work. Perhaps this Mr. Fairfield has money? Has he?" she prompted when Lily did not answer.

"I don't think it matters, does it?" Isobel intervened. "All these questions, Mildred . . ."

"I have a perfect right to question Lily. I have her interests at heart."

"That doesn't give you the right to pry."

"Pry?"

In her scenes with Harry, Mildred always began by determining not to interrogate him about some fancied rival, and then deciding he could not take offense if she asked one or two casual questions. His monosyllabic answers trapped her into forgetting the advice given in magazines. When Harry shouted, "Oh, for God's *sake*, Mildred!" and slammed out of the house, she went over his answers one by one, seeking some hidden meaning.

"I'm certainly not *prying*," she said in an injured voice. "I hope it's not unnatural for me to be interested in Lily's friends."

"How do you expect Lily to know anything about Mr. Fairfield's finances? Do you ask your friends how much money they have?"

"What difference does it make, anyway?" Lily came out of her trance to say. "I have money, and will have more when Papa dies."

Mildred put her hands over her face in shocked protest. Before she could pull herself together sufficiently to evaluate this remark, she was left alone. "I must unpack," Isobel said. "I'll help you," Lily offered, and the two went upstairs together.

Mildred looked around the empty room. This feeling of being deserted was a familiar one to her, other people being so much less considerate than she was. Her friends gave parties and failed to invite her; her husband forgot anniversaries; her sisters, on her first day at home, left her alone with a cup of cold tea.

Isobel opened her suitcase on the bed and watched Lily take the dresses out one by one, holding them up against herself, her eyes envious.

"Would you like to keep that one?" she asked when Lily picked up a green wool. "I think it will fit you if we take a few tucks in the waist. It's far too small for me. I bought it when I was dieting."

"Oh, can I?" Lily began to pull off the dress she was wearing, not bothering to undo all the buttons. When a button caught in her hair, she jerked it free.

"Careful, darling!" Isobel said, helping her. "You're pulling

51

out all your pretty hair. Look, a great long strand of it." She eased the green dress over Lily's head and stood back. "That color's good on you."

Lily twisted before the mirror. "I never have clothes like this. Fanny never lets me buy anything."

"Oh, darling!" Isobel protested mechanically. Her words held no reproach, though she knew that Lily's closet was bursting with clothes, many of them never worn. "Stand still," she commanded, dropping to her knees. "We'll shorten the belt and take up the hem . . ."

Lily said with a sidelong stare, "Fanny's not very nice to me, you know."

"I know, dear." Isobel sat back on her heels. It was always best to humor Lily when her mind took an inventive turn. "Who is this Mr. Fairfield?" she asked in a careless voice.

"Oh, Theodore!" Lily laughed. "He's a silly little man."

"Don't you like him?"

Lily's glance slid away. "He's all right."

Isobel knew better than to press for details. "Have you got some pins, honey?" she asked. "I think if we shortened this about an inch . . ."

"In the workbasket in Fanny's room," Lily said, and flew away. She returned a moment later with a box of pins. "I wish you'd stay home all the time," she said wistfully, but she was watching her own reflection in the mirror.

Fanny stayed upstairs so long that Mildred finally went looking for her. She found her on the wide balcony over the front door, where trailing vines screened out the sun and potted geraniums gave the air a spicy fragrance.

"I was just coming down," Fanny said, jumping up.

"I did want to talk to you." Mildred sat in a wicker chair and pulled out her cigarettes. She waited reproachfully for Fanny to be seated again. "Why didn't you tell me about this man—this Mr. Field or whatever his name is?"

"Fairfield," Fanny corrected. She looked down at her hands. "I couldn't be sure it meant anything—his coming here."

"I don't see how you could think it *didn't* mean anything, when he calls her on the telephone and comes to the house to see her. I couldn't believe my ears when I heard that—I simply couldn't *believe* that all this was going on and you hadn't told me."

Fanny reached over and helped herself to a cigarette. "At first he seemed . . . well, sort of a family friend. And different from the sort she usually . . . He used to bring me flowers. I thought he was too old to interest Lily."

"How often does he come here?"

"Quite often. Almost every night. He takes her driving sometimes, too. One Sunday he rented a car and they were away the whole day."

"What does he do? What do you know about him?"

"He doesn't talk much about himself. He did tell us that he's from Boston, that he owns some factories and other properties there."

Mildred sniffed. "Well, one story is as good as another, I suppose. What is he doing here?"

"On a holiday, he says."

"I suppose it never occurred to you that he might be a fortune-hunter who preys upon gullible women!"

"Oh, no!" Fanny raised her hands protestingly. "There's no *reason* to think that."

"Except his looks. I've seen his kind before."

"But you've never seen him!"

Mildred glanced quickly away. "I saw him this morning, on the way home from the station."

"Just a glimpse. How could you tell anything?"

"You must remember that I know a bit more of the world than you do. I believe I'm better qualified to judge people. Even his name sounds fictitious. Do you know what he reminds me of? That man in England—I read about him somewhere—

who drowned all his wives in the bathtub. I thought it the minute I saw him."

"Now you're being unreasonable. And unfair."

"I presume he has made inquiries, and knows exactly where we stand financially. I presume he's been told about the money Papa settled on each of us girls. He should never have given Lily all that money," Mildred went on. "Hers should have been put in trust. I said so at the time."

"Why should he be interested in Lily's money? He's got more than she will ever have."

Mildred gave an exasperated sigh. After a silence she looked at Fanny severely and asked, "What steps have you taken to discourage him?"

Fanny shifted uncomfortably. "What could I *do*?" she demanded, puffing on her cigarette, blowing smoke out through her nose. Though she smoked much, she did it awkwardly, as if she had never tried such a thing before, holding the cigarette between her thumb and first finger.

"We must do *something*," Mildred said decisively. "We must do something at once. I can't think why you didn't tell me, why you deliberately kept me in ignorance. Didn't you know I'd want to share your burden?"

Fanny rubbed her forehead, frowning. "It was all so gradual," she explained. "I didn't realize . . . and he seems so nice . . ."

"Perhaps you thought he was interested in you," Mildred observed, watching her.

It was what Fanny had thought. When she was much younger, before she had given up the idea of marriage, the one or two boys who seemed attracted to her had been large and boisterous, too much like her father, while she had liked gentle, wistful men. She could not understand why Mildred mistrusted Theodore. To Fanny he seemed above reproach: thoughtful and understanding, but rather pathetic, too, needing comfort. She had once—when she thought he might ask her to marry

54

him—even gone so far as to build up the rejection scene in her mind; for of course it was out of the question to think of leaving Lily. In the night she rehearsed how she would word her refusal so as not to hurt his feelings and, though she would hardly admit this to herself, so that he would not give up hope entirely. The picture of herself envied by other women— such a thing had never happened before—of being gossiped about because of a man, perhaps even teased because of his dejection when she refused him, the thought of letters he would write during the winter months, his return the following year to renew the proposal, had buoyed her up and colored her days, but for a very short time. She had accepted the collapse of her dream philosophically, and now even refused to acknowledge that she had been foolish enough to entertain such a fantasy.

"Don't be a damned fool," she muttered, stabbing out her cigarette.

"There's no need to be *insulting*! The question is," Mildred went on reasonably, "how are we to deal with him? I'm sure you realize that he must be gotten rid of, at once."

"I don't see how. You know Lily when she thinks people are interfering."

"Naturally we'll use tact," Mildred said firmly, standing up and brushing off her skirt as if readying herself for battle.

## CHAPTER FOUR

THE DINING ROOM AT HAWKREST HAD A VAULTED CEILING FROM which were suspended two chandeliers that cast an unflattering yellow light on those seated at the table. A row of plates hung around the wall, which was papered in white and gold. Near the head of the table a number of bleached spots stood out on the blue rug. These had once been stains, and the largest was made by a bowl of soup that King Jameson had thrown on the floor in a rage because it did not happen to suit his fancy. A dark splotch on the wall near the china cabinet had been made by a boiled egg which Mrs. Pringle had cooked less than the required four minutes.

The sun had dropped behind the trees in the garden. The curtains were drawn back to let in the cool evening light. During dinner, Isobel's husband telephoned.

"It's nice to be using the dining room again," Fanny remarked. She was filling up gaps in the conversation to prevent herself from listening to what Isobel was saying. "Since Papa's been ill, Lily and I have been eating off trays. It hardly seemed worth the bother of setting the table, just for the two of us."

Mildred bent her head in a listening attitude, her eyes on the hall door. She frowned, not so much at Fanny, whose voice she could shut out, as at the steady stream of racing results coming over Mrs. Pringle's radio in the kitchen. "In the second race, the winner was Prairie Flower, paying six ninety-five; Princess Pat was second; Irish Lass third. The daily double of Galaxy and Prairie Flower paid thirty-nine seventy-five."

"Then if you don't mind being alone, Eliot," Isobel was saying, "I'd like to stay on for a day or so . . . perhaps a week . . . Yes, of course I'll miss you, Eliot . . ."

"I knew I had the double worked out." Mrs. Pringle came in on a strong wave of French perfume—a present from Isobel —to take away the plates. "Galaxy and Prairie Flower. I told Ernie; but he said Princess Pat."

"Did you win?" Fanny asked.

"Win? I lost two dollars. That Ernie and his system. Two dollars down the drain when I could have had a nice little nest egg if I'd used my own common sense."

"Good-by, Eliot. Yes, I promise . . . Good-by."

"I'll fetch the coffee," Mrs. Pringle said, seeing that Isobel had finished her conversation. "How's your husband, dear?" she asked, returning with the tray.

"Poor Eliot!" Isobel sighed and pushed aside her dessert, as if talking with him had spoiled her appetite.

Lily stopped eating. She was wearing the green dress Isobel had given her, but had spoiled the beautiful lines of it by adding a looping necklace of imitation emeralds and dangling earrings to match. Each stone in the necklace was the size of a marble, the earrings slightly larger. The cheap green glass in its tarnished setting gave her an overdressed, burdened appearance. Her pale hair flowed to her shoulders. Her skin looked transparent, ghostly, in the unflattering light. She pushed back her hair with delicate fingers. "He wants you to go home, doesn't he?" she said to Isobel in an accusing voice.

"He never knows what to do with himself, alone," Isobel said.

"I wish you'd stay here with us," Lily said plaintively.

"Perhaps I will, soon."

Fanny looked up, wondering what Isobel meant, then decided that she was merely placating Lily.

"I'm off, girls." Mrs. Pringle paused in the doorway, skewering on her hat. She had rouged her cheeks, given her mouth a dash of lipstick, and changed into a polka-dotted crepe dress. Her ankles bulged over patent-leather pumps. Her day ended at seven, whether the dishes were washed or not. She had her own room at Hawkrest—the old kitchen at the back of the house—but rarely stayed overnight.

"Now I'll have to wash up," Fanny grumbled. She began to gather up the coffee cups, scraping a soggy cigarette butt from Mildred's.

Jessie Hutchins appeared silently on rubber-soled shoes, a carefully arranged look of composure on her face. "I don't want to worry you, girls; but could one of you give me a hand upstairs for a moment?"

57

Mildred jumped up, one hand to her throat. "What is it? Has something happened?"

"Now, it's *nothing*, Mildred!"

"Is he dead?"

"Now, now! It's nothing but a little accident."

"I'll go up," Isobel said after a questioning glance at Fanny. She started for the stairs.

"I think you should call Dr. Randolph, Fanny." Jessie spoke with frightening professional calm. "And Mildred, please don't come up as well as Isobel. Having so many around might excite him."

"I'm the oldest. If anything has happened to him, it's my place—"

"You'd only upset him. I couldn't take the responsibility."

"He is dying!" Mildred dropped back into her chair and covered her face with her hands.

"Now the doctor's out," Fanny reported, slamming down the receiver. "They're trying to locate him."

"I'm not sure he could do anything, anyway," Jessie consoled, from halfway up the stairs. She paused to say over the banister, "Now, girls, *promise* you won't worry!"

"Not worry!" Mildred sat on the edge of a chair in the living room and lit another cigarette, puffing nervously. Automatically, Fanny reached for her knitting as she listened for some indication of activity upstairs. Lily went to the window and threw it open. The sun had just set. The garden and the green wings of dragonflies circling above the grass were touched with rosy light from the western sky. A nighthawk swooped down silently past the pine trees and rose again, then dozens of them appeared at once, until the air was a pattern of swift wings. Beyond the river bank a blue mist dropped away. A shrill chorus of crickets sang monotonously. One cricket, somewhere inside the room, near the fireplace, repeatedly practiced its broken protesting chirp.

The low clock on the table in the corner ticked softly. It gave a startled little gasp, paused, and chimed the half hour, then resumed its hurried whisper. Mildred glanced at it, then at her watch.

"Why should I upset him more than Isobel?"

"Isobel could always manage him."

"It's really your place to be with him, after going through so much."

Fanny, who was thankful to be spared a repetition of last night's ordeal, went on knitting furiously.

"Must we put up with that damned insect?" Mildred demanded.

Lily turned from the window. "It's only a cricket."

"Only? Now we have crickets in the house, on top of everything."

"I'll put it out if it bothers you. It's under the rug." Lily lifted the edge of the rug, and immediately the cricket jumped high in the air and landed near Mildred, who drew her feet up in a panic.

"It won't hurt you, for heaven's sake!" Lily went after the cricket, which jumped again.

"Where . . . ? Where . . . ?" Mildred clutched the arms of her chair and heaved herself sideways.

"It's over here!" Lily's face crinkled mischievously. She caught the cricket between her cupped palms. "It wasn't even near you. See!" She held out her hands, the insect's head poking up between her thumbs.

"Take it away!" Mildred moaned, shrinking back in her chair.

"Put it outside, darling, please," Fanny begged.

Lily went to the window. "You naughty thing!" she said to the cricket in a babyish scolding voice. "You frightened Mildred." She opened her hands. "There, he's gone," she said cheerfully.

"You know I can't stand bugs and creeping things," Mildred complained. "You did that deliberately to frighten me."

"It's gone now," Fanny said pacifically. "Why don't we all have another cup of coffee? Perhaps Lily will make some."

"Of course," Lily agreed. She smiled innocently as she went off to the kitchen.

"She didn't mean to frighten you," Fanny said, depressed by Mildred's tears, which she felt would be better saved for later on.

"It's not that. It's just the worry. Not knowing what's happening . . ."

"He's seventy-nine. We've known for weeks that it's only a matter of time."

"And wondering what should be done afterwards. About the house, and everything. Whether to sell, or . . ."

"Lily and I will have to live somewhere, though we certainly don't need such a big place. But I'd miss this house."

"If you bought a smaller place, it would mean splitting up the furniture."

"And selling some things, I suppose."

"We'd never get what they're worth. Everybody wants modern things nowadays. Of course, there are some things we wouldn't want to keep, even if you stay here."

"Bedroom furniture, perhaps," Fanny said, thinking of her father's brass bed.

"Remember, I'm to have his pearl cuff links. That's already been agreed."

Dr. Randolph let himself in and shambled past them with a brief nod. He was a thin old man with a neck like a turtle's, and pale bloodshot eyes under crooked gray brows. He smelled of brandy. Soon after he had gone upstairs, Isobel came down, and Lily came in from the kitchen with the coffee and some cups on a tray.

"He fell," Isobel explained, pushing back her hair. "Jessie

says he insisted upon getting out of bed, and when she tried to stop him he flew into a rage."

"She could have called one of us. What do we pay her for, except to prevent . . . ?"

"I'm afraid he's in pretty bad shape. A stroke, the doctor says."

Mildred clasped her hands against her forehead. "We sit here doing nothing—!" she moaned.

"Drink your coffee," Fanny urged. "Dr. Randolph will do everything he can."

"Now I know what you've put up with these past weeks," Isobel said to Fanny. "If he dies, he will have killed himself with his senseless tantrums. I almost hoped he would die."

"Your own father!" Mildred gasped.

"He's old and sick. In pain. And not in his right mind any more."

"I don't know how you can be so heartless!" Mildred picked up her handkerchief. "Saying such a thing, when he may be dying at this very minute!" She could not cry without talking, giving reasons or heaping reproaches. "After the way he's pampered you and spoiled you and treated the rest of us sometimes like . . . !" She could not think of a suitable comparison, and in any case she was crying too hard to say more.

She was always a great martyr, Isobel thought. Her sighs and reproaches were meant to point up the cold-heartedness of others. She watched Mildred going through the various stages of distress. A diminishing flow of tears, then the mopping-up, the brave determination to carry on illustrated by a straightening of the shoulders, but with an almost-suppressed catching of the breath to show how difficult this was; then the last sniff, the comforting cigarette, the lipstick out to repair damages.

While this was going on, Fanny knitted steadily, as if pressed for time, and kept her eyes on her work. Lily sat on a low stool with her hands clasped round her knees, regarding Mildred with a faintly suspicious air.

When the doorbell rang, Fanny immediately laid aside her knitting.

"Who can that be?" Mildred wondered. "I suppose it's that man," she remembered, pulling out her lipstick again. "That queer-looking foreigner with the beard. But this is no time to see him." She glanced at Lily, who immediately turned aside and picked up a magazine, pretending to have heard nothing.

Fanny pushed herself up clumsily and brushed off her skirt. She wore a pale twin-sweater set of fine cashmere, a skirt of gray hand-loomed material, one strand of pearls round her neck, and expensive calf oxfords on her feet. It was funny, Isobel thought, how Fanny could spend the money she did on clothes and be so completely lacking in style. She bought all the right things. It was only when she put them on that they assumed the provincial shapeless look usually associated with English women's clothes.

Fanny ushered Theodore into the room and introduced him with gauche briskness. "These are my sisters—Mrs. McKinley, Mrs. Whitmore. This is Mr. Fairfield."

He ought to be in the movies, Isobel thought. He'd make a perfect foreign diplomat. Or a hairdresser, she added, for he reminded her of Lucien, who did her hair. But Lucien's manner was haughty. Theodore's attitude at the moment was one of humble respect. He smiled sadly. He was extremely polite, holding his hat, gloves, and a bouquet of French marigold in both hands, bowing over them, giving an impression of clicking his heels together, though he did not actually do this. The flowers were clumsily put together, with a bit of striped grass wound round their stems, and they looked suspiciously like some Isobel had noticed earlier, growing in a border along the driveway.

He turned to Mildred first, and Isobel noticed an odd thing: Mildred was blushing. Very faintly, but still . . . Fanny did not see this, and neither, presumably, did Lily, who was now leafing through her magazine, and paying no attention to anybody. But Theodore, whose face had begun to brighten with recognition, suddenly assumed a formal expression as he acknowledged the introduction. Queer, Isobel mused. It was almost as if they had met before, as if he were playing along with Mildred in concealing this fact.

Theodore now turned to Isobel, and his gaze for a moment was frankly admiring. She was not displeased. He was really rather appealing, though she herself usually preferred a more masculine type. As she looked at him, she realized why he had reminded her of Lucien. His hair was dyed a deep navy blue, and so were his mustache and little pointed beard. She thought vanity prompted this deception, that his hair was turning gray. His pale face suggested a poet. His hands were white and slender, like the hands of a musician, or someone who did card tricks. His dark-blue suit was neatly pressed, though slightly worn. Isobel, trained by Eliot, whose taste was impeccable, could not help noticing his tie, which was a particularly flashy shade of green with variegated coin dots. In his breast pocket he carried a matching handkerchief folded neatly into three points.

The introductions over, he presented the modest bouquet to Fanny with a deprecatory smile, hardly expecting her to think well of it.

"Oh, thank you," Fanny said dubiously, looking down at it. The room was filled with flowers already: great bunches of roses arranged in bowls, gladiolus in pottery vases on the floor beside the fireplace.

"Your father is better?" He nodded, answering his own question. No one corrected him. "Poor old gentleman. It must be a great relief to you all. I've grown quite fond of your father," he added shyly, as if he were afraid of being thought presumptuous.

That's overdoing it a bit, Isobel thought. He must know the

old man's a perfect tartar. "Won't you sit down?" she suggested, seeing that he would not do so without being asked.

"I'll get a vase," Fanny murmured.

Theodore crossed the room and took a chair near Lily.

"Oh, hello." Lily looked up from her magazine at last.

He gave her a charming smile, asked how she was, complimented her appearance, and finally, in desperation, it seemed, touched on the weather. Lily answered him with the greatest indifference, smothering yawns with the tips of her fingers.

Mildred, noting this, looked at Fanny with a hopeful expression. "Are you visiting St. Charles, Mr. Fairfield?" she inquired.

He turned to her at once, giving the impression that he looked forward to nothing so much as a conversation with her. "Yes, for the past month. I really intended to stay at the Falls —in fact, I did stay there for a week. Then one day, as I was driving through St. Charles, I noticed Mrs. Kinch's place, the Willows, and remembered that some friends of mine from Boston had stayed there last year. The Willitsons, no doubt you remember them," he interposed, glancing at Fanny. "It seemed just what I was looking for. Quiet—and that beautiful view of the river. I made inquiries at once. Fortunately, Mrs. Kinch had a room to spare."

He paused, a look of concern on his face. "You've been crying. Has something upset you?"

The question was so unexpected that Mildred simply stared at him.

"I'm afraid we're all a bit upset tonight," Isobel began.

Mildred raised one hand to her trembling mouth. "Our father is dying!"

Our Father, Isobel thought impatiently. As if she were talking about God.

"I'm so terribly sorry!" Theodore said, rising. He did look genuinely distressed. "If I had known . . ."

"We should have told you at once," Isobel said. "He seemed so much better this afternoon."

"Yes, I was happy to hear that. Is he very ill?"

"I'm afraid so. The doctor's with him now."

Theodore shook his head regretfully. "I can't tell you how sorry I am." He turned to Fanny. "Is there anything I can do?"

Mildred answered, forcing him to turn to her again. "Dr. Randolph is very capable. I'm sure he's doing everything possible."

"I'm quite sure he is," Theodore nodded. He gathered up his hat and gloves. "You must think me heartless, calling at a time like this—"

"Oh, no!" Fanny said quickly.

"I had no idea, of course, that you were going through such an anxious time. I think, if you'll excuse me . . ."

"Oh, don't go," Isobel said. "We need someone to talk to. You can help us take our minds off ourselves. I think we could all stand a drink, don't you, Fanny?"

Mildred said firmly, "I'm sure Mr. Fairfield understands that we want to be alone."

"I do understand," he said with great sincerity, and gave Mildred a comforting half smile that made her look the other way. "No, no, please don't bother," he entreated, as Fanny rose to see him to the door. "Will you promise to telephone me if I can help in any way?"

"Of course."

They listened to his footsteps hurrying down the walk.

"As if he cares whether Papa dies or not!" Mildred exploded resentfully. "It's probably what he's waiting for."

"I think he's rather sweet," Isobel remarked, to antagonize Mildred. "He fascinates me."

"Sweet!" Mildred glared at her. "Good God!"

Lily laid aside her magazine and stared pensively at Mildred. "You don't like him, do you?" she said at last.

"Anyone can see what he *is*!" Mildred said scornfully. "All that bowing and scraping doesn't fool me. I'm surprised you were taken in by him, Fanny. What business had he coming here tonight, intruding on our sorrow?" She caught Fanny's warning frown and stopped. Then, glancing at Lily, she tried to backtrack. "I suppose it was kind of him to offer to help . . ."

But Lily was gazing into space with a faint secret smile.

That's done it, Isobel thought. That's all Lily needs. If Mildred's against him, she's for him. What a fool Mildred is.

"What are they *doing* up there?" Mildred flung one knee over the other, drumming with her fingers on the arm of her chair. Fanny, her hands idle in her lap, sat biting her lips and frowning. Isobel moved to the window and leaned out, breathing the pleasant summer smell of damp leaves and cut grass. The garden was now in darkness. A street lamp, screened behind the laurel bushes, only intensified the shadows.

"Did Dr. Randolph recommend that Jessie Hutchins?" Mildred demanded.

"She's a good nurse," Fanny said.

"I never liked her. At school she was always giggling and talking about boys . . . Telling *me* I'd upset him! I'm going up," Mildred decided suddenly. "It's not her place to say who's to be with him and who isn't."

"I believe she was only trying to spare you," Isobel said. She closed the window and drew the curtains.

"To spare me? I don't know what you mean. He's our father, not hers. What does she care about him? Letting him get out of bed when we pay her to keep him quiet."

"He threw his supper tray on the floor, and while she was trying to clean up the mess, he got hold of his stick and hit her with it. If you had seen him, you would have been upset. You don't take things as calmly as Fanny does, or as I do."

"I *expect* to be upset!" Mildred protested. "What am I here for? Why did I come all the way from New York, except to be with Papa when he's—?" She could not say "dying" again. She went purposefully upstairs.

"She's worse than she used to be," Isobel sighed. "How old is she—fifty? Poor Harry must have a devil of a time with her."

"He always did," Fanny said, then looked conscience-stricken at this disloyalty. "I'll wash the dishes," she decided abruptly, rising.

"Let me . . ." Isobel began.

"No, please. I want to do them."

Isobel relaxed, sensing that Fanny wished to be alone.

What a day! Fanny thought as she piled dishes beside the sink. She worked quickly and efficiently, not conscious of being physically tired. Her mind felt keyed-up, anticipating change, as if she had been traveling for years along a straight familiar way and now suddenly had come to a place where a dozen roads branched off and she could take her choice. While she scraped off the plates and ran hot water into the sink, she tentatively explored one or two of these roads. Sell the house? Nobody wanted old houses any more; and though Hawkrest had been kept in perfect condition and modernized from time to time—the bathrooms gleamed with pink and green tile, a button in the hall regulated the furnace—it was probably too big and hard to manage for the average family. People wanted ranch bungalows with picture windows and no doors between the rooms, little birdcage houses with no privacy. Like living in a shop window.

Selling the house would mean disposing of all the lovely furnishings: the chairs in the dining room, the rugs, the old china pieces that were never used but displayed in a graceful glass cabinet, the *little* things, like tapestry footstools, inlaid boxes, vases, figurines, even the quartz paperweight in the study under the stairs where her father had once conducted his profitable but illicit business.

67

She could not bear to see the house in the hands of strangers, who would neglect the garden and paint the hand-rubbed paneling in the hall. Perhaps it was a bit large for two persons —three, counting Pringle—but they could shut off some of the rooms upstairs. Perhaps the north bedroom. Or else sell the brass bed and all the furnishings in that room and turn it into a den. She saw herself and Lily sitting there in cozy comfort on winter afternoons, looking down through the trees to the river. Lily's apathetic reception of Theodore, just now, had made her hopeful. Perhaps all our troubles are coming to an end at once, she thought on a wave of optimism.

When she had dried the last dish and rinsed out the towels, she wiped down the stove and the pale-blue counters, then looked around for something else to do while she waited for word from upstairs. The rosy sheen of copper pots hanging over the stove seemed a bit subdued, so she took them down one by one and polished them. She had not finished this task when Mildred came in. Fanny saw at once that something had happened.

"The doctor has gone." Mildred sank into a chair and supported her forehead with her hand. She closed her eyes as if exhausted.

Fanny placed the pot she was holding on the sink and wiped her hands on her apron. "If it had to be . . ." she began. She was no good at saying these things, but felt it would comfort Mildred to hear them. "He was seventy-nine," she went on, getting the hang of it now. "He was old. He had lived his life. In a way, it's a mercy he was taken like this, before he suffered too much."

"But he's *not*—!" Mildred cried, opening her eyes.

Fanny sat down. Both stared dejectedly at the wall.

"It's so unfair!" Mildred broke the long silence. "Making him live on, when it only means prolonging his suffering. When he can't *want* to live."

Fanny was silent.

68

"The doctor says he may live for years if he is cared for properly. *Years!*"

"But it was only yesterday that Dr. Randolph said he was dying!"

"That old fool! If he hadn't come meddling!" Mildred was too upset to care what she said.

"Have you told the others?"

"I came straight to you. After all, it's you who have borne the burden all this time."

"Well!" Fanny heaved herself up. "We had better get some sleep. Will you tell the girls? And when I've finished here, I'll bring you up some aspirin." She began methodically to hang up the pots.

But as soon as Mildred had gone, she leaned her head against the cupboard and burst into tears.

## CHAPTER FIVE

WHEN MISS ANSTICE, THE REGULAR NIGHT NURSE, ARRIVED AT twelve, the house was quiet. A dim light burned in the downstairs hall. Jessie Hutchins was waiting in the sickroom.

"Am I glad to see you! That substitute they sent over last night! Didn't know beans. Fanny had to stay up half the night. Well, now, did you have a nice weekend? How's the folks?"

"They're fine." Miss Anstice glanced at the sleeping figure on the bed. "He's still with us, I see. How did things go today?"

"Oh, Lord!" Jessie sighed eloquently.

"Bad, huh?"

"A stroke," Jessie explained. "I thought he was done for,

69

but there he is, sleeping it off. You just can't kill him. One good thing—he won't be getting out of bed for a while. Whole right side paralyzed. Voice gone, too. You know how some people get with a stroke."

Miss Anstice picked up the patient's slack hand and let it drop again.

"He'll sleep for maybe a couple of hours," Jessie said.

"Are the others asleep?"

Jessie nodded. "You want to see if there's anything to eat in the kitchen?"

"All right to leave the old boy alone, I suppose?"

"Oh, sure. What can he do if he does wake up? He can't hardly make a sound, and I'm damn sure he won't be getting up." Jessie jerked up a corner of the sheet, which was trailing on the floor.

In the kitchen, over tuna-fish sandwiches and a pot of coffee, they settled themselves for a chat. Jessie had slept until long past noon, and now felt wide-awake, gossipy. Since the death of her husband she hated night time, going home to her empty house.

"Did the others come?" Miss Anstice asked. "The sisters?"

"Oh, God, yes. All fuss and feathers, ready to weep over the corpse. They might as well go home. He's got nine lives."

"What are they like—the sisters?"

"You don't know the family, do you? You haven't been here long—in St. Charles, I mean?" Jessie leaned back and propped her feet on a chair.

"I've heard stories."

"Ha! Who hasn't?"

"Somebody was saying about the old man—the King, as everybody calls him."

"That old reprobate! Oh, God, I forgot his medicine! Every hour on the hour he's supposed to have three drops of that new stuff. He's half an hour overdue."

"I'll give him a double dose at one o'clock."

70

"Lord, you'll kill him! Old Randolph warned me to be careful about measuring. Three drops to half an ounce of water."

"Think I should go up and give it to him?" Miss Anstice set down her cup reluctantly.

"Never mind. You'd have to wake him up. He'd probably start fussing. Much better to let him sleep, don't you think?"

Miss Anstice nodded and reached for the coffee pot. "Was he as bad as people say?"

"He was a lecherous old goat. You know what he used to do? After his wife died, he used to keep a room at the Frontier Hotel, and half the women in town used to go traipsing up there. Young girls—he liked big fat country girls; trollops is all they were. Married women, too. I could name half a dozen that you wouldn't *believe* . . . ! Makes you sick, doesn't it? The *look* of him. If I couldn't get anything better than that, I'd go without."

"It takes all kinds . . ."

"And, Lord, what a temper. He was bad enough before his wife died. Did you know that he once shot a man—right in this house—that he caught carrying on with his wife? Yes," Jessie nodded at Miss Anstice's wide-eyed stare, "practically killed him. Of course, if he'd gone around killing every man she carried on with, he'd have had his hands full. It was after she died he really turned into a tartar. Look!" She pulled up her sleeve. "See that? It doesn't show much now, but wait until morning—it'll be black and blue. That's where he hit me tonight. He's nuts, of course," she added comfortably, reaching for another sandwich. "Has been ever since Hazel was killed."

She took a bite and continued with her mouth full. "They're all queer, if you ask me. Fanny's not bad, but stiff . . . you know . . . not what you'd call friendly. Of course, she's had a hard life."

"Is that his wife—the picture in his room? She must have been quite pretty."

"Well, people said she was. I myself could never see it. Sexy-looking, maybe, and the way she got herself up you'd have to be deaf, dumb, and blind not to notice her. Oh, she had a great opinion of herself. She thought every man in town was in love with her." Jessie's eyes glittered. "It's her fault that Fanny's an old maid. What chance did poor Fanny have when she was around? She was always after the girls—Mildred and Fanny—about not getting married, and every man that showed up around here she'd start making eyes at herself. Even Harry. It took him five years to make up his mind about Mildred, simply because Hazel had him bedazzled. He didn't marry Mildred until after Hazel killed herself, when Mildred was thirty-one."

"You mean Hazel was in love with him?"

"Love? She didn't know the meaning of the word. No, I mean she was always rolling her eyes at him, oh, Harry darling this and Harry darling that; oh, Harry, you're so clever, would you do this that and the other thing for helpless old me? What man wouldn't be flattered? They're all human. And you can say what you like, Mildred was the damnedest prude I ever saw. If a boy so much as looked at her, she acted as if he was out to rape her. I just can't imagine her getting into bed with Harry, but she must have, because they had a child, a boy; died some years back. Harry was real cute when he was younger," Jessie went on wistfully. "He had an awful crush on me. That was before he ever thought of coming here, of course, before I married Albert. I married practically out of the cradle," she said, looking her companion shamelessly in the eye, remembering that she had been past twenty-six and really worried about being left on the shelf when Albert finally proposed. "That's one reason Mildred dislikes me. She knows Harry asked me first. I was going with Albert at the time, as well as with Harry, and like a fool picked the wrong one. Harry was working in the bank, and you know what they make: hardly enough to feed themselves. Albert was making three times as much laying bricks, so . . ." Jessie spread her hands helplessly. "If I'd known

I was going to be left like this, without a cent of insurance at my age, I'd have thought twice." She gazed sadly into space.

"You'll marry again," Miss Anstice comforted.

"Yes, I see myself!" Jessie thrust up one leg and disconsolately eyed her swollen ankles. "Some rich executive type, no doubt. They're hanging around in droves, waiting for my answer . . . If only he hadn't waited so *long*," she continued bitterly. "Ten years ago I was still passable. Then I had all that trouble with my Fallopian tubes, and my operation . . . And just when I thought there was no more need to keep up the struggle—dieting and trying to keep young—then Albert died and left me like this."

"There's worse things than being single."

"You'd say that, naturally."

Miss Anstice flushed. She was past thirty, a plain, flat-chested girl with large teeth.

"It's different for anyone who's been used to attention," Jessie went on cruelly.

Miss Anstice decided to pass this off with a careless laugh, since she was anxious to hear more of the Jamesons.

"What about the other sister?" she prompted. "The one that came on the afternoon train."

"Isobel? She's settled down *some*," Jessie conceded grudgingly. "It must be a great relief to the others, and to her husband's family. The Whitmores weren't too pleased when Eliot married Isobel, though God knows he was old enough to think for himself. She'd already divorced two husbands, see, and then of course her father being what he is. The Whitmores are *the* people around here. Old man Whitmore—dead now—just about owned the whole town. The old lady's still living—you know that big stone house past the hospital, with the high wall in front of it?—but I haven't noticed her rushing over to greet Isobel with open arms. Never even called up, as far as I know. Isobel's been married to Eliot Whitmore for ten years now, and people *say* she's behaving real well. She wouldn't dare do anything else. If you ask me, she's lucky to get a man like Eliot after the life she's led, though I wouldn't care, myself . . ." Jessie paused thoughtfully. "He's quite a bit older," she explained, "and kind of set in his ways. But pretty well fixed, from all accounts. Not that she *needed* money. Makes you sick, doesn't it, to think of them all living in the lap of luxury when you consider the old man was nothing but a crook. Isobel's only got the one child: a daughter by her first husband. The daughter's married now, and *she's* got a child, though she can't be more than eighteen or nineteen."

"She doesn't look old enough to be a grandmother—Isobel, I mean."

"She's not bad-looking. More sexy-looking than pretty, wouldn't you say? She takes after her mother. I don't know where Lily gets her looks."

"What about her?"

"Well, Lily . . ." Jessie tapped her forehead solemnly with one finger.

"Yes . . . ?" Miss Anstice picked up the coffee pot and filled Jessie's cup, then settled back with her elbows on the table, her eyes expectant.

"You noticed that scar on her face? She got that when her mother was killed—an automobile accident. Lily was almost killed, too. She was in bed for months, never left the house for three years. She hasn't been quite right since."

"You mean she's really touched in the head?"

"They won't admit it. I happen to know the whole story because a friend of mine nursed Lily after the accident."

"She looks a little—oh, vacant, sometimes."

"They never let her go back to school after the accident. Hardly let her out anywhere. I used to drop in sometimes to see the girls, and I kept my eyes open. They'd *watch* Lily every minute. She did act queer, sometimes, too."

"In what way? What did she do?"

74

"Oh, moody, unpredictable. One minute she'd be sweet and loving to everybody, and the next, when anyone spoke to her, she'd pretend not to hear. It was uncanny, in a way, how she'd sort of go off in a world of her own. Did you ever notice her eyes—that sort of blind stare? Well, Mildred was married by this time; she married Harry shortly after the accident, before they suspected Lily wasn't right. She was living in a flat down near the bank—this was before Harry was transferred to New York—but she spent half her time here. That old cat Pringle was here, too; she's been here since the year one. (She drinks like a fish, did you know that?) The three of them were always on tenterhooks, as if they were afraid of what Lily might do next. I don't know how bad she really was; whether they imagined . . . you know, because they were *afraid* she wasn't right, they may have interpreted her actions differently."

"Yes, I see." Miss Anstice considered this.

"I think myself Lily was just plain spoiled, and who wouldn't be? Anything she wanted, *anything*, Fanny and that Pringle would rush out and buy it. She knew they'd give her the moon if she asked for it. And if something didn't just suit her, they were all apologies and promises, Lily dear this and Lily dear that. Of course she was bored; she didn't have any friends her own age, or lessons to take up her time, so naturally . . . She kind of turned against Mildred—no doubt she had good reason. Mildred's enough to get anyone's goat. I think myself it would have been better for all concerned if she'd kept her nose out of things; but no, she had to be running over here every whipstitch, telling them how to manage Lily, bossing everybody around." Jessie paused to finish her coffee. "And you know, Lily was such a pretty little thing, rather appealing, with that transparent skin and yellow hair. She still is, though she doesn't look *natural* to me. I mean, she reminds me of a china doll or something."

"Mmm." Miss Anstice pursed her lips judiciously. "How old is she?"

"Lord!" Jessie did some mental arithmetic. "She must be twenty-eight now, though you'd never guess. Lucky she doesn't have to work and worry and wear herself out like the rest of us. She certainly doesn't look heartless, does she? I mean, you'd never dream of her doing anything cruel. But do you know— I happen to know this for a fact—one time when Mildred came home from New York she brought her dog, a nasty little Pomeranian. It was always yapping around, nipping at people's heels, except when Mildred was cuddling it. Well, naturally, Lily hated the thing. So do you know what she did one day?" Jessie's eyes widened. "She picked that creature up and threw it over the garden wall into the river. Without a word of a lie, that's exactly what she did! Fanny saw her."

Miss Anstice shuddered. "Did somebody tell you all these things?" she inquired tactlessly. "I wondered . . ." she added, seeing her mistake.

Jessie gave her a hostile stare. "It just so happens that I was nursing the old man when that happened—the time he broke his leg."

"Oh, I see . . ."

"You may have noticed I'm more observant than the average person, that I understand people better. I flatter myself that I have a pretty good knowledge of psychology." Jessie tilted her head proudly. "I happen to have read the complete condensed works of Sigmund Freud." She waited for a minute, then said coldly, "Perhaps you think I'm making up all this about the Jamesons?"

"Oh, no, of course not! I was just curious to know . . . I didn't think *they'd* mention anything outside. But naturally, if you were here . . ." Miss Anstice smiled disarmingly.

"Naturally," Jessie agreed haughtily. She was enjoying herself too much to break off her narrative in the middle. "Where was I? Oh, yes—about the dog. Well, as I said, Fanny *saw* her do it, but . . . and here's the funny part . . . Fanny never let on to anyone. Never opened her mouth when Mildred discovered the dog was missing; even went around the garden pretending to hunt for it, and helped Mildred compose an ad for the lost and found in next day's paper. She was protecting Lily, see? I never let on, either, though I'd seen the whole thing from an upstairs window. I wouldn't give Mildred the satisfaction, and besides, I figured the least I could do for poor Fanny was to keep my mouth shut. As for Lily . . . this just shows how bad she is . . . two hours later she couldn't even remember what she'd done. She had absolutely no memory of it."

"Lord!" Miss Anstice breathed.

"Makes you feel kind of sorry for her, doesn't it?" Jessie mused.

"So what else did she do?" Miss Anstice prompted after a time. "Did other people know she was queer? What did people think?"

"Well, as I told you, the family watched her like a hawk, never even allowed her to walk downtown by herself. Most people thought she was a little odd, but the world's so full of crackpots these days that nobody notices. We all knew that she'd been ill for a long time after the accident, that she was still delicate, and we made allowances."

"If they didn't let her make friends, how did she happen to marry? She was married, wasn't she?"

"I'm coming to that. Are you going to eat this?" Jessie eyed the last sandwich.

"Go ahead." Miss Anstice pushed the plate toward her. "There's more coffee, too."

"Oh, God, I shouldn't! What the hell, I can starve tomorrow."

"I don't think you're overweight. How'd you like to be a beanpole like me?"

Jessie glanced over her cup at the bony chest, the thin, unattractive face opposite her, and was comforted. She looked down at her own breasts. Really just a nice handful, she thought.

"So, Lily . . . ?" Miss Anstice laced her fingers together, leaning forward.

Jessie swept the last crumbs on the plate into a pile between her fingers and popped them into her mouth. "So when she was about sixteen or so, she got out of hand. They couldn't keep an eye on her *every* minute, and she got so she'd sneak off downtown by herself. Naturally, the boys noticed her. Well, the first thing the family knew, here was Lily inviting these characters up to the house to visit her—boys she'd met on street corners. Fanny and Pringle almost had a fit, but they couldn't simply order these boys out of the house. No telling how Lily would react if they did that. No, they had to be subtle about it." Jessie was so warming to her story that she began to invent what she supposed had happened. "They had to be nice to Lily's friends, at the same time freezing them out. Mildred came running over every night to help. They froze out half a dozen before Lily twigged. Then she cut loose with a few tricks of her own: sneaking out her bedroom window and down the porch roof, running off to meet them. You can imagine what went on—the tearing around in jalopies, parking in dark lanes. Oh, Lily went to hell with herself, believe you me! Late at night you'd see poor Fanny driving around the country roads looking for her, coaxing her out of cheap dives . . ."

"Over-sexed," Miss Anstice hazarded.

"No, that's the funny part. It wasn't sex. It was just plain contrariness. I'm not saying she didn't go the whole hog, mind, but it wasn't because she couldn't get along without, like some women: her mother, for instance. It's my belief she doesn't like men. No, it was just plain cussedness, and whose fault was it? If they'd allowed her to live a normal life, it never would have happened. They must have begun to wonder, too, if they'd been doing the right thing, for after a while they took her to this doctor—psychiatrist—over in Buffalo. (Nobody

78

knows this but me, naturally; they didn't tell anybody.) He must have advised them to give her more rope; it stands to reason the life they wanted her to lead wasn't natural—cooped up like the princess in the tower . . . So, anyway, Fanny arranged for her to have lessons with one of the high-school teachers—she hadn't been to school since the accident, you know, only what they'd taught her themselves—and taught her to drive the car, too; kind of encouraged her to do things for herself. See, the idea was to keep her so busy she wouldn't have time for nonsense, but it was too late. The funny part was that for months at a time she'd be meek and mild, just staying at home every night or going to the movies with Fanny; then, bang, off she'd go on another tear. Do you know that once she stayed away for two days, and Fanny finally tracked her down to this cheap hotel in Buffalo, exhausted, without a cent, deserted by this creature she'd gone there with—a traveling salesman, I believe."

"My God!"

"My God is right. Mildred and Harry had moved to New York by this time, so poor Fanny had to bear the whole burden. She and Pringle. They didn't even tell Mildred, which in my opinion was a wise thing, considering how Mildred would probably have come rushing home, raising a fuss. I happen to know the whole story because they kept Lily in bed for two days and got me in to nurse her after they brought her home. The story they gave *me* was that she'd caught a chill; but I kept my ears open. So you see Fanny hasn't had an easy time of it. And all this while, too, the old man was rampaging around, adding to her misery. He didn't give a damn about Lily—too busy with his own affairs. Of course, old Pringle stuck by, through thick and thin. I don't know what Fanny would have done without her."

"You never know how the other half lives."

"You can say *that* again!"

"You'd never dream, to look at Lily . . ."

"I know what you mean. She looks like an angel, sometimes. It just goes to show that appearances are deceiving. It's kind of pathetic, though . . ." Jessie shook her head.

"What about her husband? Where did she meet him? Was he a local man?"

"He was a drifter. I doubt if he ever said where he came from. He worked in Sweeney's garage. Lily was pretty cagey about him—Joe Nicholson his name was. The family didn't suspect a thing until she turned up missing one night, and the next day they got a letter saying she was married to him, staying at the Honeymoon Motel over at the Falls. Fanny high-tailed after them, of course, and brought Lily home that very morning. But she couldn't get rid of Nicholson that easy. He followed Lily back, all set to live on her money, and moved right in with the family. He was here—oh, I'd say three weeks before they got him out. I used to drop in occasionally to see how things were going. There he'd be with his feet up on their best upholstered chairs, dropping ashes on the rug, drinking the old man's liquor. I have an idea it was the King who drove Nicholson away in the end; perhaps he staged so many tantrums he *scared* him away. Of course, Lily could hardly stand the sight of him herself by this time. She's like that, you know, very fickle. Or—I couldn't swear to this—it may be that Fanny *paid* Nicholson to get out. She wanted Lily to herself, see? Someone to mother. She'd thought up a good excuse for being an old maid. I honestly think that Fanny believes now she turned down half a dozen proposals because she had to take care of Lily."

"Did anyone ever want to marry her?"

"I never heard of it if they did . . . Well, they booted Nicholson out at last, but it was a long time before they got enough evidence for a divorce. Mildred had this detective agency in New York working on it. So, anyway"—Jessie scratched her head and yawned—"they got the evidence at last. So that was the end of him."

"Queer . . ." Miss Anstice murmured. "I see her around with that man who's staying at the Willows."

"Isn't he the cute thing?" Jessie shivered deliciously. "How'd you like to be tickled by that beard?"

Miss Anstice ignored the question. "Do you think she'll marry him?"

"Not if the girls can stop her, she won't."

"I should think all they'd have to do would be to tell him she's not quite right. That'd scare him off."

"They won't do that. They'd never admit to anybody that there's anything wrong with Lily. I doubt if they'll even admit it to themselves. Don't ask me why. Pride, maybe. It's a damned shame, though, a nice man like that. Somebody ought to tell him," Jessie said grimly, wondering what Theodore would say if *she* warned him. Would he turn to her for sympathy? She stared at her watch for some minutes before she realized what time it said; then her face froze. "My God, we've forgotten the old man again! It's ten after one."

Miss Anstice scowled at her watch as if it had betrayed her. She held it up to her ear, shook it, and examined it again. "Well . . ." she sighed. "I suppose I'd better go up and give the old billy-goat his medicine. Three drops to a half ounce of water?"

"That's right. The directions are printed on that sheet of paper on the wall over the table. I stuck that up for the girls. Every hour he's supposed to get it."

"See you tomorrow night, then, if he hangs on that long." Miss Anstice went up the stairs, yawning.

Jessie had left her battered little car on the driveway near the front door. As she climbed in and started the motor, she thought how lonely everything looked—not a light showing in any house. Dark shadows across the lawn were faintly menacing. A cat prowling under the hedge made her jump. She hated all the wives who were safe at home, in warm beds with husbands who, unlike Albert, had been considerate enough to remain alive.

"He never gave a thought to me," she said aloud, dreading the return to her empty house, the night silences filled with imagined scuttlings, looming shadows. Tears of self-pity filled her eyes. "To be left alone, at my time of life, when a woman needs someone!"

## CHAPTER SIX

"SO THE OLD BASTARD'S FOOLED US AGAIN," MRS. PRINGLE SAID to the night nurse, who was eating breakfast. "That's twice he's got us worked up over nothing. Perhaps the third time . . ."

"I don't know what's keeping him alive," Miss Anstice marveled.

"Spite, that's what. Anybody with common consideration would have died long ago and got it over with. Not him!"

"He has a terrible temper."

"Temper! You haven't seen anything. Before he took sick, he kept things hopping around here, I can tell you. Ranting all over the house at the least thing."

"He won't rant again, after last night," Miss Anstice said with satisfaction.

"Lord, I *heard*—! Is it true that he can't speak a word?"

"Oh, he makes mumbling noises. Nothing that makes sense."

"Well, that's something. We won't have to listen to him, at least. He's helpless now, too, is he? It looks like the beginning of the end, wouldn't you say?"

"Not necessarily. Doctor says he may last for years."

"No!" Mrs. Pringle stared, aghast.

"Doctors always say that." Miss Anstice plunged her fork into a fried egg, spreading the yolk about evenly. "And of course there's a possibility that he *will*. I had a patient once lasted seven years, absolutely paralyzed; had to be given a liquid diet through a tube."

"My God!" Mrs. Pringle sat down. "And we've got to put up with that for maybe seven years?"

"In the end, he'll probably die of old age."

"He's old enough to die of that now." Mrs. Pringle began to enumerate the extra work in store for her. "Running up and down stairs, fetching and carrying . . . I'll give my notice. I'd have quit long ago except the girls needed me. But this is too much."

"Doctor *could* be wrong," Miss Anstice comforted. "If you want my opinion, I don't think the old man will last the week. Though I hate to say it, it will be a blessing if he does go. I don't think his mind will ever be right again."

Mrs. Pringle, glimpsing a ray of hope, brightened a bit. "He was always a little—you know—" She tapped her head.

"Does it run in the family?" Miss Anstice asked, greatly interested.

Mrs. Pringle looked sharply at her. Are you trying to be snoopy, or what? she asked silently. "Well, Mildred . . ." she offered conversationally as a diversion. "You haven't met her, have you, dear? Mind, I'm not saying for a minute that she's . . . but bad-tempered! Always carrying on. Nothing's ever done right for her. To give the devil his due, I think it's nothing more nor less than the change of life right now. Some women get funny."

"My mother used to cry," Miss Anstice said. "One of the girls in town was telling me about Lily . . ."

"Was she, now?" Mrs. Pringle said pleasantly.

"She looks rather—different. I just wondered . . . Does she

83

often go for walks this early? I heard her go out this morning." Miss Anstice paused. Receiving no enlightenment, she gave a disappointed laugh and added, "I wouldn't mind being different, myself—all that money."

"No danger of them starving to death," Mrs. Pringle conceded.

"How did Mr. Jameson make his money? Somebody said real estate."

"Real estate!" Mrs. Pringle hooted. She folded her arms more comfortably and propped her elbows on the table, for this was a subject she was prepared to discuss, and had discussed many times over drinks with her friends. Her loyalty to the girls—excluding Mildred—was unwavering, but she had never considered gossiping about their father a disservice to them. "You're not a local girl, are you, dear?" she asked. "I thought not."

"Then he wasn't in real estate? Somebody said he had an office on Main Street."

"So he had; but if he took in more than a thousand a year there . . . No, dear." Mrs. Pringle smiled, enjoying this. "He had money when he came to St. Charles over thirty years ago. Some money, that is. Don't ask me how he made it. To hear him talk you'd think he was born rich. But after he came here he made a fortune on the river."

"I don't think I understand," Miss Anstice said, laying down her fork.

I've an idea you know more than you're letting on, Mrs. Pringle thought, eying her. If you've been in St. Charles two months and never heard how King Jameson made his money, then you must be deaf. But as long as you want to play innocent . . . "Look, come here to the window a minute, dear. Now, see the river down there, with the international border line running right up the middle? Well, of course you can't actually see the border line, but it's there. And the summer-house on the edge of the bank?"

"Yes . . . ?"

"We don't use the summerhouse nowadays. Does it strike you funny the way it's built so near the edge, with that old butternut tree growing right up through it, sort of bolstering it so it can't fall over the cliff?"

"I never really noticed it before."

"Hah, that's just it. Nobody ever does notice it. Looks pretty innocent sitting there, doesn't it? Just an old summerhouse—weeds growing up all around it, and the bushes hiding what's beyond. But step inside and you'll see that it's built right on a jog in the cliff—a little cove, practically hidden from the river until you're right on top of it, and big enough to wedge a boathouse in. There *is* a boathouse down at the bottom of the cove, and steps zigzagging down to it from the summerhouse."

"For heaven's sake!" Miss Anstice craned her neck.

"I've never been down—catch me risking my neck on those steps! It gives me the willies just to *look*—straight down—like looking into a well. That's where he kept his boat: the *Lilybell*."

Miss Anstice glanced over her shoulder, her eyebrows raised.

"If you were a local girl, you'd know all about the *Lilybell*. A gray launch—she was gray then, he painted her white later on—the finest boat money could buy. She's still down there; falling to pieces, no doubt. A crying shame when you consider what she cost. *He* hasn't been down to the boathouse for years. Too fat to climb the steps. Well, I suppose he figured he got his money's worth out of her . . ." Mrs. Pringle paused. One of these days she must ask Ernie to go down and have a look at the *Lilybell*, see what kind of shape she was in.

"What do you mean, his money's worth?"

"Well, Lord, I thought you knew. In prohibition days he used to do a roaring business shipping contraband across the border. Every night they'd go shuttling back and forth. The cases of whiskey! It'd make your mouth water."

"But didn't anybody—? I mean, wasn't it against the law?"

"Depends on how you look at it. The way *he* looked at it, the Americans wanted whiskey, and he supplied it. Those were the days!" Mrs. Pringle sighed. "Then, of course, they got in that repeal or whatever they called it. Things were never the same after that, though he still made money, bringing in stuff the Canadians wanted and taking across stuff the Americans wanted. What he should have done was quit as soon as he'd made his pile, before that repeal took all the respectability out of it. But, no, he couldn't be content."

"I don't see anything respectable about *smuggling*."

"We don't generally use words like that around here," Mrs. Pringle said with fine restraint.

"I should have thought the police . . ."

"The police! Hah!" This statement was not clarified, though Miss Anstice waited.

"Were you here then?" she asked after a moment.

"I've been here since the family moved to St. Charles. Mrs. Jameson, the younger girls' mother, was my best friend," Mrs. Pringle said proudly. "Naturally, I don't *have* to work. I only stay on to keep the girls company, since they consider me one of the family. Ernie used to work for the old B. too. Half the men in town did, as far as that goes, but Ernie was one of his top men."

"I shouldn't think you'd want to tell people," Miss Anstice said virtuously. "After all, it was against the law."

"Oh, the law!" Mrs. Pringle snapped her fingers. "If the government's going to think up these damned tariffs and what not, they'll get what they deserve. They make me sick, with their customs officers and prying. Why, only last month I took the bus over to Buffalo to pick up a few things: some nice cotton undies and a hat. You know the price they want for cottons on this side. Well, coming back: 'Got anything to declare?' this customs officer asks me. I looked him straight in the face. 'Not a thing,' I said. 'Mind coming inside?' he asks me. What could I do? So what have they got inside but this woman. 'I'm very sorry,' she says, so bloody polite I could have hit her, 'but I'll have to ask you to take your clothes off.' Was I flabbergasted! Take my clothes off in front of a strange woman! I was never so humiliated in my life. My mother used to say to me, 'Daisy, always keep your underwear mended, in case of accidents,' but . . ." Mrs. Pringle shrugged helplessly. "To get back to this woman. 'What's this hat doing inside your brazoo?' she asks me. (It was my old one.) 'It just so happens I always carry an extra hat in case of rain,' I told her. 'And I suppose you always wear three pairs of bloomers?' I could have murdered her. Me standing there without a stitch. 'Can I help it if my behind gets cold?' I said. August, mind, ninety in the shade, but I could be as snippy as she was. Well, the upshot was they made me pay duty, even on the hat, though I swore up and down I'd bought it three months ago. Wouldn't take my word for it!" Mrs. Pringle said bitterly. "And cigarettes. I forgot to tell you. I had them inside my girdle. So what can you do if the blasted government's going to treat you like that? It ruined my whole day, I can tell you."

"You could have declared everything in the first place," Miss Anstice reminded.

"That's just what I couldn't do, with this law saying you can only bring back one lot every four months. I'd been over the week before to buy sheets. I'd declared those, like a fool. What I should have done is stuffed them in my girdle and walked right past. They'd have thought I was pregnant."

Miss Anstice looked doubtful, but said nothing. Mrs. Pringle would never see fifty-five again.

"Them and their damned tariffs! Always going on about being friendly with our neighbors to the south, as they put it, cementing relations and all that; and won't let us do a little friendly shopping."

"What did you mean when you said he should have quit—Mr. Jameson, I mean?"

"Listen to her, letting on she doesn't know!"

"Well, I did hear something . . . I didn't like to mention . . ."

"Why not? *He's* not ashamed of it. What if he did spend six months in the county jail? Politics is all it was. It wouldn't have happened in prohibition time. Why, he had the chief of police working for him then."

"No!"

"You needn't look so scandalized. Nothing wrong with making an honest living."

"If you call that *honest*!"

"Look, dear, let me give you a little advice. You won't get anywhere talking like that around here. Calling people dishonest when all they're doing is taking advantage of opportunities. There's some narrow-minded bigots in this town might look down on it, but the ones with brains know which side their bread is buttered on. If the government wants to provide the butter, who's fool enough to complain? My God, the way the government goes around robbing people; that finance minister or whatever they call him that they got in there now, with his hands in everybody's pockets, passing the hat every time I make a dollar at the races, even—you call that honest?"

"I was only thinking—"

"It don't pay to think too much," Mrs. Pringle warned darkly. "That's the trouble with people nowadays. I was only telling you about the old man because I thought you'd be interested, but if you're going to quibble about trifles . . ." She turned her back and began to stack dishes in the sink.

"No, really . . ." Miss Anstice was apologetic. "I didn't *mean* anything. It was just—well—it struck me kind of funny, that's all."

"I fail to see the funny side of it, myself. But everybody to his own opinion, as the saying goes. Now, where was I when you interrupted?"

"You were telling about Mr. Jameson going to prison."

"Lord, it was only the county jail! As I said, it would never have happened in prohibition time. This was afterwards. They caught him on the road with a shipment of goods. Naturally, since he had friends on the force, they never found out how he got the shipment across the river. They never found the *Lilybell*, though half the town could have told them where to look if they'd had a mind. Poor Fanny almost died of shame, though there was no *need* for her to, as I told her at the time."

"I should think she *would* be ashamed. I'd die, myself."

"It's all in the way you look at it. As I said at the time, the girls can't be held responsible for what their father does. It's no disgrace to *them*. And besides, it was nothing but politics. It wasn't as if he'd done something to be ashamed of. He kept right on with his business while he was in jail—catch a little thing like that stopping him! But shortly afterwards he decided to retire. He painted the *Lilybell* white and fixed her up as a pleasure boat. Used to go cruising down the river to Youngstown and places, all decked out with flags like Commodore Vanderbilt."

"Well, all I can say, I'm glad he's not my father. And think of them living in this big house, in the lap of luxury, on what amounts to stolen money."

"I'm sure I don't know what you mean by stolen money." Mrs. Pringle's eyes had a glint.

"Good heavens, after what you've just told me—!"

"I wouldn't go casting aspersions if I was you, dear," Mrs. Pringle said with dangerous calm. "There now!" she exclaimed, as the door opened and Lily came in carrying an untidy handful of wildflowers. "Been for a nice walk, have you, honeybun?"

"I must go." Miss Anstice buttoned on her cape.

"Yes, it's past your bedtime," Mrs. Pringle agreed with a minimum of sarcasm, holding the door open. She was certain that Miss Anstice had slept through the entire night without interruption.

"The way they train nurses nowadays!" she grumbled to

Lily. "Giving them college educations and God knows what. In my day a nurse knew her place. It didn't take a college education to teach them how to empty slops and make beds. Now they got eight-hour shifts and, oh, my, no, they can't soil their pretty hands carrying a bedpan to the toilet. They cover it with a nice clean cloth and leave it for other people to do. Well, now!" she went on in a more cheerful tone, "What have you been up to this morning, ducky?"

Lily shook her hair back from her forehead and placed her flowers—loosestrife and blue chicory among tendrils of vetch—in a water glass. She was dressed like a gypsy this morning, in a printed cotton skirt and scarlet blouse, with jangling bracelets on each thin arm. "Nothing much," she said. "I went for a walk."

"That's nice; work up a good appetite for breakfast." Mrs. Pringle nodded. "Went by yourself, I suppose?"

Lily looked up with a teasing expression. "You are a nosy old thing!" she said, throwing her arms round Mrs. Pringle's neck. "Who did you think I was with?"

So that's your mood for today, Mrs. Pringle thought, returning the hug. Now, I wonder . . . This mood of affectionate teasing was one Lily adopted when she was planning to go against someone, was set on having her own way. Now who, Mrs. Pringle wondered, was she preparing to balk today? Mildred was the most likely candidate. Had Mildred been sticking her nose into things already, interfering where she had no business to?

Lily leaned over the table, pushing her little bouquet around in the glass, trying to arrange it better; but the stems were broken, and the leaves were crushed where she had held them. When she pulled out a spray of vetch, long tendrils caught on the other flowers, spilling the whole bunch onto the table. She pushed them aside, exasperated.

"Here, sweetie, let me . . ." Mrs. Pringle said placatingly. She rearranged the flowers in the glass and placed them in the center of the table. "Now, isn't that pretty? If you had your little paint box, you could make a lovely picture for Fanny's room. She was saying to me only yesterday, she said. 'Oh, I wish Lily would paint a nice little picture for my room!' Those were her very words."

"I'll do one some time," Lily said absently. "I'm busy today."

It's not Fanny, then, Mrs. Pringle thought. So it must be Mildred. Now what's Mildred been saying? Has she been after her already about Mr. Fairfield? She'll ruin everything if she doesn't watch out. She ought to know by this time how contrary poor Lily is. "What's keeping you so busy, today, dear?" she asked in an offhand voice.

"I may go for a drive with Theodore later on."

"That should be nice." Mrs. Pringle tried to sound enthusiastic. "You didn't happen to meet him when you were out walking, did you, honey?"

Lily looked at her suspiciously. "What makes you think that?"

"Well, I know he does go walking before breakfast. Here's your orange juice, now. Drink up, dear. Put roses in your cheeks."

Lily drank, gazing thoughtfully into the garden. "Do *you* hate him?" she asked suddenly.

"Mr. Fairfield? Lord, no, dear! I think he's a lovely man. Hate him!" Mrs. Pringle laughed gaily. "What a question!"

An expression crossed Lily's face—was it disappointment? It was gone so quickly that Mrs. Pringle couldn't be sure.

Hate Mr. Fairfield! she was thinking. If poor Lily only knew. It's a good thing she isn't a mind-reader. The most fascinating man I ever met. It must be that beard. He makes every other man in the world look ordinary . . . When Theodore met her on the street, he raised his hat and bowed as if she were a duchess. It was years since anyone had treated her with such respect. The only thing was that she found herself making comparisons between him and Ernie. She had never been really dissatisfied with Ernie before. He has his faults, same as everyone else, she had told herself. We can't all be perfect. She had lived long enough to know that nothing in this world comes up to one's expectations, so you might as well make the best of what you get. Like most wives, she camouflaged reality with dreams, her husband's shortcomings with tolerance. In time she had grown so accustomed to Ernie's table manners, his general sloppiness, that she scarcely noticed. But lately she had become critical. Ernie came to the table in his undershirt, and complained about his wind. Sometimes, looking across the breakfast table on Sunday mornings, she just simply wondered why, out of all the men in the world, she'd been fool enough to get tied up with this draggletailed old party who belched over his kippers and never even had the decency to fold up the comics after he'd read them.

Though she felt such admiration for Theodore, she worried just as much as Fanny did about his interest in Lily. A man like him don't chase after a woman unless he means business, she told herself. We might as well make up our minds to it: Lily'll go off and marry him one of these days. And we can't say he isn't suitable, because he is. If they searched the world over, they couldn't find a more suitable husband for Lily. Even Fanny saw that. Theodore was quiet, respectable, and rich. (Though he never said so, one got the impression that he had so much money it was a bore to talk about it, even to spend it.) He was older than Lily, which was another point in his favor, for she needed someone stable and understanding. No, there wasn't a thing in the world you could say against him except that, if he married Lily and took her away, there would be nothing left for Mrs. Pringle to live for.

Fatalistically, she was already visualizing the desolation of her life without Lily, though she was unselfish enough to admit that Lily would be better off married to some nice respectable man who would treat her right. Though she couldn't very well say so to Fanny, Mrs. Pringle firmly believed that a woman might just as well go out and drown herself if she couldn't find a husband. I won't stand in Lily's way, she thought, feeling martyred. It's just what she needs—a man to sleep with and relax her tensions.

Mixed with her sadness over losing Lily was a vague yearning for what she had missed herself, and a depressing conviction that, having once compared Ernie with someone faultless, she would never again be able to overlook his shortcomings. She could never make excuses for him again, or console herself with the thought that hardly anyone was perfect. She looked back regretfully to what might have been. If I'd been a bit more choosy, she thought, who knows? I might have met someone like Mr. Fairfield.

I'll quit, she decided disconsolately. If the old B.'s going to live forever, if that Mildred's going to be nosing around . . . They needn't expect me to wear myself out running up and downstairs with trays, cleaning up after *her*, being treated like a bloody servant . . . If I had a good excuse I'd give my notice this minute.

Mildred came downstairs in her pink negligee, her curls still pinned up. In the kitchen, all the breakfast things had been cleared away; the coffee pot was empty. Mrs. Pringle, going about some business of her own in the next room, stuck her head round the half-opened door and immediately withdrew it.

Mildred yawned and yawned until tears came into her eyes. She wiped them away with the back of her hand and opened the refrigerator, staring blankly inside. At home, Harry always prepared breakfast. As soon as he had gulped his own and hurried off to catch his bus, Mildred would climb out of bed and paddle out, bleary-eyed, half asleep, to find a pile of buttery toast in the oven and coffee perking on the stove. Now, looking vaguely about the tidied-up kitchen, from which even the smell of breakfast had disappeared, she felt neglected.

"Oh, you're up," Fanny said, coming in from the garden.

93

"I'm afraid we've thrown out the coffee, but I'll make some more in a jiffy. What else would you like?"

"I don't want much." Mildred sat down and watched Fanny as she sliced bread, set out cups, opened a jar of honey. "I thought perhaps you might have kept something hot for me. Has everybody eaten?" she asked in an accusing voice.

"Breakfast at eight-thirty." Mrs. Pringle appeared briefly with a pail of soapy water, which she emptied into the sink. "If everybody ate at odd hours, we'd never get our work done up."

"Perhaps you'd rather I went without breakfast altogether," Mildred suggested.

"Just so long as you clean up your own mess," Mrs. Pringle said airily. She refilled her pail, shook soap flakes into it, and went out again.

"I will not tolerate her insults!" Mildred clenched her thin hands on the table. "What have I ever done to her?"

"She really doesn't mean to be rude. And it's no use saying anything—getting her all upset."

"Whose house is this, I'd like to know? Whose feelings are more important, hers or mine?"

"Was that the postman?" Fanny turned her head, listening, and Mildred hurried into the hall to see if there was a letter from Harry; but the postman was nowhere in sight.

Later, when she had dressed, Mildred went into the garden to help Fanny cut the flowers. Armed with a pair of garden shears, and carrying a flat wicker basket, Fanny went around snipping a bloom here, a spray of leaves there. Both of them saw Theodore walking along the dappled pathway through the wood, but neither would acknowledge that she had seen him. Mildred pushed up her curls; Fanny straightened her skirt and tucked in her blouse.

"Good morning!" He stepped over the hedge with that mixture of deference and watchfulness that Mildred had noted

94

before. He wore the same dark-blue suit. In the bright sunlight it looked shiny, worn at the cuffs. "I'm not intruding?"

"Of course not," Fanny said.

"How is your father?"

"Dr. Randolph says he's out of danger for the time being."

Mildred allowed Fanny to do the talking. She held herself aloof, idly plucking the petals from a chrysanthemum, trying not to stare at him, glancing away quickly whenever he turned to her.

Just before he left, he said, smiling and addressing her directly, "Are you feeling better this morning, Mrs. McKinley?"

"Yes, thank you." She threw away the chrysanthemum.

He nodded. "You look happier, more rested." It sounded like a compliment. In spite of herself she flushed, and touched her hair again.

But when he had gone into the woods again, she said to Fanny, "If he has money, as you seem to think, why does he dress like that? Did you notice his suit? It's years old."

"He always wears that one dark suit. Mrs. Kinch thinks it's because he's eccentric."

"Or because he's too poor to buy another."

"It can't be that. Some rich men are funny about clothes."

"What makes you so sure he's rich?"

"Mrs. Kinch showed me some letters he'd written to his lawyers. She found them in his wastebasket—some with lines scratched out as if he'd made a mistake and had to start all over again. I shouldn't be telling on Mrs. Kinch," Fanny interposed, "but since you seem to doubt him . . ."

"What did the letters say?"

"They were all to some legal firm in Boston—instructions about stocks and bonds. I remember one in particular—about placing an order for ten thousand shares of U.S. Steel, and paying for them out of his personal account."

"Ten *thousand* !"

95

"I saw the letter myself."

"Well . . ." Mildred plucked a yellow cone off the fir tree and split it with her thumbnail. She frowned, not knowing what to think. Later, when she had dug yesterday's paper out of the ashcan and read the market quotations, she said, "I don't *believe* it!" in a tone of great conviction. But she was not quite sure.

"We could all drive out to the cemetery," Mildred suggested at lunch time. "Mrs. Pringle will keep an eye on Papa."

"Perhaps later on," Isobel said.

"I thought right after lunch." Mildred refused to be put off. She felt that Isobel was waiting for something—a telephone call or a message of some kind. When the postman had finally arrived, Isobel asked, "Is there anything for me?" and seemed disappointed when there was not. There was nothing from Harry, either. Later it seemed to Mildred that Isobel hovered near the telephone. When it rang twice in mid-morning, she hurried to answer it.

"Unless you have something more important to do"—Mildred put on her glasses and looked disapprovingly at Isobel— "then I think right after lunch will be the best time," she said firmly. "Lily, if I were you, I'd put on something different. That dress is hardly the thing to wear to the cemetery."

"Oh, *I'm* not going." Lily patted her mouth delicately with her napkin.

"Why not?"

"I'm going for a drive with Theodore."

"Oh? And when did you plan all this?"

"This morning."

"I see. You made plans to spend the afternoon with a perfect stranger, when Isobel and I have come all this way—"

"Theodore isn't a *stranger*!" Lily said in a smiling, indulgent voice, as if Mildred had made a ridiculous statement.

"We know nothing about him," Mildred said sharply. "He

96

that the desperate note in Mildred's voice meant something, quite apart from her concern for Lily. But what was it? And why did she hate Theodore so?

"I found a piece in a magazine this morning." Mildred, calm again, touched her face with her handkerchief. Her hands still trembled, but her voice was firm. She thrust one hand down the front of her dress and drew out a folded clipping. "I cut it out because it seemed—well—the same sort of problem, in a different way." She felt in her pocket for her glasses, and put them on. "The mother wrote in this case, asking advice about her daughter who has become infatuated with a married man —separated from his wife, but you can imagine. Here's the answer." She smoothed the bit of paper on her knee, adjusted her glasses, and read: " 'Dear Mrs. J. B.'—I won't read the whole thing, just the part where it says what to do—'This is a situation where you must employ great subtlety. You must be careful not to appear critical or disapproving at this stage, for that will simply drive your daughter in the wrong direction.' " Mildred paused and looked at Fanny, remembering what she had said to Lily a short time before. "All I said was he's a perfect stranger," she defended herself. "You needn't look so critical."

"What else does the letter say?"

Mildred read on. " 'The next time this man calls for your daughter, suggest that they spend the evening at home with you instead of going out. You might plan some wholesome entertainment, games, etc. Talk to him. Draw him out skill-fully. Your letter indicates that you are clever enough to do this without arousing his suspicion or antagonizing him in any way. On this first visit, do not mention his wife, but allow him to understand that you consider marriage a sacred trust . . .' "

"Not much to go on," Fanny said dubiously when Mildred had finished the letter. "It's not the same sort of problem at all. Theodore is not married, for one thing."

"How do you know? He may have a dozen wives."

"He's a widower. He told Mrs. Kinch."

"He may have told Mrs. Kinch any number of things. That doesn't necessarily make them true."

"I see no reason for him to lie. Besides, he doesn't seem the sort of person . . ."

"I hope I'm not going to have to do all this by myself," Mildred said, looking over her glasses.

"I don't know what you mean."

"You seem bent on defending him."

"I merely said—" Fanny began, exasperated, and stopped. "What do you think we should do?" she asked in a normal tone.

"I thought, when he calls for Lily this afternoon, we could ask him to visit the cemetery with us. He can hardly refuse to do that. And bring him back to the house for tea. We don't want him to get the idea he's not welcome here." Mildred glanced down at the clipping as if for guidance. "It certainly wouldn't seem unnatural for us to show an interest in his past life. We can draw him out."

"We mustn't ask too many questions."

"We can do it without seeming to. That's the whole point."

"Well . . . I suppose it's the only way."

"As it is, we have nothing to *go* on," Mildred pointed out. She glanced at her watch and rose. "We had better go down."

In the living room, Isobel was lying on the couch eating grapes, dropping the seeds into a potted fern.

"Where is Lily?" Mildred asked from the doorway.

"Gone." Isobel rolled over lazily and scooped another handful of grapes from the silver bowl on the floor. "She went out with Theodore."

Mildred frowned. "Why didn't you call us?"

"Did you want to see him? I thought you didn't like him."

Mildred walked across the room with an offended expression. It was like Isobel to take the whole bowl of grapes and put them where nobody else could get at them. She had always been greedy, wanting more than her share. Selfish, too, never sharing the family burdens. Running off with that cheap trombone player before she was out of school!

"By the way," Mildred said casually, "who was it that telephoned you at lunch time?"

"A friend," Isobel said, spitting seeds into her hand.

Mildred gave her a good long look, noting that the remnants of a smile lingered about her mouth, as if she were remembering something pleasant. I just wonder what Eliot would say if he knew you were getting long-distance calls from strange men —running around with God knows who the minute his back's turned, too, probably, she speculated silently. Aloud she said, "Well, if you don't care to say, it makes no difference to me, of course."

"I didn't think it would," Isobel said with her maddening sensuous smile.

## CHAPTER SEVEN

THEODORE DROVE THE RENTED CAR—A SMALL ENGLISH ROADSTER with the top down—along a country road bordered with vineyards. He drove slowly, for he was not accustomed to handling a car. From the highway he had glimpsed the dusty road dipping into a valley, had been lured by the panorama of vineyards and orchards, farmhouses nestled under tall elms, and, far off, alternating squares of plowed earth and yellow stubble. The sunny landscape had looked inviting from the top of the hill. Now he regretted his decision to explore it, for the road was narrow and full of bumps, and he could see nothing but rows of grapes. Blue butterflies rose from the dust ahead of them and settled again when they had passed. There was no room to turn. Every little side road had a "No Trespassing" sign.

Lily, sitting beside him, selected an apple from the basket he had bought at a roadside stand and polished it on her skirt. "Where are we going?" she asked idly.

Theodore stopped the car in the middle of the road. He smiled ruefully. "I haven't the faintest idea. The view from the highway enticed me, but now that we're here I see nothing but those vines, which look quite unromantic at close quarters."

Lily nibbled at her apple. "There might be something over the next hill," she suggested.

"Shall we go on, then?" He pressed the starter. The engine coughed asthmatically and stopped. To add to his annoyance a farm boy on a horse now appeared on the brow of the hill. The horse came lumbering along, its huge feet raising spurts of dust, its stomach rumbling and swishing like a barrel of water.

"Trouble?" the boy asked, reining in. His mount towered over the little car, snorting, blowing foam. Theodore was afraid of horses; but Lily leaned forward and offered the core of her apple to the prancing monster, which backed away suddenly, throwing up its head.

"We don't need help," Theodore said sharply.

"Okay." The boy grinned, slapped his bare legs against the horse's flanks, and was off. Theodore took out his handkerchief and mopped his forehead.

"Were you frightened?" Lily asked.

"I dislike animals." He put away his handkerchief carefully, giving himself time to regain his composure. After a moment he was able to smile and say, "And I'm afraid I know nothing about these English cars. What is wrong with it now? Why won't it start?" He looked appealingly at Lily, noting that it pleased her to be asked advice. Yes, he decided, she would like helpless people, those who failed in many things. Perhaps she would even like people who were afraid of horses. The thought reassured him.

He had always considered himself an expert at understanding women; but Lily had baffled him from the very first. He was beginning to think he had made a great mistake in allowing his heart to rule his head. He had no business falling in love.

In the beginning he had thought that Fanny would be the one. It was true, as he told Mildred, that he happened to be passing through St. Charles one day, saw Mrs. Kinch's guest house—a sign on the gate informed him that she was the proprietress, and that her house was called the Willows—and decided it would be a fine place to stay. It was an August afternoon, and a number of Mrs. Kinch's guests were sitting in the garden. Noting the predominance of middle-aged women, Theodore deduced that half of them, at least, would be spinsters or widows. And they must have incomes; otherwise they could not afford to stay there. Though the Willows was a far cry from an expensive resort hotel, it had an air of refinement about it. The owner of such a place would be choosy about her guests, and would probably ask a good price for her rooms. The ladies sitting on the lawn would lead quiet dreary lives. Theodore knew that women are able to lead such lives because they are optimists. The spinster never gives up hope that she will some day meet a man who will want to marry her; the widow is always on the lookout for someone to share her insurance and her home. He was not looking for a rich woman; one with a steady comfortable income would do.

He surmised, correctly, that Mrs. Kinch would not consider taking a guest who came unrecommended. He therefore went back into town to pave the way by making inquiries. When he presented his card to the postmistress—always, in small towns, the best source of information—he ran into an unexpected bit of luck.

"Boston?" Miss Peoples examined the card with such curiosity that he began to feel uneasy. "You wouldn't happen to know the Willitsons, would you?"

"The Willitsons?" He assumed the expression of helpless puzzlement that was so handy for getting out of tight corners.

"They came from Boston," Miss Peoples rattled on in a friendly way, dispelling his uncertainty. "Stayed at Mrs. Kinch's place last year. Real nice people. No, they didn't come back this year. Went to Europe. I happened to read a post card they sent—oh, three weeks ago. They weren't what folks around here call 'regulars.' Some people come back year after year," she explained. "The Willitsons just came the once. Willitson had something to do with shipping. Got his address around here somewhere." Miss Peoples fished some yellowed slips of paper from a pigeonhole. "Here it is. J. B. Willitson, Vice-president, Eastern Line." She glanced up. "Did you say you knew them? Stout man about sixty-five; wife had a thyroid condition."

"Oh, the *Willitsons*!" Theodore exclaimed, with a great burst of enlightenment. He had decided that J. B. Willitson and his wife, whoever they might be, were tried and trusted friends. "Of course I know them! I know them very well. As a matter of fact, it's on their recommendation that I'm here in St. Charles. They were so enthusiastic about a little hotel they stayed at last year. Would that be the place you mentioned?"

"That's it. Mrs. Kinch's place. The Willows."

"Could you direct me to it?"

"Just go out the River Road. You can't miss."

"Thank you." He lifted his hat.

The Willows was just what he had expected, for he was well acquainted with guest houses. A great air of respectability and gentility had been achieved through the use of red carpeting, polished woodwork, and muddy oil paintings in gilt frames. An afghan thrown over a settee gave a touch of homey color, as did the flowers arranged artistically in a copper bowl under the antique mirror. Over all hung a smell of furniture polish and soap.

His dear friends the Willitsons stood him in good stead when it came to dealing with Mrs. Kinch. "Any friend of the Willitsons . . ." she said with her broad smile. But she had nothing left except a small back room. Theodore assured her that it would suit him admirably. He wanted only to rest, to lie in the garden. He represented himself as a lonely widower whose wife had died the previous year.

"Have you been ill?" Mrs. Kinch inquired solicitously.

He nodded, hoping to enlist her sympathy.

"We'll soon have you feeling fit again," she said in her motherly way. "Plenty of eggs and milk—we'll get rid of that prison pallor in no time at all."

He started, then realized that her words were not meant to be taken literally.

It took him only a day to realize that the eligible ladies at the Willows were an impossible lot: a librarian who was collecting data for a history of the Niagara frontier (no money, interested only in such dead and gone things as the battle of Lundy's Lane); two spinster sisters, over fifty, who had already lost half their income on the market; and a clergyman's widow. But he was heartened to discover that Mrs. Kinch, a kind-hearted woman of sixty-five, was an inveterate matchmaker. He took to visiting her in the little sitting room where, after dinner, she made up accounts. He had only to employ a few phrases such as "a lonely widower like myself" and "when one is all alone" to send her mind scurrying through a list of names.

"You ought to marry again, Mr. Fairfield. You're the kind that needs a woman to look after you."

He smiled sadly. "Yes, I would like to marry. Unfortunately, so few women want to settle down with a quiet fellow like me."

She protested at once, as he knew she would. "You're the very kind they do want! Someone steady and dependable, with nice manners; but with a look—" She paused, fearful of offending, then decided she was old enough to speak her mind. "Well, a *look*. You've got a way with women, Mr. Fairfield. I saw it the first day. You're too shy; that's your trouble. Why, I know any number of nice girls." She looked thoughtfully at the ceiling. "There's Miss Abbott and the Miss Baxters"—she was referring to the librarian and the two spinster sisters—"but somehow I don't fancy them for you. I think one of the Jameson girls . . ."

"Who are the Jamesons?"

She pulled back the curtain and pointed past the red umbrellas and metal bird baths on the lawn. "They live right next door. You can just see their roof over the trees. Lovely girls, both of them."

"There are two?" he asked, with just enough interest in his voice to keep her talking. Though he could see nothing but the chimneys of the house next door, he had already appraised it from the street and wondered about its occupants.

Mrs. Kinch settled back in a way that indicated she was prepared to discuss the Jamesons thoroughly. "Lily's a funny little thing. A bit too—" He thought she had been about to say that Lily was too young for him. "Fanny's the one I had in mind. A really lovely girl, Mr. Fairfield. So friendly and agreeable. Dresses well. Not a fashion plate, but everything the best. Like the royal family. You know what *they* look like sometimes, but you can tell their clothes cost a pretty penny, just the same. Of course, Fanny can well afford it."

He pricked up his ears.

"I remember when I bought this house, right after the war. A lot of people along the River Road raised a fuss about my opening a hotel here. Said it cheapened the other properties. But Fanny was as nice as anything. Came to see me the first day, asked if there was anything she could do."

"She sounds like a wonderful person," Theodore said encouragingly.

Mrs. Kinch needed no encouragement. During the next half hour she recounted everything she knew about the Jamesons. "There's some people look down on them because of the way the old man made his money," she said, and explained this statement fully. "I wouldn't go so far as to say he's a millionaire, but according to local standards, he's pretty well fixed. He's already settled an amount—I couldn't say how much—on each of the girls. He's getting on in years, he can't last forever, so they'll each get another tidy sum before long." She became so engrossed in her story that Theodore was afraid she would forget why she was telling it.

"I should like to meet this Fanny," he said during a pause in the monologue. He had heard enough about the Jamesons to be sure.

"And so you shall!" Mrs. Kinch's round face beamed up at him. "Tomorrow afternoon, I'll call Fanny and ask her to pop over—I'll think up some excuse—early, before the ladies want their tea. Then I'll leave you two alone."

Fanny came the next afternoon, and, as planned, Mrs. Kinch invented an excuse to absent herself from the room. While he made polite conversation, Theodore took stock of Fanny. Not particularly clever, he decided, agreeing with her trite comments about the weather; a bit tall and awkward, but really not bad-looking. Actually, he preferred women who lacked grace and beauty. They were much easier to get along with, more appreciative of attention. He questioned Fanny, encouraged her to talk about herself, and finally walked back to Hawkrest with her to see the garden. "I love flowers," he confided.

This was in early August, a hot afternoon with the sun beating down, making dark shadows under the trees. He inspected every inch of the formal front garden, was lavish with praise of Fanny's green thumb.

"I can't take all the credit," Fanny protested, flushing with pleasure. "We have a part-time gardener. He does all the work. Would you like to see the view from the back garden?"

"Very much," he said promptly.

"We can go this way," Fanny said, and led him through the front door and down a long hall which opened onto a screened porch at the back of the house. In the back garden Mr. Jameson and Lily were reclining in canvas chairs. Lily was asleep with her hands behind her head and her bare legs stretched out. She had kicked off her sandals, and her slender feet were crossed, the insteps arched as if she were posing for a picture. Theodore thought at first that she was a little girl, a pretty fragile child whose hair needed combing. King Jameson was reading a newspaper, which he cast aside. "It's damned hot out here," he said petulantly, as if he were blaming Fanny for the weather.

"Papa, this is Mr. Fairfield."

Mr. Jameson nodded and made a groaning movement as if to rise, then sank back. He was grossly overweight, asthmatic. "I'm damned thirsty," he complained. "That old bitch in the kitchen won't exert herself to bring us a drink. All afternoon she's been sitting in there guzzling my best rye."

"Now, Papa, you know Mrs. Pringle doesn't drink," Fanny said, greatly embarrassed.

Theodore saw that Lily was not really asleep, only pretending to be.

"Hellish weather!" Mr. Jameson grumbled. "Sit down, Fairfield. Fanny, bring us a drink."

"Shall I make tea?" Fanny asked uncertainly.

"Tea! My God!"

"I thought perhaps Mr. Fairfield would rather . . ."

For practical reasons, Theodore elected to side with Fanny. "I find a cup of tea most refreshing on a hot day," he said.

Mr. Jameson glared at him and muttered, then picked up his paper, and though he did not read it, frowned at it and maintained an irascible silence. As soon as Fanny had gone inside,

evenings in bed. They could hear him fuming away in his room, occasionally shouting down for something he wanted. Lily was always there, aloof and bemused, rarely contributing to the conversation. Theodore wondered how she occupied her time. She seemed to possess a great faculty for doing nothing. One night she had a butterfly, a painted lady, in a glass bottle containing some whitish powder, and was making a water-color sketch of it.

"So you're an artist," he said, bending over her.

She glanced up at him briefly and made no comment.

"That's good. Very good." He cocked a critical eye at the picture. In truth it was not good at all. The drawing was careless, the paint muddy. "Have you more like this?" he asked.

"Lily's always drawing, when she isn't collecting flowers or bugs," Fanny said. Why don't you show Mr. Fairfield your flower pictures, dear?"

Lily moved her shoulders impatiently. "They're upstairs."

"She has a lovely picture of a yellow lady's-slipper that she found on the river bank," Fanny said encouragingly, smiling down at Lily's bent head.

"Do you mean that you climbed down the bank to pick it?" Theodore asked. "Isn't that rather dangerous?"

Fanny waited a moment for Lily to answer, then did so herself. "It does seem dangerous. But there's a place along by the beechwood where the bank slopes down gradually to the water, and there are little paths, one above the other. It's a beautiful spot, but I never go down myself. I worry about Lily going." She moved closer to Lily and smoothed back her hair.

Reluctantly, that evening, Theodore decided that he would never get anywhere with Lily. She was simply not interested in him. Fanny, on the other hand, was displaying all the symptoms he knew so well: the flustered downcast look when he pressed her hand in parting, the touch of complacency in her smile when she thought no one was watching, the subdued glow that animated her features. There's no doubt about it, he thought, nothing whips up the circulation like falling in love.

So, when he said good night, he held Fanny's hand longer than usual, then suggested that they take a turn in the garden.

Fanny blushed and withdrew her hand from his. She glanced at Lily as if seeking encouragement from her. Lily laid down her brush and watched as he picked up a chiffon scarf that lay over a chair and draped it tenderly round Fanny's shoulders.

Fanny took the precaution of turning on the outside lights before they began their stroll, so that they walked up and down the curving path in a yellow glare. Their shadows went ahead of them or dropped behind, and the trees shrank back into darkness. Theodore placed one hand under her elbow, but she walked so quickly and crooked her arm so rigidly that he soon made an excuse to remove his hand. On the second turn, Lily came out and sat on the steps.

"I wanted to show you my drawing," she said reprovingly, when they paused beside her. "Look, I've finished it." She held it up for Theodore to see.

"It's very beautiful," he said with false enthusiasm.

"Do you really like it?"

"It's lovely, darling!" Fanny exclaimed. "The best you've ever done. We must buy a frame for it right away."

Next morning, as he sat in Mrs. Kinch's garden reading the paper, the Jamesons' car stopped at the gate, and Lily called to him. She was driving into the country to pick up some fruit for preserving that Fanny had ordered, she said, and invited him to go along with her. He was immensely flattered, and strove to make the outing as enjoyable as possible. Lily drove so badly on the narrow roads that he was afraid to divert her attention with anything more entertaining than remarks about the weather and the beauty of the landscape. He even gave that up after a time, for whenever she took her eyes off the road to admire the view, the car meandered from side to side like a drunken pedestrian. In the fields, reapers were cutting grain and stacking it into sheaves; low clouds sent shadows flying over the hills. The vineyards were festooned with plump clusters of purple grapes. At the farm where they picked up the fruit, cattle lay in the meadows or stood knee-deep in rush-grown streams. But it was not the summer day that made Theodore feel so gay and adventurous. Glancing down at his clothes, he wondered if he could possibly afford a new suit, and knew he could not.

Returning home by another route, they passed a wayside inn. Theodore felt in his pockets and secretly counted his money before he suggested stopping there for lunch. The garish little dining room of the inn was empty, and he imagined the chatty companionable meal they would have, the confidences they would exchange. He hoped to engage Lily's sympathy with a reference to his own loss, thus perhaps enticing her to talk about the husband she had divorced (he could then offer sympathy in return), and about other phases in her life: what accident had caused that scar, for instance, and all the things that a man on the brink of infatuation wishes to know about the woman who attracts him. He had received scant enlightenment from Mrs. Kinch, who had acquired all her information from Mrs. Pringle. "She never talks about the girls," Mrs. Kinch told Theodore. "Shuts up like a clam when you ask anything about them. And of course, since I'm not here in the winter and am kept so busy during the summer, I don't get to know the townspeople well enough to ask questions."

"What a poky little place," Lily said. She propped her chin on her hand and read the beer advertisements on the wall.

He felt deflated. "Would you rather go somewhere else?" He had already ordered chicken sandwiches and coffee. The waitress had gone behind some curtains and left them alone.

"Oh, no. This will do. We could go home, except that Fanny will be fussing around." She interrupted her study of the posters to glance at him. "Do you like Fanny?"

"Why, yes. I like her very much."

"I wondered . . ." She looked away again.

He began to speak of himself, testing the story of his life which he had invented. After several references to his bereaved state, he said, "I understand that you have recently lost your husband."

"Lost?" She looked at him blankly, then gave a little metallic laugh.

The waitress placed the sandwiches and coffee on the table. When she had gone back to the kitchen, he tried again. "Were you very unhappy with him?"

"With Joe?" Lily pulled her sandwich apart and picked out the meat.

"Was that your husband's name?" He waited a moment, then said, "I hope you don't mind—that you don't think I'm prying . . ."

She went on eating as if she had not heard.

"Were you?" he persisted. "Unhappy with him, I mean?" With any other woman he would have put the question in a roundabout way, since he would be less interested in hearing the answer than in establishing himself as a sympathetic listener. Now he simply wanted to know.

"He was quite handsome," Lily said in a musing voice. "But rather stupid. Tiresome . . ." She frowned slightly, as if describing someone she had met once, and whose features she could not quite recall.

In the evening he went again to Hawkrest. Assuming that Lily would have told Fanny about the drive in the country, he began to speak of it.

"Oh, look, Fanny!" Lily cried suddenly. "Someone's broken my little shepherdess!" She picked up the pieces of a figurine that had been lying broken on the mantelpiece for days, and cradled them pathetically in her palms.

Theodore found this little ruse—though appealing—a trifle obvious; but Fanny didn't seem to see through it. "Never

116

mind, darling," she said. "We'll buy another one. You mustn't fret about it."

It was some days before he realized that the problem of choosing between the sisters was being settled for him. It could not be mere chance that Lily so often happened to be taking walks at the same time and along the same route as he took his morning constitutional; or, in the early evenings when he walked through the beechwood toward Hawkrest, that she should be wandering in the woods also. When he bought three tickets to a play presented by a summer theater group in a neighboring town, Fanny was in various unobtrusive ways made to assume the appearance of a chaperone. As they were being shown to their seats, Lily paused to search in her bag for a handkerchief. Fanny, following the usher in her usual brisk fashion, was already seated when her sister and Theodore came down the aisle. Then, of course, Lily sat next to her, leaving the outside seat for Theodore. All through the play, Lily sat forward with her hands clasped on her knees as if spellbound, so that if Theodore wanted to address Fanny, he was forced to lean far forward, or else lean back and speak over Lily's shoulders. Whichever he attempted, Lily immediately shifted her position.

That she should employ subtlety to avoid sharing him with others seemed to him quite touching, for he was now at the fatuous stage where he considered everything she did quite wonderful. Having no basis for comparison, he believed the sentimental protectiveness he felt for Lily to be love, and the sensation was so new to him that he did not quite know how to deal with it.

Fanny's attitude puzzled him somewhat. As the days went by and it became evident to her (and to everyone else in town) that he went to Hawkrest to see Lily, Fanny withdrew more and more into the background. But at the same time she maintained a hovering watchfulness, an anxiety that Theodore could not account for. It was not the attitude of a woman who has been rejected in favor of another.

And then, having disposed of Fanny, Lily became elusive. He could not be sure whether she simply lost interest, or whether she was playing a coy game; but over and over again, just at the moment when he thought he was getting somewhere with her, closing in on the quarry, so to speak, he found himself standing foolishly back at the beginning. He began to feel that he had wandered into a strange looking-glass world where everything had been turned round, for he had never before been obliged to implore and placate. It had always been a simple matter of standing still and allowing himself to be caught. Twice during the past week, having taken pains to select a suitable time and place, and to pave the way with what he considered to be great finesse, he had been on the point of asking Lily to marry him; but on each occasion, before he got to the actual question, Lily had had one of her quick changes of mood, and he had thought it wise to await a more favorable opportunity.

He could not postpone the question much longer, for time was running short. Though the room he occupied at the Willows was the cheapest one Mrs. Kinch had to offer, living there was eating into his funds at an alarming rate.

Fate seemed against him in other ways, too. King Jameson's illness was no hindrance in itself—Theodore hoped, merely, that if the old man must pick this particular time to die, he would get it over with quickly—but the arrival of Mildred and Isobel was; for now—like Prince Charming, he thought—he had four sisters to contend with instead of two. He believed that Isobel would not interfere. She would live and let live. He rather admired her, though she represented a type of woman he did not know well, or understand, since he was unacquainted with passion. Mildred's type, on the other hand, he knew well. If circumstances had been different, if *she* had been Cinderella instead of Lily, he would know exactly how to deal with her. But circumstances had placed Mildred in the role of the wicked stepsister, which altered the picture considerably.

In spite of the additional obstacles, Theodore now glimpsed a ray of hope. For today—was it because of Mildred's disapproval, he wondered—Lily seemed a shade less indifferent. It was she who had suggested this drive into the country.

When he had succeeded in getting the car started, they continued along the narrow road, which now appeared endless, flaunting more "No Trespassing" signs than ever. He had hoped to find some secluded glade beside a stream, with a rustic bridge and a little path leading off into the woods, which they would explore. He had brought along a bottle of wine, and a blanket to sit on. When he finally stopped, it was beside a shallow brook running through a pasture, not at all the sort of place he had in mind, but it would have to do; they could not go on driving forever. He parked the car under some elm trees. On the other side of the fence, under the same trees, cows were lying about in a much-trodden, dung-caked semicircle. Across the very unrustic concrete bridge, another car was parked, and a family was unpacking a picnic basket. In the farmyard at the top of the hill some men were winnowing grain, and a clacking machine blew the chaff onto a huge stack beside the barn. Two farm dogs ran down the hill, barking, but keeping at a distance.

"I thought Canada was such a vast country," Theodore complained, "but every inch of ground is marked 'private.' Where do people go when they want to have a picnic?"

"To city parks. To places like this." Lily tossed an apple over the fence, and all the cows started and heaved themselves up, turning their heads reproachfully.

"Not a particularly secluded spot," Theodore remarked, glancing at the family across the stream. The mother had opened a thermos, and was handing around sandwiches.

"What do we care about people?" Lily gave the picnickers a brief glance.

"I wanted to be alone with you," he said sadly, spreading the blanket on the grass, placing cushions against a rock.

Lily sat down, yawning and stretching her hands over her head. Her hair was blown into tangles. She combed it back with her fingers and yawned again.

Not much hope of getting anywhere with her today, Theodore thought pessimistically. "I hoped we could have a long talk," he said, "but this hardly seems the place."

"I think it's a lovely place." Lily took a lipstick and a small mirror from her bag and began to make up her mouth.

He watched her, debating with himself whether to risk saying what he had in mind, or to wait until she seemed in a more receptive mood. The trouble was, he could never tell when her mood was receptive and when it was not. He said firmly, "I have something rather important to say to you."

Lily looked up quickly, then went on examining herself in the mirror. After a minute she put away the lipstick and mirror and took his hand. "Come and sit down," she invited, pulling him down beside her. "Now, what did you want to talk about?"

She was smiling, though not exactly at him. It was more as if she had thought of something amusing. However, it gave him confidence.

"I wanted to talk about us," he said, enfolding both her hands in his.

Lily leaned back against the rock and closed her eyes, still smiling. "Well, go on," she urged, when he hesitated. "What about us?"

"It must be apparent to you why I've stayed on in St. Charles all these weeks—why I've spent so much time at Hawkrest."

"Of course. You wanted to see me."

"I hope you will do me the honor of becoming my wife."

Lily opened her eyes and stared at him.

"Does that surprise you so?" he asked. "Surely you must have guessed that I love you."

"Oh, yes. I knew."

"Then why are you laughing?"

Lily was instantly contrite, but could not stop smiling. She put one hand over her mouth and assumed an exaggerated expression of penitence. "It was only the funny way you said it. So old-fashioned."

"I'm sorry," he said with dignity. "I wasn't trying to be amusing."

"Now, don't mope!" Lily shook his hand coaxingly, trying to cheer him. "I was only teasing. Of course I'll marry you."

All his confidence returned with a rush. He moved closer and put one arm about her shoulder. He had never really made love to her, though he had gone through all the preliminaries: holding her hands and kissing them, making tender protective gestures, occasionally throwing in an endearing name. This system of approach had been most successful in the past. Women, wishing to feel cherished, had accepted such engaging exhibitions of self-restraint as evidence that they were indeed considered rare and precious, and were touchingly grateful. At the same time they had concluded that a man of such sensitive perception must possess all other good qualities as well.

From force of habit, he had employed these dependable tactics with Lily. Now, however, he put both arms around her and drew her head down to his shoulder. "When?" he asked, kissing her hair. "Tomorrow? The next day?"

"I don't care. Whenever you say." Lily was neither yielding nor unyielding in his arms. She simply drooped against him, her back half turned. The woman across the stream called sharply to her children.

"You don't want a big wedding, do you?" he asked. "I thought we could go to some little country church where nobody knows us. I want you all to myself," he added, and hoped this explanation sounded reasonable.

121

"It doesn't matter where," Lily said.

"When your father is so ill, it seems better to keep everything simple—not have notices in the paper, and so on. I wonder," he continued, feeling his way, "if it would be better not to tell your sisters until afterwards. I'm not sure how they feel about me. Mildred, especially."

"Oh, Mildred!" Lily moved her shoulders impatiently.

"You're not fond of her?" Theodore suggested.

Lily sat upright, turning to look at him. "Are *you*?"

He felt he was on safe ground. "Not particularly. In fact, I rather dislike her."

Lily settled back, satisfied. "I hate Mildred," she said calmly.

"I feel that she rather dislikes me, too." Theodore gave a rueful smile. "I wonder if it is because she knows I want to marry you, and she has guessed that I'm not rich," he said sadly.

Lily looked up, interested. "Are you poor?"

"I really have no business asking you to marry me." He glanced humbly down at his hands, then with a brave smile faced her again. "I never intended to tell you my troubles . . . but the fact is, I have recently suffered a severe financial loss."

"Did you lose everything?"

He hesitated, studying her face for a moment before answering. He could always tell how women were going to take it. Their eyes gave them away. A sudden wariness, or a lowering of the eyelids to cover any expression, meant trouble. Lily looked up at him so encouragingly that he gave her the full treatment.

"I haven't a cent."

Lily's face fell, and he added hastily, "I have money at home, of course, but at the moment it's tied up—in real estate and so on. My lawyers tell me it will be months before they can dispose of the properties. In the meantime . . ." He spread his hands, gamely minimizing his predicament.

"Couldn't you borrow?"

"I could, I suppose. But, you see, I haven't told my friends of my loss. One hates to admit failures, even temporary ones. I am rather proud." He threw back his shoulders to illustrate that this was so. "Too proud to let my friends know. Besides," he went on with a rallying smile, "I'll soon be on my feet again. I've lost fortunes before, and managed to build them up again."

Lily looked thoughtful, but said nothing.

"It humiliates me beyond words to have to tell you all this," he said, watching her closely. "Mildred has every right to hate me—to protect you from me."

Lily said sharply, "I never tell Mildred anything. If you need money, I can lend you some. How much do you need?"

"Oh, *no*!" He raised his hands in shocked protest. "I couldn't borrow from you!"

"Why not?"

"What would your sisters think? No . . ." He put one hand to his forehead as if the idea of such a thing, even, pained him. "I can't tell you how grateful I am, but I could not. It wouldn't be right. Your sisters . . ."

"What business is it of theirs?" Lily demanded. "It's my money. I have a checkbook in my bag. I'll write you a check."

"They might see the withdrawal and ask to see the canceled check."

She considered this while she wound a strand of hair about her little finger and chewed the end of it.

"If you made the check out to yourself . . ." he suggested at last.

"Yes, I could do that. And then give you the money." Lily felt around in her bag and pulled out a roll of bills, which she counted. "Here's forty dollars." She opened his hand, placed the money on his palm, and closed his fingers over it. "And tomorrow we'll go to the bank and get some more."

"I can never thank you enough," he said fervently, pocketing the bills.

"You won't tell anyone, will you? This will be our secret."

"I'll pay you back, of course. The minute my money comes through."

"Don't be silly," Lily said, and added, "I used to give money to Joe. He never had any."

"I have never borrowed money before," Theodore said. His voice sounded sincere, even to himself. "I had hoped to take you on a wonderful honeymoon, and to buy a beautiful home for you. All that will have to come later." He opened the bottle of wine, and when they had drunk he pulled her toward him and kissed her. She lay against him for a moment, then sat up and smoothed her hair. "It's time to go home. We have to drive along that dusty road, and I think we're lost, anyway."

## CHAPTER EIGHT

"LOOKING FOR SOMETHING?" MRS. PRINGLE INQUIRED. SHE WAS seated in the rocker beside the kitchen window and had no intention of exerting herself, though Mildred made a great point of stepping around the chair on which her feet were propped.

"The garden shears." Mildred's expression implied that not everyone was fortunate enough to be able to sit around doing nothing all afternoon. Some people had duties to perform.

"Well, you won't find them in my broom closet." Mrs. Pringle stopped rocking and half rose, then dropped back as Mildred, seeing only the dusters on the shelf and not what was behind them, shut the closet door.

"I want to cut some flowers for our mothers' graves," Mildred explained.

124

How many mothers can a person have, for God's sake? Mrs. Pringle asked herself. If there was one thing she couldn't stand, it was people rummaging through her kitchen, upsetting her routine. She had grumbled all morning about the extra work and the lack of consideration displayed by certain people. Seeing Lily drive off with Theodore after lunch had depressed her spirits further. What she needed was a drink, and as soon as Mildred left she intended to cheer herself up with a double gin fizz, while she read a magazine article entitled "True Facts About Flying Saucers." Mildred's presence alone irritated her. The opening and closing of cupboard doors, the sliding in and out of drawers that were not as tidy as they might be, infuriated her. To show her indifference, she leaned back and half closed her eyes, while phrases went through her mind: always pushing herself in where she's not wanted; never thinks of anyone but herself; if there was one place I thought I was entitled to a little privacy, it was my own kitchen . . .

Mildred opened the breadbox and looked inside. She took out a moldy crust and laid it on the counter.

If she says one word! Mrs. Pringle thought. Just one word; I'll give my notice.

Finally she remarked caustically, "I don't know where else the garden shears would be but in the potting shed. It's where they're always kept."

"If you had told me that in the first place . . ." Mildred said with great patience.

"I wouldn't go cutting all Fanny's flowers without asking," Mrs. Pringle remarked with calculated reproof.

"*Fanny's* flowers?"

Mrs. Pringle shrugged, absolving herself from blame. "I merely mentioned it, dear. No need to get in a huff."

"I think you're forgetting yourself, Mrs. Pringle."

"Am I, dear?" Mrs. Pringle smiled airily. "Perhaps you'd like to give me my walking papers. Perhaps you'd like to take over the kitchen, not to mention all the waxing and scrubbing and cleaning up after other people; washing cups that people have thrown their filthy cigarette butts into, emptying bedpans that Miss Whatsername leaves for other people to empty. Since you own the garden, I presume you own the house, too, and have every right to give me notice if you so desire. If you're dissatisfied," she added, crooking her fingers daintily and examining the chipped red polish on her nails.

"I said nothing about being dissatisfied," Mildred protested.

"Then pardon me, I'm sure!" Mrs. Pringle raised one hand with a mincing gesture and flattened down a spit curl. When Mildred had gone, she made the gin fizz and carried it to her sitting room, where she kicked off her shoes and lay back on the sofa. She opened her magazine with pleasurable anticipation, though she knew from experience she was in for a letdown. The trouble with writers, they were too cautious, afraid to come right out and say; always qualifying, evading. Mrs. Pringle wasn't born yesterday. She knew as well as the next one that strange little men from some planet or other were continually making trips between wherever they lived and Earth, though the government did its best to keep this fact from the general public. If the author of this article, for instance, came right out and told everything he knew, he'd likely find himself clapped into jail for alarming the populace. But there was one thing the government couldn't do: it couldn't prevent people from reading between the lines.

The first Mrs. Jameson was not buried in the churchyard at St. Charles, but her tombstone was there. King Jameson had bought the cemetery lot some years after his arrival in St. Charles—at about the time he began referring to Hawkrest as "the old family mansion"—so that if the occasion ever arose to mention "the family plot in the churchyard," he could do so. He encircled the lot with a garland of iron chains running through ornately carved stone posts; then, feeling that it needed something more, decided to erect a monument to his first wife.

The tombstone marking the burial place of his second wife was an exact replica of the other, and was set a little way off, to make room for himself in between.

Mildred arranged the flowers impartially, making sure that the same number of blooms rested against each stone. When everything was in place, she sat on a campstool with her head slightly bowed, while Fanny and Isobel wandered among the other graves, waiting for her. She looked as if she might be praying, or lost in sorrowing thought, but in reality she was thinking about Theodore Fairfield.

She had been thinking about him more or less constantly since yesterday morning, though she tried not to. He seemed to wait at the back of her mind, ready to jump in the minute she relaxed her guard. When she closed her eyes, she saw his wistful smile and felt his hypnotic glance. If Harry had taken the trouble to write, or telephone, she felt sure she would have been able to stop thinking about Theodore. But Harry had let her down, and this reminded her of other times when she had looked to him for comfort and encouragement and he had not been discerning enough to see her need.

She could not have explained why she was so sure Theodore was not the respectable businessman he pretended to be. She told herself it was intuition, but in reality this belief was born of fear. She needed some weapon with which to fight her own obsession, for in her mind Theodore was becoming identified more and more with the magician she sometimes dreamed about, and a sense of shame accompanied all her thoughts of him. She had even begun to feel that he knew what she was thinking.

As she sat beside her mother's gravestone, she considered ways and means of exposing him. She decided to see what information she could get from Mrs. Kinch.

"Come, girls," she called, folding up her stool. It was three o'clock, and her mother-in-law was coming to tea at four. Harry's mother was a wiry old woman who clung to her

127

Cockney ways despite her fifty years in Canada. Mildred considered her stupid and common. Her class-consciousness prevented her from even presuming to rise above the station in life to which she had been born, and was responsible for Harry's lack of ambition, for she considered his commonplace job a much better one than a person of his rank was entitled to. In her words, he had "done well" and "got along in the world."

"This *is* a surprise!" Mrs. Kinch said pleasantly, though in truth she was rather annoyed. "I hope you don't mind sitting in the kitchen, Mrs. . . ." She had forgotten Mildred's name. "You've caught me at my busiest time, my baking day. No rest for the weary when you've got hungry mouths to feed three times a day." She led the way into the kitchen and invited Mildred to sit down, first removing a pile of folded sheets from a chair. "Well, now, your father's having a time of it, poor creature. I know how it is. My mother went the same way. You think they won't hang on another day, yet something keeps them alive. Will-power, that's my opinion." She tossed a great lump of dough on the kitchen table and attacked it with floury fists, glancing at Mildred over her glasses, trying to guess why she had come. Being a relative newcomer to St. Charles, she did not know Mildred well, though she had heard a great deal about her from Mrs. Pringle. "A run-of-the-mill bitch" was one description Mrs. Pringle had given.

"The girls have told me what a wonderful help you've been." Mildred leaned forward with her elbows on the table, giving such a warm smile that Mrs. Kinch began to wonder if the reports she had heard were true.

"Glory, dear, I haven't done a thing!" she protested.

"You've offered to help. We always knew that you were here, that you were thinking of us."

"Well, I try to be a good neighbor. What's the use of *being* neighbors, I always say, if we can't help one another? I don't

128

know what I'd have done when Willie died—Mother, too—if it hadn't been for the people next door. We lived in Buffalo then. I'll just stick the coffee pot on," Mrs. Kinch added, turning for a moment to the stove. "Nothing like a cup of coffee to keep your spirits up."

" I really only dropped in for a minute, to thank you for your kindness."

"Oh, go on!" Mrs. Kinch was highly pleased. "You just call on me any time, any old time at all. I'm never too busy to lend a helping hand." She folded the dough expertly into small rolls, which she arranged on a pan. "There, now. One more job finished. Will you be staying in St. Charles long, Mrs. McKinley?" She had just remembered that Mildred was the daughter-in-law of old Mrs. McKinley, who had a flat over the florist's shop on Main Street.

"Until the end of the week, I expect, if Papa continues to improve." Mildred prepared to rise, then dropped back into her chair. "By the way, how long has Mr. Fairfield been staying with you?" she asked in a conversational voice.

"A bit more than a month, I'd say. Let's see, he came on a Tuesday." Mrs. Kinch glanced at the calendar on the wall. "August fourth, five weeks to the day. Such a nice man!" She looked archly at Mildred. "From what I hear, you've reason to be interested in him. Well, he'll make Lily a fine husband. The only thing I regret is that Fanny didn't get him."

"Naturally I'm interested in him." Mildred's voice was strained. "We know very little about him, you know—where he comes from, or what he does."

"He's a friend of those people who were here from Boston last year—you wouldn't know them, the Willitsons. Do you know, I never thought to ask Mr. Fairfield what he does. I assumed he was sort of a financier, or whatever you call them. I believe he mentioned owning some stock in Mr. Willitson's steamship line—that's what *he* does, something to do with steamships. I know Mr. Fairfield owns considerable property."

"Did he tell you that?"

"Naturally. I don't pry into people's affairs behind their backs," Mrs. Kinch said with dignity.

"He doesn't *look* particularly prosperous."

"You mean that one suit he wears all the time? Well, some men are like that, you know. He told me his wife used to have a terrible time with him. She was an aristocratic type, I gather —used to be at him all the time about buying clothes. What he needs right now is a woman to take care of him."

Mildred looked away.

"Some men are absolutely lost without a woman to fuss over them. Mr. Fairfield's that kind."

"I wonder if he's really as well off as he pretends to be."

Mrs. Kinch's manner cooled somewhat. "I really couldn't say."

"I hope you'll forgive my questioning you," Mildred said quickly. "But you can understand our concern, I'm sure. You apparently know how often he comes to see Lily. We don't want her to make a mistake."

"Believe me, I know!" Mrs. Kinch warmed again. "When it's your own family, you take a different view. Well, now, as far as I know, Mr. Fairfield's a perfect gentleman. I'd trust him with my own daughter. Such nice manners. You can tell he comes from a good family."

"Do you know anything about his family?"

"Well, now, I don't. I don't believe he's got any. His wife died about a year ago. I feel real sorry for him, losing his wife so young. She was a beautiful creature, according to him."

"Doesn't he have pictures of her?"

"Now, there's a funny thing. He's got a phobia against picture-taking. Can't stand to face a camera himself. He was quite put out when Miss Abbott wanted to take a snap of him for her scrapbook."

"I see . . ."

Mrs. Kinch looked up, wondering if she had revealed something without knowing it. She was not a mystery-story fan, and missed the significance of her own words. "Miss Abbott did take a picture of him one day when he wasn't looking. I've got it here somewhere." She searched behind some cookbooks at the end of the counter. "There, doesn't he look handsome?"

Miss Abbott's camera had caught Theodore at the moment he was folding back the pages of his newspaper. He looked preoccupied, unaware, as he sat neatly upright in the hard garden chair, one knee over the other, his polished shoes reflecting the light.

"Miss Abbott called it a candid camera study," Mrs. Kinch explained. She chuckled. "Oh, my, wouldn't he be annoyed if he knew!"

"I'd like to keep this," Mildred said peremptorily, leaning back, away from Mrs. Kinch, the picture held up to her breast as if she defied anyone to take it.

"Well, I'm sorry," Mrs. Kinch said with great politeness, "but it happens to be the only one I have." What's got *into* her? she asked herself. What's she blushing about?

"You must have the negative. You can get another print made."

"Miss Abbott took the negative with her when she left," Mrs. Kinch explained patiently. "Why on earth would you want a picture of him? Lily's got one. I gave it to her myself. She'd let you have it, I daresay, if you want it that bad."

Mildred laid the snapshot on the table. Mrs. Kinch seized it at once and replaced it in the folder behind the cookbooks. Coming into a person's house, snatching their possessions from under their very noses! she was thinking.

"It strikes me as rather strange that he's so reluctant to have his picture taken," Mildred said. "What do you really think of him, Mrs. Kinch? You're too sensible to be taken in by flattery and fine manners."

Mrs. Kinch, detecting a note of condescension in her voice,

was immediately on the defensive. "I'm not a suspicious person," she said with dignity. "I consider myself a good enough judge of character to know a gentleman when I see one."

"I wonder . . ."

Mrs. Kinch pressed her lips together in a hard line.

"Have you got his home address?"

"Naturally. It's in my guest book."

"I'd like to have it, please."

It was the wrong tone of voice to use on Mrs. Kinch. Her gorge rose. "I don't like people casting aspersions on my guests," she said sharply. "Mr. Fairfield has always been a perfect gentleman, paid his bills on time." She paused, remembering that he was behind with his rent. "I have no reason to suspect him of not being what he says he is," she continued firmly. "The Willows is a respectable guest house. I never take people that aren't dependable. Now, if you'll excuse me, I'll get back to my baking." She plucked the coffee pot, which was now perking merrily, off the burner and set it aside to cool.

There's ten cents worth of coffee wasted, she thought resentfully as she watched Mildred take the short cut through the wood. Casting aspersions on my guests! I wish I'd told her what I really think of her. Coming in here all smiles and thank you for this, thank you for that, you've been so kind, I'm sure, when all she wanted was to pry and ask questions. And poor Mr. Fairfield, of all people. I wonder what he'd say if he knew.

Mrs. McKinley—Harry's mother—arrived just as Mildred emerged from the wood. Fanny had driven into town to pick her up.

The old lady stepped from the car with her usual jauntiness and stood on the driveway looking about her, delighted with everything, holding a bundle of magazines to her chest as if she hugged her pleasure, too. She was quite unlike Harry, being small and thin, with a brown inquisitive face. She was dressed in neat rusty black with touches of white, a saucy jabot at her throat, and a pair of cheap lace gloves on her hands. Going out for tea was a great occasion for her, since she had outlived most of her friends.

Her flat over the florist's shop on Main Street was bursting with souvenirs of bygone days: seashells, paper fans, carved wooden figures. Squares of pink silk with tasseled corners were draped over the lampshades. A pair of lovebirds hung in a cage beside the window. There were plants everywhere, too: ivy and philodendron, geraniums and African violets. It was a depressing little place, but she loved it and thought it cozy, and would never dream of giving it up to live with Mildred and Harry, as he often suggested. Few people came to see her. Fanny was her most frequent visitor, dropping in at least once a week with flowers from the garden or a box of cakes. And once a month Fanny invited her out to Hawkrest for the afternoon. The rest of the time she had her television set, which Harry had given her. She spent so many hours of the day watching it that sometimes when she went out into the light she blinked, feeling herself to be in unreal surroundings.

She accepted Mildred's kiss gingerly, holding the magazines before her as a shield. "How are you, dear?" she asked. Traces of Cockney accent still clung to her speech. "These magazines are for you, Fanny," she went on, leading the way into the house, for she liked being indoors better than out. "Some lovely pictures of the royal family that I knew you'd want to see."

"How nice!" she said of everything, her glance darting about the room, noting the smallest changes as Fanny poured tea. How nice that Mildred was home, how nice to see Isobel, that Mr. Jameson had survived his latest attack, that Harry was getting along so well. In the end, her conversation always came back to Harry. "He always had a head for figures. When he was a bit of a thing I used to say, 'Harry, with your head for figures, you might get into the bank when you're older.' Never thinking he would! And look at him today."

"He makes five thousand a year," Mildred said.

Her sarcasm was lost on Mrs. McKinley, who thought this a very good salary. "His dad wanted him to take up tailoring, but Harry couldn't see it. 'No, Dad,' he said, 'nobody ever got rich making suits for other people. I'm going into the bank.' And he got the job by hisself. Walked into the manager's office and asked for it, and they took him on within the fortnight. What lovely little tarts, dear," she interposed, speaking to Fanny and holding a tart up to look at the bottom. "Oh, my, he did cut a figure when he got his first week's salary. He was always quite a one for the girls, you know." She looked apologetically at Mildred and added, "He settled down when he got married, of course, but in his young days he was quite a Cassanovia" (she gave the name five syllables)—"had half a dozen on the string at one time . . ." She went on and on, making the most of the opportunity, which seldom came her way, to talk about her son.

But when Fanny mentioned the royal family, Mrs. McKinley immediately seized upon this topic, for she loved royalty almost as much as she loved Harry. "There's an interesting article here on Princess Margaret," she said, picking up one of the magazines she had brought with her. "And look at this: the latest portrait of the Queen." She held the picture up to the light. "My, she does look lovely, doesn't she? Did you see the Coronation, dear?" she asked Mildred.

"Parts of it. I thought it was rather tiresome."

"Tiresome, oh my!" She laughed delightedly at this joke. "I never took my eyes off the television the livelong day. When Edward the Seventh was crowned I sat on a campstool for eighteen hours. Did you know that I once stood as close to Queen Mary as I am to you this minute? That was when she was Duchess of York." Mrs. McKinley looked from one face to another to observe the effect of this statement. "She was on her way to open a bazaar."

"It must have been an experience, I'm sure," Mildred said.

134

Her mother-in-law nodded. "I've always been sorry we moved out here before Harry had a good look at a royal wedding or a funeral. The only funeral I ever saw was old Queen Victoria's. I used to take him down to see the changing of the guards, but he wouldn't remember. He was only five when we left the old country. I always hoped I'd get back for a last look at things," she mused sadly, drinking her tea, which had grown cold while she talked.

Jessie Hutchins came downstairs on a mythical errand. She had heard voices, and wondered if she was missing anything. On her way back from the kitchen she glanced into the living room, and paused long enough to be noticed.

"Why, there's Jessie Hutchins!" the old lady exclaimed.

"I didn't know you, Mrs. McKinley!" Jessie smiled, now free to join the party. "All dressed up! My, don't we look chipper today!"

"You're nursing the old gentleman!" Mrs. McKinley announced, having figured out the reason for Jessie's presence in the house. "Well, now! He's in good hands, I'll say that."

"Oh, go on!" Jessie said in the teasing voice she reserved for her patients and for old people. "Why, yes, thank you, perhaps I will," she said to Fanny, who offered her a cup of tea. She sat down.

"We were just talking about Harry. I was telling the girls I used to take him down to Buckingham Palace to see the changing of the guards, when he was a bit of a thing, before we left London."

"He's grown a lot since then."

"My, hasn't he? Why—" Mrs. McKinley's eyes brightened suddenly. "*You* used to be an old flame of his, Jessie. When he first started in the bank. I remember it so well."

"I wasn't the only one. Remember the Litchfield girls? And that one with the red hair—I forget her name—and the blonde who won the Charleston contest over at the Falls?"

They laughed immoderately.

"Oh, that Harry!" Mrs. McKinley wiped her eyes. "I was just telling the girls—a regular Cassanovia when he was young."

Jessie looked sideways at Mildred, who was smoking furiously. "If I was Mildred, I'd be afraid to leave him alone in New York, wouldn't you? All those pretty girls—no telling what might happen."

"Harry was always a *good* boy," Mrs. McKinley said reprovingly. She felt that Jessie had overstepped the line when she insinuated that Harry had carried his boyish inconstancies into middle life. She had a nice appreciation of a mother-in-law's rights and privileges. The time before Harry's marriage belonged to her, and she had every right to reminisce as much as she pleased about his life and habits then; but his doings from the time of his marriage on were his wife's concern. His mother would never presume to mention them. "Why, he wouldn't dream!" she protested, suddenly noting Mildred's offended expression. She looked anxiously around at Fanny and Isobel.

"I wonder if Papa should be left alone so long," Isobel said pointedly, looking at Jessie, who rose at once.

"Well, ta ta. I'm off to my patient. Nice to see you again, Mrs. McKinley."

"Good-by, dear." The old lady smiled uncertainly. She fancied that an accusing silence fell as Jessie went up the stairs, and tried her best to make amends. "My, I *am* sorry she said that. So thoughtless. I'm sure she has no cause to suspect—"

"Of *course* not!" Fanny gave her a rallying smile and cut off another great slab of cake. "She was only teasing. She didn't mean anything."

The smile erased Mrs. McKinley's uneasiness. She accepted the cake greedily, for she never had such food as this at home, and meant to eat enough to do for her supper, too. Fanny was such a nice girl, so kind and good. A pity Harry hadn't married

136

her instead of . . . Oh, what am I thinking? she asked herself, glancing around guiltily.

"Lily isn't here," she remembered suddenly, a little later. She was beginning to become forgetful of late, and had just now noticed that one of the family was absent.

To her surprise, this mention of Lily seemed to have much the same effect as Jessie's thoughtless remark about Harry. Mildred stiffened perceptibly, and exchanged a look with Fanny.

Isobel answered. "She's out with her new beau."

"Oh, really? I believe I heard something . . . Yes, somebody did mention about her and that rather distinguished-looking man . . . a visitor to St. Charles, I believe . . . How very nice!" Mrs. McKinley waited, hoping to hear all the details of this romance, but nothing more was said.

She was thoughtful on the way home, not quite as buoyant as she had been on the journey out, realizing—as she had often suspected—that other people's lives were not as uncomplicated as hers. Behind the front they presented to the world, all sorts of secrets were hidden. People like the Jamesons—now who would dream they'd have a worry in the world? They had everything they wanted: security, a nice home, and even poor Lily, who was thought to be a trifle peculiar, was finding herself a nice husband at last. Mrs. McKinley's fears had always been tangible ones, something you could put your finger on, like her husband losing his job or, more recently, anxiety over investing the bit of money he'd left. (Just now she worried about getting home in one piece. Driving with Fanny was hard on the nerves, though she was too kind-hearted to say so.) If she was in the Jameson girls' shoes, she'd be hard put to it to find a bugaboo. And yet she had sensed this afternoon a tension in the air as if they all expected something unpleasant to happen. It wasn't their father. His death would not upset them that much. Besides, whatever was bothering them wasn't a collective thing. Each had her own private anxiety. If anybody in the world had reason to be happy, it was Mildred, married to Harry, who was doing so well, and with money of her own besides; yet there she was, moping and fretting as if her life had been one long tragedy. And Isobel, when she thought nobody was looking, examined some disturbing thing in her own mind. What it could be Mrs. McKinley was unable to imagine. Everybody in town said how lucky Isobel was, finding a nice husband like Eliot Whitmore after getting herself talked about the way she had.

I don't know what gets *into* people, she thought. As if there isn't enough trouble in the world, they have to go and invent their own.

Passing a candy shop on the way home, Fanny saw a box of hazelnuts in the window and remembered how Isobel used to love them. She went in and bought half a pound. While she waited for change, she wondered if Mildred would think she was showing favoritism, and ordered a pound of chocolates as well. She had been thinking about Isobel all afternoon. She had an idea that, though Isobel had seemed happy about that telephone call at lunch time, it had disturbed her, too—presented her with a new problem or renewed an old one.

Then, a little later, Mrs. Pringle had beckoned Fanny into the kitchen to impart some information she had received in confidence from Isobel. Listening, Fanny was sadly aware that Isobel never told *her* things. She had not the courage to offer herself as a confidante, though she often thought wistfully how nice it would be if Isobel would come to her for advice or help, if only about trivial things.

"I'm afraid we're in for trouble, dear," Mrs. Pringle had said, scratching a match on the bottom of a kitchen chair and lighting her cigarette with great pleasure. "I've just had a nice little talk with Isobel about that so-called man she married. I've been afraid all along," she continued, settling back and undoing the top of her corsets. "When a woman in her thirties

—just when she's at her best—goes and marries a man twenty years older than she is, watch out for trouble. I said that when she married him. I never did believe in all this talk about women wearing out faster than men. It's nothing but a fairy tale, made up by men, no doubt, to help their conceit. My glands are in *better* shape than they were twenty years ago, but Ernie—my God! you'd think he had one foot in the grave . . . But what's happened is far worse than anything I imagined. You remember that operation Whatsisname had a year or so ago?"

"Eliot? It wasn't terribly serious, was it?"

"Well, mind you, Isobel didn't say right out, but I wasn't born yesterday. From what I can gather, he's lost his . . ." Mrs. Pringle looked modestly away and tried again. "You remember Lady Chatterley's husband?"

Fanny blushed painfully.

"I don't need to explain, I see. So you can imagine the quandary the poor girl's in, through no fault of her own. She can't help the way she's made," Mrs. Pringle said quickly, as if defending Isobel, though Fanny had said nothing. "Some women's got more active glands than others, that's all. It's natural for her to be telling me her troubles," she added, reading Fanny like a book. "She's been telling me things since she was knee-high. And of course, me being married, having gone through the mill, so to speak. It takes an experienced woman to really appreciate . . . But the question is, how is it going to end? She's only thirty-eight, the full flower of womanhood, I read somewhere once. The only thing she *can* do, as far as I can see, is get rid of him and start fresh with someone else."

"She's had three husbands already."

"Well, there you are. She's been unlucky with men. Why she ever married that dried-up creature is beyond me. If the truth were known, I'd hazard a guess he didn't have much to lose in the first place."

Fanny bit her thumb, frowning.

"I thought I'd warn you, dear, so you could get yourself braced for a little unpleasantness. His mother's going to have the grandfather of all conniptions; and Mildred—I tremble to think!"

"Isobel didn't actually say anything about leaving Eliot?"

"Not in so many words. But no doubt you've noticed by now that I've got a better understanding of human nature than most people. It helps in drawing conclusions," Mrs. Pringle said with satisfaction. She had never liked Eliot.

"You may be making a mountain out of a molehill."

Mrs. Pringle shook her head vigorously, unwilling to tolerate such a thought. "Of course she could go on living with him, and get herself a friend, but them affairs are always dangerous. And you know how possessive he is. He'd catch on in no time. Maybe he has caught on, for all I know," she added meaningfully. "That telephone call at lunch time didn't fool me. I happened to be just inside the dining room door, dusting."

"She didn't say anything about him—that man who telephoned?"

"She will in time. She'll confide in me." Mrs. Pringle could not help preening herself a little. She, not Fanny, was the one people told things to.

"If anything does happen, we must try to be understanding. There will be enough people to criticize her," Fanny said.

"I hoped you'd say that, dear." Mrs. Pringle beamed. "I said to her myself, 'You know you can always count on me.' I'd like to be the one to tell old Mrs. Whatsername myself."

Old Mrs. Whatsername, otherwise known as Mrs. Whitmore, telephoned Isobel later in the afternoon. Eliot's mother always gave the impression that she expected anyone who received a call from her to be properly cognizant of the honor thus bestowed. Eliot was like his mother in many ways. The air about them always contained a faint—perhaps even

140

imagined—atmosphere of disapproval. When Isobel had finished her conversation with her mother-in-law, she said, "I've been asked to dinner, a royal summons," and her sigh had a new significance. Fanny said nothing, since she could not very well assure Isobel of understanding when she was not even supposed to know that Isobel needed it; and in any case she would not have known how to express what she wanted to convey. So she bought a box of hazelnuts, a gift being the best she could think of in the way of encouragement.

She did not recognize the English roadster that was parked by the front door when she returned home. She put her own car in the garage and went through the kitchen.

Mrs. Pringle, scrubbing potatoes at the sink, which was already piled high with dirty cups, was in a rage.

"I'm not an unreasonable woman," she began, the minute the door opened. "I've put up with more than my share; all the extra cleaning and people leaving their dirty underwear in the bathroom, never a hand raised to help. I've kept my peace, with His Majesty sick and those nurses running up and down, Mrs. Pringle this, Mrs. Pringle that, trays for this one and trays for that one, washing and ironing and scrubbing. But I've reached the end of my rope. I'm not paid to run a hotel." She kept her back to Fanny and scrubbed away viciously at the potato.

"Daisy, dear, what is it?" Fanny went up behind her and took her arms.

"Don't Daisy dear me!" Mrs. Pringle thrust her elbows out angrily, shaking off Fanny's hands. "I've stood all I'm going to stand. There's a limit to human endurance, though some people don't seem to think so. I'd quit this minute, except I've got more consideration than some people. No, I'll work out my two weeks' notice, unless you can find somebody in the meantime."

"Oh, no!"

Mrs. Pringle turned on the tap. Water gushed into the sink.

"Come and sit down," Fanny coaxed. She shut off the tap, took the potato from Mrs. Pringle's hand, and turned her round.

Mrs. Pringle allowed herself to be led to a chair. "And what happens when dinner time comes?" she asked, looking offendedly down at her hands as she dried them on her apron. "When people sit down at the table expecting to be served so they can pick and poke and complain?"

"I know you've had all this extra work, and we haven't been very helpful. Look, why don't you leave all this and go home? Get a good rest. I can clean up here and put the dinner on."

"I'm not complaining about you." Mrs. Pringle relented a bit. "You've had your hands full. You know I'm the last person in the world to make a fuss over nothing, but when people deliberately sit in there on their backsides, knowing full well I'm out here working my fingers to the bone, and ask to be waited on hand and foot, then that's carrying things too far. I'm not running a bloody tea shop. I can't get meals at any hour of the day or night on a moment's notice."

"Has anybody asked you to?" Fanny said, puzzled.

"Asked me to? *Ordered* me to, like Lady Flounderface talking to her chimney sweep. 'Another tea tray, Pringle. Another plate of sandwiches.'" Her voice rose in mimicry. "What am I, a short-order waitress, for God's sake?"

"Who is in there?"

"Mr. Fairfield, and I heard him with my own ears saying he didn't *want* tea. But she had to have it. Oh, my, yes. 'Oh, Mr. Fairfield, we wouldn't *dream* of letting you go without a cup of tea. Oh, Mr. Fairfield, we're going to have such a lovely chat, and you can tell us all about yourself.' What the devil is she up to?" Mrs. Pringle wondered abruptly.

"I'd better go in," Fanny said, glancing toward the door. She bent over and patted Mrs. Pringle's plump shoulder.

142

"Now, I want you to promise you won't touch a thing here, or bother about dinner. You're to go straight home and rest."

"I haven't got the strength to walk home," Mrs. Pringle said resignedly. "No, I'll rest my poor feet for five minutes, then carry on. I'll work out my two weeks' notice."

"Don't say that, *please*!" Fanny begged.

"I can't put up with *her*. Ordering me around . . . and if the old man's going to live forever . . ."

"Don't decide now."

"I have decided." Mrs. Pringle remained inflexible.

"Just rest here until I get back, then, and we'll talk about it. We can arrange something . . . We *will* be more helpful, I promise." Fanny looked into the mirror behind the door and ran her fingers through her hair before she went into the living room.

Theodore was standing with his back to the fireplace, as if he had retreated as far as he could. Both he and Isobel looked up with relief when Fanny entered the room. Mildred, presiding over the tea things, wore her most sociable smile, but behind it there lurked a suggestion of uncertainty. It was the expression she had worn as a child when the suspicion first crossed her mind that, because of something she had said or done, she was about to be excluded from the other children's game. Lily sat on a footstool with her hands clasped round her knees, daydreaming.

"Oh, there you are, Fanny!" Mildred said brightly. "Mr. Fairfield has just been telling us about himself."

"And now I really must go," Theodore said.

"Oh, but you can't leave yet!" Mildred chided playfully. "When we're just getting to know you." She gave Fanny a significant look, demanding her cooperation. "Mr. Fairfield says he comes from Boston, Fanny."

"I know," Fanny said.

"Did you know that he's a friend of the Willitsons, who visited St. Charles last year?"

Fanny glanced apologetically at Theodore. "Yes, I believe he did tell us that."

"You know, I *thought* that name rang a bell. Now I remember. I *met* the Willitsons last fall, through some friends of ours in New York. Isn't that a coincidence?" Mildred was lying, Fanny saw. "It just shows you what a small world . . . Well, if you must rush away," she added reproachfully, seeing that Theodore could not be induced to stay longer. "You must come again soon." She smiled, extending her hand, which he shook rather stiffly. "It's been lovely having this little chat with you."

Lily went to the door with him, and a moment later they heard her going up the stairs.

"*Not* very diplomatic," Isobel remarked.

Mildred glanced across at her but made no reply.

"And rather embarrassing for the rest of us."

"I haven't the faintest idea what you're talking about." Mildred shuffled a pack of cards and, pushing aside the tea things, began to lay out a hand of solitaire. "I was merely trying to be agreeable."

"I don't think it was necessary to ask so many questions. I suppose you thought you were drawing him out in a subtle way. It sounded more like a cross-examination."

## CHAPTER NINE

AFTER DINNER THEODORE TOOK THE PATH THROUGH THE BEECH-wood and stood for a moment looking at the house before he stepped over the low hedge into the garden. It was nothing new for him to be prowling about in the dark, waiting to keep a rendezvous. Slits of light came through the partly drawn curtains of the downstairs rooms and lay in pale bars across the lawn. Inside, he could see Fanny and Mildred drinking coffee and smoking their eternal cigarettes. The air was blue with smoke.

Keeping to the shadows, he skirted the house and went round to the back garden. This side of the river bank was almost in darkness, though the houses on the opposite shore were clearly visible, catching the last pink light from the sky behind him. The old summerhouse in the corner attracted him. Grass and shrubs had been allowed to grow up around it, so that it seemed cut off from the rest of the garden. It was neglected and unused. Cobwebs hung from the beams, and seedlings grew between the floor boards, which creaked under his weight. When he touched the railing he drew back at once, not because it seemed insecure, but because the river bank dropped away so sharply a few feet beyond.

Far below in the blue dusk, the ruffled current reflected the afterglow. Three gulls circled upward like pale ghosts. To his left, the butternut tree grew up through a hole in the floor-boards of the summerhouse and disappeared again through the roof. The summerhouse must have been built when the tree was much younger, for the trunk had expanded until the timbers around it were heaved up and pushed aside. Theodore laid his hand on the ridged bark as he went by. He saw a little gate in the railing beyond. It was open, swinging on rusty hinges, and it led to a narrow wooden platform with steps going down. Leaning over, he found himself looking into what seemed at first to be a bottomless chasm: a break in the rocky cliff, about twenty feet across at its widest point. The steps zig-zagged down one sheer face of it, and at the bottom he could make out some sort of roof, with the dead branch of a tree fallen across it.

When Lily came silently up behind him and touched his arm, he started.

She laughed. "Did I frighten you?"

"What are these steps?"

"They go down to the boathouse. They're safe enough," Lily assured him. "I've been down hundreds of times." She leaned on the railing and looked over. "Do you know why they were built?" she asked, looking back over her shoulder.

"Please be careful!" he begged, grasping her arm. Remembering the source of Mr. Jameson's income, he now realized the purpose of the steps, but did not like to say so. He listened while Lily told him the whole story.

"When I was young, I used to come out here in the middle of the night and hide. It was so dark, and sometimes I'd have to wait for hours before the men came up. They never spoke. They'd creep up the steps in the dark, like ghosts, carrying boxes on their shoulders, and go across the lawn to the side door. They never used lanterns, or any kind of light; so that's why the steps had to be made strong. Let's go down. I'll show you the *Lilybell*. She was named after me and Isobel."

He looked fearfully over the railing. Below, the shadows were deepening by the minute. "No," he said firmly, drawing Lily back into the summerhouse and pulling the little gate to behind him. "I have no desire to risk my neck when I have so much to look forward to. Come and sit down."

She resisted with the stubborn tilt of her chin he was beginning to know. "Why can't we go down tonight?"

"Because I want to talk with you. Because the thought of going into that yawning chasm frightens me to death, even in daylight. But we'll look at your boathouse tomorrow, if you insist. Now will you come and sit on this bench, like a good girl?"

"Oh, all right, if you're frightened." Lily pouted, then laughed. "You are funny. You're afraid of a lot of things, aren't you? Nothing frightens me." She swept away a cobweb that hung from the roof, and taking his hand led him past the tree to a wooden bench. "You're safe here," she said in a mocking voice.

146

He glanced over his shoulder at the house. "Where are the others? Will they wonder where you are?"

"They'll never think to look here."

Through the screen of bushes he saw the curtains being drawn back in an upstairs room. The nurse opened the French doors, stepped out on the balcony, and lit a cigarette.

"She can't see us," Lily whispered.

Theodore moved along the seat, close to her, and held her hands. "How soon can we be married?"

"Any time. I don't care."

"Shall we buy the license tomorrow?"

"Not in St. Charles. We'd have to buy it from old Mr. Ramsay, and he'd tell everybody. We can go to another town, and give fictitious addresses. Then we must wait three days after that."

He wondered how she knew so much about it. "Perhaps we could get a special license." They both spoke in low tones, because of the figure on the balcony.

"It's an awful nuisance. Joe and I tried, then decided it was simpler just to wait the three days. We didn't want the others to know," Lily explained. "Where shall we go afterwards?"

"Not far, on my present finances."

"*Will* you stop worrying about money?" Lily said impatiently. "There, she's gone," she added. On the balcony, the nurse threw away her cigarette, yawned, and went inside, closing the French doors after her and drawing the curtains. "We'll buy a car and drive—oh, to Mexico, or California. Somewhere far away."

"It's wonderful of you to be so understanding about my difficulties," he said.

Lily shrugged. She turned, listening to the rustlings in the underbrush below. A dark shape detached itself from the shadows and went sailing off over the trees. "Look, there's an owl," she said. "All kinds of animals live down there. Foxes and rabbits, even skunks. Once we had a flock of white

147

pigeons. They kept disappearing, and one night Mildred saw a red fox come up over the bank and kill one. She cried for hours."

"Why does Mildred dislike me?" he asked.

"Because I like you."

"This afternoon I felt that she hated me, though she pretended to be so cordial. And the way she questioned me—as if she suspected me of some crime! Would your other sisters object if they knew we plan to be married?"

"Who cares what they think?"

"It would be more pleasant if they liked me." He stood up and looked over the railing at the river. "I believe Mildred will try anything in her power to prevent us from being happy."

"What can she do?"

"She came to see Mrs. Kinch today." Theodore grasped the steel railing with both hands. "She asked a great many questions." When Mrs. Kinch had told him about Mildred's call, he had been so upset that he had paced about his room for an hour, trembling with anger. He began to tremble again now, remembering. "To have her questioning people about me . . . As if I were a common criminal! Prying into my life. What does she expect to find?"

"Mildred pries into everybody's life."

"How dare she pry into mine! What does she hope to gain by it?"

"Just to find out all about you. She and Fanny have had their heads together ever since you telephoned yesterday."

"But surely you're capable of choosing your own friends."

"They don't think so." Lily hooked one finger in his buttonhole and looked up at him pouting. "They're not very nice to me, you know."

He was flattered to think she would employ such an obvious falsehood to invite his sympathy. "Then it's high time somebody rescued you, my darling!" he said. "*I'll* be good to you!" He added, "If Mildred should find out anything about me,

148

would it make any difference to you? You wouldn't let her turn you against me, would you?"

"What could she find out?"

"Well—about the money, for instance . . ."

"I wouldn't believe anything she said, ever." Lily lifted her arms appealingly and laced her fingers together at the back of his neck. "If she told me you'd been in jail, I'd know she was lying. If she said you were Bluebeard with twenty wives locked in a dungeon, I'd marry you anyway. Nobody can stop me from doing what I want to do!"

"Mildred will try," he reminded.

"Let her try!"

"Hush!" he soothed. "Somebody will hear us." He drew her head down to his shoulder and smiled into the darkness.

Mildred had been trying to telephone Harry all evening.

"I'm sorry, madam, your party does not answer," the operator kept saying.

"But he must be there!" Mildred protested. "Are you sure you're ringing the right number?"

"Do you wish me to keep on trying, madam?"

"Of course keep on trying!"

"She *can't* be ringing the right number," Mildred said, moving restlessly about the room.

"Harry could be out," Fanny reasoned.

"Out? Out where? I told him I'd telephone tonight."

"He may have gone out to buy a paper or something."

Mildred threw herself into a chair with a long sigh. She had taken three aspirin tablets for her headache, but her temples still throbbed; the dull ache went down the back of her neck and fanned out over her shoulders. When the telephone rang ten minutes later, she pounced on it as if it were an animal that might get away. But the caller was Eliot. She almost cried with vexation as she explained that Isobel was having dinner with his mother. How unfair, she thought, that Isobel, who

149

didn't *care*, should have so devoted a husband, while she, who had never given Harry a moment's worry . . . She shaded her eyes with her fingers, contemplating this injustice.

She thought perhaps another cup of coffee might cheer her up, and went into the kitchen to put the kettle on. While she waited for the water to boil, she rested her elbows on the sill and stared into the garden, which looked unfamiliar in the dying light. She would never go out into the garden by herself at night, for every shadow, every leaf movement, terrified her. The houses across the river were like ghosts, their lighted windows dimly yellow. Was that something moving in the deep shadows of the summerhouse? She drew back quickly and pulled down the blind.

She felt tired, weighted down with all her cares. She should be at home with Harry (where *is* he? she asked herself impatiently, straining her ears toward the silent telephone in the hall), but she could not return to him when she was so needed here. Lily had slipped away again after dinner. One moment she had been sitting innocently in the living room, yawning over a puzzle, and the next minute she had disappeared. Where was she now? Was she sitting in some lovers' lane with that man? Were they lying together in the long grass? Mildred's hand shook as she poured the coffee.

The whole afternoon had gone badly for her. She had realized, while questioning Theodore, that she was not being as subtle as she had intended to be. Her own impatience trapped her, made her incautious, put questions into her mouth that she had never intended to ask (at least, not in the way they came out). She had seen the guarded look come down over his face like a shadow, but still she had kept on, unable to stop once she had started.

Mrs. Pringle had gone home directly after dinner, leaving a mountain of dishes to be washed. The extra work made Fanny unreasonable and fault-finding.

"For heaven's *sake*, Mildred!" she remonstrated when Mildred told her about the visit to Mrs. Kinch.

"You leave everything to me, and then complain about the way I do it."

"But to question Mrs. Kinch!"

Mildred accepted this unfair criticism with a sigh. "It's not the first time I've had to shoulder the whole burden," she said.

Now, sitting forlornly in the kitchen drinking her second cup of coffee, she had a sudden idea. Inertia vanished. She dropped her half-finished cigarette into the cup and went upstairs to Lily's room, drawing the blinds before she turned on the light. The room was untidy. The poppy-colored silk dress Lily had worn that afternoon was flung on the bed; a pair of linen pumps had been kicked into a corner. Blotchy water-colors were tacked on the wall, and a bunch of wild asters drooped in a glass vase on the dresser. The snapshot of Theodore was in the top drawer, tossed carelessly onto a jumble of lipsticks and spilled face powder. Mildred held it up to the light, squinting, for she had come up without her glasses. Then, thrusting it inside her bosom, she went downstairs to the living room, where she sat at the mahogany kidney desk in the corner, helped herself to notepaper, and began a letter to the Peerless Detective Agency in New York.

The Peerless had gathered the evidence required for Lily's divorce from Joe Nicholson, and Mildred was confident that the agency would be able to furnish her with all the facts of Theodore's past life.

She wrote busily, making the most of the meager information she had. All she really knew about him was that he hated to have his picture taken. She had read enough mystery stories to know that this was important. As for the rest, he *said* he lived in Boston, that he owned some factories and other real estate there, that he knew a man named Willitson who was in shipping; but these facts could be taken with a grain of salt. She wished she had thought of tricking him into leaving his fingerprints around somewhere. On a letter, a book jacket, anywhere. It would have been so easy. Too late for that now. She had his picture, anyway. She would enclose that, and write a description of him as well. With her back to the room she took the snapshot out of her blouse and studied it. She could describe his features one by one, but how convey to a stranger the *way* he looked, the sum of his features, the sorcery of his glance? She chewed the end of her pen, scratched out some words, then tore up the whole sheet and began again. By the time she had finished, it was after nine o'clock, and Isobel had returned from her mother-in-law's, looking ruffled.

"What time does the night train go through?" Mildred asked.

Fanny answered. "Around eleven."

"If I took a letter down to the station, would it go out tonight?"

"Yes, Mr. Romano will put it in the bag. Is it something important?"

"A letter to Harry," Mildred lied. "Since he won't answer the telephone . . . It's about some business that must be attended to tomorrow."

"I'll run you down to the station, then," Fanny said.

## CHAPTER TEN

IN THE MORNING, ISOBEL ROSE EARLY. WHEN SHE LOOKED INTO her father's room on the way downstairs, she found him awake, slipping sideways off the pillows. His face was contorted with frustration and anger because he could not right himself. Miss Anstice slept in a chair beside the window. Isobel placed her hands under her father's arms and tried to lift him into a more comfortable position. He complained in a broken mumble, which woke the nurse.

"Oh, heavens!" She jumped up, all apologies. Together they propped up the old man and straightened the bedding.

"All right now?" Isobel asked, bending over him.

He leaned his head against her arm and whimpered. Tears ran down his cheeks, and greasy perspiration from his forehead stained her robe. She turned her head away, thinking for a moment that this peevish old man was someone she did not know. Her father had been so lusty and arrogant, staging his theatrical tantrums and making sure no one missed the exhibition. He was common and vulgar, but honestly common and vulgar, even when he postured, even when he talked about the old family mansion and made up tales of his childhood; for these were not lies, only flights of imagination. When he raged, Isobel had never tried to avoid him, or to endure the ordeal with long-suffering calm. She listened as if he were an actor delivering lines. She knew that he *was* acting, was entranced with the mastery of his own performance. Unlike Mildred and Fanny, she had never regarded her father's numerous affairs as either disgusting or embarrassing. Women had fluttered around him like moths, and none of them had ever complained afterwards. It seemed to her that only very narrow-minded persons would resent a man of his energy and enthusiasm taking advantage of opportunities that came begging.

But this old man on the bed was bleary-eyed and sexless, smelling of age and sickness. A decaying shell, Isobel thought. Dr. Randolph had worked frantically to keep him alive last night. It would have been more humane to let him die.

She met Fanny in the hall. "Is he all right?" Fanny asked.

Isobel nodded. "Poor old thing," she said as they went downstairs together. "I hate to see him lying there."

"I'd almost rather see him in one of his old rages," Fanny agreed.

153

"It seems indecent, somehow . . . degrading. It's one of the things that frighten me about old age—being helpless and repulsive. He must know we only go into his room because we don't want to seem heartless." Isobel added, "I thought you promised to sleep this morning."

"I couldn't sleep. I was so worried about Pringle leaving."

"She's threatened to leave before. She really doesn't mean it."

"I believe she does, this time." Fanny raked her fingers through her hair. "The *years* she's been here! What will we ever do without her?"

"Perhaps if we don't mention it, she'll forget that she's given her notice."

"It will save face if she changes her mind," Fanny agreed.

Mrs. Pringle was in the kitchen, changing into the black oxfords she wore during working hours. "Well, girls," she said in a haughty voice, not looking at them as she heaved herself upright and examined herself in the mirror behind the door, pushing her curls into place with both hands. Her injured expression meant that she was not yet ready to forgive anyone for provoking yesterday's burst of temper. Showing up this morning a quarter of an hour early was intended to point up the fact that she had been meticulous in the performance of her duty these many years, though so hard done by.

"Are you feeling better?" Fanny asked her.

"I feel well enough," she admitted frostily. "Is this coffee?" she asked dubiously, lifting the lid off the pot and sniffing. She poured herself a cup, sat down with a long-suffering sigh, and lit a cigarette.

"I thought you were going to stay at home and rest today."

"I get week-ends off, not Wednesdays," Mrs. Pringle reminded self-righteously.

"Pringle, darling, what's got into you this morning?" Isobel dropped one arm round the plump shoulders and laid her cheek against the mahogany bangs.

Mrs. Pringle hunched herself disdainfully away.

Isobel ignored the snub. "What would you like for breakfast?" she asked in a coaxing voice.

"I'll have a good long rest when I've worked out my two weeks' notice," Mrs. Pringle remarked, staring into the garden.

"Oh, Pringle, you wouldn't! Not when Fanny needs you so much."

"I've given my notice." Mrs. Pringle's face was stony. "I don't fancy spending the next ten years running up and down stairs with trays, waiting on people who come visiting, listening to their complaints, being ordered about by people who have no business ordering me about."

Fanny and Isobel exchanged glances, held a silent conference over her head. Fanny nodded doubtfully.

Isobel fetched a decanter from the dining room sideboard. "What you need is a pick-me-up," she said firmly, pouring whiskey into a glass.

"My God, at this hour of the day!" Mrs. Pringle turned a shocked face from the window.

"It's just what you need, darling." Isobel set the glass on the table. "Think of it as medicine," she urged.

Mrs. Pringle looked sideways at it. A little of her antagonism melted, but it was too early for surrender. "I'd never get through the day," she said, drawing herself up primly. "Drinking before breakfast! I hope I've got some self-respect." As both girls had their backs to her—Fanny taking eggs from the refrigerator and Isobel reaching into the cupboard for dishes—she picked up the glass and turned it in her hand, then set it down hastily.

"Shall we have our eggs scrambled or poached?" Fanny asked. "Pringle, dear, what would you like?"

Mrs. Pringle glared at her. "I couldn't eat a morsel. Up all night with this pain in my back . . ."

"Your poor back! Shall I rub it for you?"

"Rubbing's no good, you know that." Mrs. Pringle was

waiting for further encouragement. When none came, she said resignedly, "Well, I suppose . . . if you really think this will help me . . ." She picked up the glass and took a sip, then drained it.

When Miss Anstice came down ten minutes later, the three were sitting around the table eating, all in high good humor. "Laugh, I thought I'd die!" Mrs. Pringle was saying. "There she was in nothing but a pair of black lace panties and two stars stuck on front . . . Good-morning, dear. You look nice and fresh. I was just telling the girls about the burlesque show I took Ernie to over in Buffalo."

Miss Anstice flicked a glance at the decanter. While she ate her breakfast, she rehearsed the story she would tell her land-lady. "Sitting there drinking and carrying on as if they hadn't a care in the world, and that poor old man dying upstairs. A bottle of whiskey right on the breakfast table!"

Mildred and Fanny were making the beds, later, while Mrs. Pringle was cleaning the bathroom down the hall and singing. Her pre-breakfast drink had cheered her considerably, but it had not had the desired effect of persuading her to retract her ultimatum.

"I don't know which way to turn," Mildred told Fanny. She had finally succeeded in telephoning Harry at the bank, but talking with him had not comforted her. "I know that my place is here with you," she went on, "that I'm *needed* here, but now Harry says he doesn't know about the week end— whether he can get away or not. When is Isobel leaving?"

"She hasn't said."

Mildred frowned. "Eliot called her this morning. And that other man. It couldn't have been Eliot again, because she'd just talked to him. Besides, her voice was different. I wonder what Eliot would say if he knew."

"It may be just a friend."

"You know what she's like, yet you always take her part."

"It's really none of our business, is it, who she talks to?" Fanny folded the sheet expertly at the corners and tucked it in, not wishing to continue this conversation, since she knew something about Eliot that Mildred did not.

"It might be Eliot's business."

"You've got too much on your side." Fanny jerked the bedspread toward her. "Those flowers go in the middle." She added after a moment, "I don't think it's our place to tell Eliot anything."

"He's so good to her. Anything she wants . . . Isobel just simply doesn't *care*!" Mildred said so vehemently that Fanny stopped working to look at her. "She's like Hazel. Every man she looks at she wants for herself. I saw the way she looked at that Mr. Fairfield the other night. Oh, you needn't try to defend her. I saw her. It's her mother's blood coming out. Hazel never cared for anybody else's feelings. She was selfish, selfish, selfish, and she ruined more lives—" Mildred broke off. Her hands were trembling.

"I always liked Hazel," Fanny said perversely. "She was gay, and she laughed a lot. I always wanted to be like her."

"Oh, she was gay enough," Mildred conceded bitterly. "That was the hellish part of it. She was always so good-humored that people couldn't see the harm she was doing."

"She's been dead for twenty years," Fanny said. "And what *harm* did she ever do? She made a lot of people happy."

"Isobel's the same," Mildred went on as if there had been no interruption. "She doesn't know the meaning of morality. She ought to be *thankful*, marrying into the Whitmores after the life she's led. I never expected her to be true to Eliot. I always knew she was incapable of fidelity. Women like that don't deserve husbands. I can't *understand* them," Mildred said despairingly. "It's just sex. Their minds dwell on nothing else."

157

"You're worrying about trifles, aren't you? Just because some man happened to telephone Isobel . . ."

"Some man she's probably running around with behind Eliot's back."

Fanny plumped the pillows into a neat bolster. "I never liked Eliot," she said. "I always thought he was a prig."

"At least he's not a drunkard," Mildred said, as Mrs. Pringle came down the hall.

"Don't say anything to her, *please*!" Fanny begged.

"If I had anything to say, I'd wait until she was sober."

"She's not drunk. If she leaves, who could we get? Nobody else would work here."

"You pay her twice what she's worth."

When Mrs. Pringle stuck her head in the doorway, Mildred at once turned to the window and gazed into the garden.

"There's the bathrooms done," Mrs. Pringle said cheerfully. "Now then, your ladyship, what's next? Polish up the spittoons? Sweep down the chimneys?" She glanced over her shoulder toward the window and with a bawdy gesture offered her plump behind in Mildred's direction.

"That's everything, I believe," Fanny said, pretending to notice nothing. "Why don't you go and have a nice rest now?"

"Yes, I'll go and have a lay-down, then." Mrs. Pringle flounced off, pausing in the doorway to say, "I'd be obliged if nobody disturbed me for half an hour; but if it's something that can't wait, something really *imperative* like somebody wanting a formal dinner for twenty people at a moment's notice"—she breathed on her nails and polished them on the cushion of her breast, her eyes on Mildred's inflexible back— "then you'll find me on the couch in my room."

"There's really no need to put up with that," Mildred admonished.

"It doesn't happen often."

"Once is enough, I should think."

"We have to overlook other people's weaknesses. Besides,

158

it's my fault. She wasn't feeling well when she came in this morning, and I thought a drink would cheer her up. And she does work hard. All the years she's been with us and shared our troubles . . ." Fanny sat down on the bed. "If she leaves, there won't be anyone . . . I'll be all alone."

"Lily hasn't married that man yet. And won't, if I have anything to do with it," Mildred said sharply. "Not that I expect much help. You complain about being left alone, yet you refuse to lift a finger. You know that you could reason with Lily, make her understand that she's making a mistake, yet you haven't said a word to her. Where is Lily?" she asked suddenly.

"She went somewhere with Theodore."

"Where?"

"She didn't say."

"Didn't you ask her?"

Fanny shook her head wearily.

"What was she wearing?"

"That little wool suit Isobel gave her. Why?"

"She wouldn't dress like that unless they had planned something." Mildred paused as the significance of her own words struck her. She stared at Fanny, then dashed across the hall to Lily's room and flung open the door.

Fanny followed more slowly. Lily's bed was still unmade, the sheets thrown back and trailing on the floor. Her nightgown was on the floor, too, in a limp circle as if she had just stepped out of it.

Mildred opened the closet door. "You know what clothes she has. Is everything here?"

"Of course." Fanny glanced at the row of dresses.

"Are you sure? When she ran away with Joe Nicholson, she took very few clothes. Is anything missing?"

"Oh, God, the way you imagine things!" Fanny said impatiently. "If Theodore wanted to marry her, he'd do it properly, with a long engagement, and notices in the paper."

"How do you know?"

"Because he's a gentleman." But Fanny turned back to the closet and, seeing a number of empty hangers, began to worry herself, trying to remember what clothes had been sent to the cleaners that week.

Mrs. Pringle spent two hours in a delicious languorous state between sleeping and waking. Rising at last, and filled with optimism, she opened the racing form she had bought the previous night and spent another enjoyable hour making notes on a slip of paper. "The double's a cinch," she told Fanny in the kitchen. "Gadabout and Miss Muffet. Ernie said Black Prince in the first, but I don't agree. You've only to look at the record. I was just going to call Mr. Flaherty."

"Who's Mr. Flaherty?"

"The bookie, dear. I'm putting five dollars on Gadabout and Miss Muffet. If they win—and I don't see how they can help it—I'll have a nice little nest egg for my retirement." She looked sideways at Fanny and was gratified to see that her innuendo was not wasted. "Why not try a little flyer yourself, dear?"

"Well . . . all right."

"Good for you!" Mrs. Pringle hid her surprise. "I'll tell Mr. Flaherty a five on the double for you too, then."

"Do you want the money now?"

"Oh, no. I have a charge account. He'll collect at the end of the week—or pay up as the case may be. Let's hope for God's sake he'll pay up for a change."

"If he does, I want you to keep my winnings—a little present."

Mrs. Pringle opened her eyes wide. "You realize how much you'll win, if they both come in? Say the odds are still five to one on Gadabout—I forget what Miss Muffet was; I can find out—but yesterday's double paid over thirty dollars on the two-dollar bet."

"That's all right. I'd like you to keep the money."

Mrs. Pringle recognized this as a bribe. She accepted it, but with no intention of being swayed by it. During the morning, while she studied the history and performance of various horses, she had built up a lovely picture of whole days devoted to such research. She had discovered what she believed to be an infallible system, which she was testing on today's race. If it worked, she might even stop doing business with bookies, who placed a limit on winnings, and follow the horses from one track to another. "Well, if you're sure . . ." she said. "It'll make a nice little addition to my nest egg."

"Has Lily come back yet?" Fanny asked.

"I haven't seen her. Went off early this morning with Mr. Fairfield, didn't she?"

"Yes. She didn't tell you where they were going, did she?"

"Why, no." Mrs. Pringle glanced up. "She didn't even mention she was *going*. I wouldn't worry about them, dear," she added, but her own voice lacked assurance.

"What do you really think of him, Daisy?"

"I don't know," Mrs. Pringle said untruthfully. "I can't make up my mind. But I do like a man to look neat, don't you? And he's got a nice way of treating people. *He* never looks down on me, like some people I know. Mildred makes an awful to-do about him coming here."

"It's only that she worries about Lily."

"I wonder if it is? Oh, I know—I heard her making a fuss before she'd ever laid eyes on him, but it's got to be a kind of obsession with her now—running him down. As if she was stuck on him herself. Have you noticed that?"

"Why, no. I hadn't noticed. I'm sure you're mistaken about that."

"You watch her the next time she talks about him." Mrs. Pringle folded the racing form and thrust it into a drawer. "Well, regardless of what anyone thinks, it won't stop Lily if she's made up her mind. Yes, it's hard to know what to do," she sighed. "Lily's been behaving so well these past two years. If she got married—who knows?—it might be the very thing. Especially someone like Mr. Fairfield."

"Mildred thinks I should try to reason with her."

"Mildred should know by this time that there's no such thing as reasoning with Lily. Besides, I don't think Mildred's got any say in the matter. It's you who'll be left alone, you poor thing."

"That's one reason I hoped you'd change your mind about leaving."

Mrs. Pringle stiffened. "You'll have the old gentleman."

"But that's not the same as having someone . . ." Fanny looked away. "You needn't worry about his trays, or caring for him. I'll do all that."

Poor creature, she'll never get over it if Lily leaves, Mrs. Pringle thought, but she hardened her heart. "An invalid in the house always means extra work. What you should get is one of those practical nurses."

Fanny said nothing.

"Of course, if the old gentleman should . . . if there was no invalid to care for . . ." Mrs. Pringle smoothed out the slip of paper on which she had worked out the daily double for the races. "I'll call Mr. Flaherty," she said abruptly, rising. "You're sure you want to bet that fiver?"

"Yes."

"Well, keep your fingers crossed."

"I will," Fanny said, but she wondered if Mrs. Pringle was really thinking about horses.

The morning began beautifully. Theodore felt buoyed up, confident, as he drove Lily down to the bank and waited outside while she cashed a check for two hundred dollars. When she came out, she tucked the roll of bills into his breast pocket with a casual air that pleased him. If it's going to be this easy, he thought. He wanted to put his hand to his pocket and feel the reassuring bulge, but did not. He gave her a quizzical smile. "You're sure you haven't overdrawn your account?"

"With this little bit?" Lily laughed. "Don't be silly!"

They drove to the crossroads at the edge of town, where Theodore stopped the car for a moment to pull out a road map. He had already made up his mind which direction he would take. Consulting Lily was only a form of courtesy, which he expected her to recognize as such.

"Straight ahead, I think," he said, tracing the route on the map and drawing a circle around some red dots. "We'll buy the license at one of these little towns."

Lily was not interested in the map, or in his decision. "Let's go this way," she said, pointing to the left. "I like the sound of those places." She began to read aloud the names on the signpost.

"I'm afraid there's nothing in that direction but tiny villages."

"How do you know?"

"They look quite small on the map. But let's take that road, anyway." He felt so lighthearted this morning that even his anxiety to please struck him as amusing. Usually it was the other way round. Women sought to please *him*. He did not mind being placed in the reverse position under the circumstances. It was a novelty, if nothing else. And none of the women who had sought to please him had been as pretty and dainty as Lily.

They drove on, through one tiny village after another, and came at last to a sizable town. The main street was lined with dingy shops; a brick hotel was wedged between the five-and-ten and a supermarket. People hurried up and down as if they really had somewhere to go, and around the corner, on a side street, an empty bus waited. Theodore drove slowly past the cars lined up along the curb. At the end of the street he saw a building set a little back from the others, with a sign which

163

said "Municipal Offices" over the door. He pulled in to the curb.

"I saw a hat in one of those shops . . ." Lily twisted round in the seat, looking back.

"The one you're wearing is very becoming," he said. He knew how women were about hats.

She pulled the rear view mirror round to see what she had on. It was a little tweed cap that she wore pushed up from her forehead. Under it, her yellow hair hung down straight, like a schoolgirl's. "Let's just walk back and look," she said, opening the door.

He held her arm. "What a time to think about buying hats!" he scolded playfully. "Have you forgotten why we came here?"

"It will only take a minute." Lily settled back against him. "You're not going to be mean, are you?" She looked up through her lashes, pouting.

"*After* we've bought the license," he said firmly, "you can buy twenty hats if you like."

"Why not now?" Lily asked in a coaxing, childish voice. But her eyes, looking up at him, had narrowed.

A small price to pay, he consoled himself, feeling the weight of the bills in his pocket. "Your wish is my command," he said facetiously, bowing.

At the little milliner's shop Lily sat in a mirrored alcove trying on hat after hat, turning from side to side, studying her reflection in a cracked hand mirror. Theodore was given a chair to sit on while she made up her mind. A harassed-looking woman with a pencil stuck behind one ear, wearing a great deal of yellow make-up—evidently the owner of the shop— hovered about offering suggestions, bringing out new models as fast as Lily threw the others aside. She looked desperately anxious to make a sale, Theodore thought, and an unpleasant picture of her life rose before him. He saw her cooking solitary meals on a gas stove in a cheerless flat upstairs, sitting in the back room surrounded by snips of ribbon, feathers, pressing

164

boards, standing at the window waiting for customers while she gazed at the unattractive store-fronts across the way. He felt uncomfortable, being reminded that a number of women he had known in the past were perhaps in no better circumstances.

"I'll take these," Lily said at last.

"Both of them?" the woman asked hopefully.

"Yes."

"That will be twenty dollars, then."

Lily opened her bag. "I haven't any money!" She caught her lower lip between her teeth, looking at Theodore as if she expected a reprimand.

I will not pay for them, he told himself. Lily and the saleswoman kept on looking at him. Just this once, then, he thought, reaching into his pocket.

Outside again, they found the streets deserted, the blinds down in all the shop windows. "I hope it isn't a half holiday in the town hall as well," he said.

"If it is, we can come back tomorrow."

She certainly doesn't mind spending my money, he thought. He had bought gasoline on the way out, and hoped it would last the day.

The little office where marriage licenses were issued was not closed. Buying the license was a simple matter. The clerk who filled out the form did so in a slapdash way, with one eye on the clock. In half an hour they were out on the street again, driving toward home.

"Do you remember the little restaurant we passed on the way in?" Theodore asked. "There it is ahead." He had caught sight of the blue sign, and pulled up in front of it. "Shall we have lunch here?"

It was a converted brick dwelling house, painted blue, with boxes of geraniums at every window. One large window showed the interior: small tables covered with white cloths, flower prints arranged around the walls, starched curtains. It looked neat and attractive. Fairly expensive, too, but he felt it was important to keep Lily happy. He remembered how she had complained about the inn where they had stopped on that first drive into the country.

Lily frowned. "I don't like that place."

He was already out of the car, opening the door for her with his usual gallantry, but she did not move. He turned to look at the restaurant, wondering what she saw that displeased her. "There may not be another one for miles," he reminded her. "But, whatever you say . . ." He walked round the car again and slid under the wheel. He was developing that technique of controlled patience he had observed in the husbands of ailing wives, and was surprised to find that this was not as vexatious as he had supposed. But Lily did have a great talent for arousing irritation. A suspicion crossed his mind that in some inexplicable way the tables were being turned on him; that all the while he had been scheming toward one end, she had with greater cunning been making plans that would cancel his. As they drove along, he stole glances at her, wondering if her actions really were, as they sometimes seemed to be, calculated and without heart. She sat with her hands clasped in her lap. Her face, lifted to catch the breeze, was serene, all innocence.

He took her hand and tucked it under his own on the wheel. "Do you realize that in three days we'll be on our honeymoon?"

They had lunch in a dingy little café in the next village: unappetizing stale hamburgers, the only thing on the menu. Lily ate hers quickly and asked for another. "Aren't you hungry?" she asked with an engaging smile of concern. "What a pity!"

"Where on earth have you *been*?" Mildred cried, opening the front door.

"For a drive," Lily said. She threw her hat on the settee and

166

smoothed her hair, then took some parcels from Theodore and placed them on the flat newel post.

"But you've been gone all day!"

"I know." Lily brushed past her and walked into the living room.

"Without a word to anyone . . . Didn't you realize we would worry?" Finding herself alone in the hall with Theodore, Mildred's voice faltered at the end of her question. She looked at him, then away. Both stepped back to allow the other to pass.

"We went for a drive in the country," Theodore explained. He put one hand under Mildred's elbow to guide her through the doorway ahead of him. Half turned, she hung back momentarily, so that his shoulder was against hers, his voice close to her ear. "I'm sorry if you were disturbed," he said.

Mildred jerked herself away as if he had been holding her there by force. In the living room, she lit a cigarette with unsteady hands and hid behind the smoke. After a time she became aware that Lily was regarding her with a steady, unblinking stare.


## CHAPTER ELEVEN


THE GIRLS AND MRS. PRINGLE WERE HAVING TEN O'CLOCK COFFEE in the kitchen the next morning when the postman came. Mildred, who had been listening for him, heard the plop-plop of letters on the hall floor and hurried to pick them up. There were two, both for Isobel. Mildred laid them on the table with a frown.

"Nothing from your husband?" Mrs. Pringle asked spitefully, glancing up from the racing form. Gadabout and Miss Muffet had won the double yesterday, and now, richer by one hundred and forty dollars, she was picking today's winners.

Isobel glanced at the letters, picked up the top one, a bulky envelope addressed in a masculine hand, and carried it upstairs.

"This one's for you, too," Fanny called after her.

"It's only from Eliot," Mildred said with sarcasm. "Naturally she wouldn't be interested."

"Perhaps Harry's decided to come up for the week end after all," Fanny said. "Perhaps that's why he hasn't written."

Mildred looked away, uncomforted. She felt neglected and forlorn. Earlier in her life, she had thought nothing of these moods of depression, had even in a way enjoyed her melancholy days, for they had given her an excuse to indulge herself in various ways: afternoons in bed with a book, toasted snacks on a tray while she read over old letters. But nowadays being unhappy frightened her, she kept watching for symptoms of change in herself, for she had always heard that women her age shed unnecessary tears and felt themselves abused without cause, made much of trifles.

Everyone's turned against me, she thought. Harry neglected to write, Isobel was mocking, Mrs. Pringle was openly malicious, Lily went out of her way to be provoking; even Fanny, who could usually be counted on for sympathy and understanding, had changed. There's no one to turn to, Mildred thought unhappily. Nobody understands.

She sat down at the table opposite Lily. "I hope you're not planning to spend another day in the country with that man."

"This isn't getting the shopping done," Fanny interrupted briskly, taking a pad and pencil from a drawer. "We need eggs, I suppose?" She looked inquiringly at Mrs. Pringle.

"Eggs, butter, bacon . . ." Mrs. Pringle opened the refrigerator and looked inside.

"Where did you *go*?" Mildred persisted, raising her voice and looking at Lily.

"Olives . . ." Fanny said loudly, writing on her pad.

"A nice rib roast for the week end, wouldn't you think?" Mrs. Pringle suggested.

Mildred waited, tight-lipped, but before the shopping list was finished, Lily had gone upstairs. "Why shouldn't I question her?" Mildred demanded.

Fanny looked anxious. "You'll only antagonize her."

"I mean to find out where she was yesterday—why she was away the whole day."

"She won't tell you anything. Questioning her will only make her stubborn."

"You're all against me!" Mildred burst into tears. "You don't care what happens. You sit there doing nothing, and interfere when I try to prevent disaster."

"Don't cry!" Fanny begged.

"No one cares! I'm the only one who tries to do anything. And then to be criticized at every turn . . ."

"I didn't mean to criticize."

"I haven't anyone to turn to." Mildred sobbed, her hands over her eyes.

"You mustn't cry so," Fanny pleaded. She put one arm round Mildred and patted her shoulder. "Why don't you go upstairs and lie down? I'll get you some aspirin."

"What was that all about?" Mrs. Pringle asked, when Fanny came downstairs.

Fanny shook her head. "I don't know, unless it was not hearing from Harry."

"My God, she talked to him on the phone yesterday. Does she think he's going to run off with some burlesque queen the minute her back's turned?"

"I don't understand her," Fanny sighed.

"Well, dear, I wouldn't worry about it." Mrs. Pringle nodded sagely. "She's just at that age, you know. Best to take no notice." She folded up the racing form and studied the sheet of paper on which she had jotted down notes on the past performance of horses in today's race. "You know what I'm going to do?" she said recklessly. "I'm going to put the whole lot I won yesterday on Piccolo Pete to win."

"Not the whole hundred and forty!"

"I am so!"

"But what if Piccolo Pete doesn't win? What if you lose the whole lot?"

"He's got to win. He's due. And only carrying one fourteen."

"But you can't be sure."

"I am sure. I've just got a feeling today's my lucky day. I've worked out a new system. Fool-proof, this time. You saw how it worked yesterday. I'm going to call up Mr. Flaherty this minute, before I lose my nerve."

When Fanny returned from shopping, the letter from Eliot was still on the kitchen table. She carried it up to Isobel's room. Isobel turned it over in her hand, then laid it aside. The other letter she had received that morning was now a pile of torn scraps in the ashtray.

"You won't mind if I borrow the car for half an hour?" she asked, outlining her mouth with lipstick. She had changed into a dark street dress, and combed her hair up into a knot at the back.

Handing over the keys, Fanny could not help giving Eliot's letter a worried side glance. Seeing this, Isobel slit open the envelope and removed the closely written sheet of creamy paper, but did not read it. "Don't go away," she said, smiling into the mirror. "I haven't really talked with you since I came home." She turned, leaning against the dresser. "What was Mildred crying about?" Her face, though beautifully made up, looked a little damp around the eyes as if she had been crying herself.

"She worries about Lily."

"What *about* Lily? It seems to me she's behaving in a perfectly normal way. Normal for her, that is. I know Mildred worries about her interest in Theodore, but I can't help feeling sometimes that he's the one we should be concerned about. I believe he's very fond of Lily."

Fanny bit her thumb, frowning. "Mildred can't get over the idea that he's a fortune-hunter. I don't know why. He seems so nice . . ."

"You'd hardly call the bit of money Lily has a fortune."

"It might seem a great deal to some people."

Isobel said thoughtfully, "I'm not sure, myself, that he's really the man of the world he pretends to be. I have an idea he's just a harmless little man who likes to masquerade."

"What makes you think that?"

"I don't know. It's just a feeling. But he is rather nice, as you say, and don't we all like to masquerade once in a while?"

Fanny stood up and walked to the window. This room faced the beechwood, where yellow leaves were beginning to drift down, one by one. She had rejected Mildred's theory that Theodore was not what he pretended to be; but now she began to wonder.

"Why did you say he's the one we should be concerned about?" she asked.

"Because, whatever Lily pretends, I believe she's completely indifferent to him. She's encouraging Theodore just now simply because Mildred disapproves of him. Which is rather hard on him, if he likes her. Lily has no heart," Isobel said, dabbing perfume on her wrists. "I've been thinking about her since I came home," she went on after a moment, replacing the glass stopper. "Last night I evolved a crazy kind of theory: that the reason we feel as we do about Lily—I'm talking about you and me and Pringle, not Mildred—is because she doesn't return our affection, so we have to give her twice as much, to make up. They say there's a funny quirk in people that makes them love better those who don't return love."

Fanny mulled this over. "It sounds all wrong."

"It probably is, like all my theories. But I'm convinced that

Lily is simply using Theodore for her own purpose." Isobel picked up her letter and glanced through it. "Eliot says he's coming up for the week end."

"Oh, that's nice. Would you like to move your things into the spare room?"

"He can sleep there. I'll stay here."

"When is he coming?"

"Saturday morning, he says." Isobel folded the letter. "I wish I had the courage to tell him not to come."

Fanny looked away. She thought that this might be what she had hoped for; Isobel was about to confide in her. But repeated failures in dealing with other people had made her cautious. Instead of offering encouragement, she waited uneasily for what was coming next.

"It doesn't matter, really." Isobel glanced at the scraps of paper in the ashtray. "I had made other plans for the week end. Someone else was coming up—not to stay here, of course, but at the hotel. However, he seems to have changed his mind."

He! Fanny thought, feeling her cheeks go red. She looked wildly at the door, then at her watch. "I must see if lunch is ready," she said, and almost ran from the room. At the head of the stairs she stopped in dismay, realizing that by behaving like an outraged Mrs. Grundy she had destroyed forever all hope of the cozy woman-to-woman talks with Isobel that she sometimes dreamed about. She wanted desperately to go back into the room and be given a second chance, but did not have the courage to try.

She was not shocked. Twenty years ago, the knowledge that her sister was having an affair with a strange man would have upset her terribly, but since then she had read a great many novels and plays, and knew that fashions were changing. Today, even the best people, morally and financially, threw everything overboard in the name of love, and popular opinion condoned their actions. The sin nowadays was in not having enough of whatever it is that drives men and women into each other's arms. Sometimes in the middle of reading a novel Fanny would feel inadequate, out of place in this world where everyone else—if you could believe what the authors said— seemed capable of such overriding passion that all reason was swept away; where men and women, exchanging one look, suddenly found their pulses racing; where hands, touching under a table, set up an electric current that wrecked homes, left careers in ruins, tore people's hearts to shreds, drove them to suicide. *I must be queer,* Fanny often thought. *I never felt like that.* Even when she was younger and still dreamed of marriage, the most she had felt was anxiety to please, to prepare favorite meals, lay out slippers. Holding hands made her feel silly. Kissing was something to be done in pitch darkness and got over with quickly. In her imagination she had never approached anything remotely resembling a bed.

She went to her room and sat with her hands in her lap, trying to think of some way to patch up the mistake she had made, but decided at last that she could do nothing.

*If I were like those women in magazines,* she thought, *I would know exactly how to act.* She had always admired, in stories, those women who with great wisdom and understanding went about the business of setting everybody on the right track, as if by magic they recognized and evaluated the difficulties that beset their friends and families, saw through the masks that others wore, salved wounded vanities and broken hearts, reconciled people to the inevitable, brought estranged lovers together, solved every kind of problem with dispatch and tact; and found, in the end, peace of mind for themselves. As well they might, after such achievements.

Isobel stood for some minutes looking at the door, which Fanny had left partly open. She had wanted to talk with Fanny, and was impatient with herself for not realizing that Fanny would be upset by such an abrupt disclosure of marital unrest.

173

She sighed, picked up the car keys, and went downstairs. She had no specific errand in the town, though earlier in the morning, before the letter came, she had intended to look around the shops for some absurd gift, something that two persons could laugh over now and think about fondly in later years. Each time she fell in love she thought it was forever and, dreaming of long companionable years stretching into a serene old age, would misquote lines of poetry:

"When we are old and gray and full of sleep
And nodding by the fire . . ."

Marital fidelity she looked upon as a cardinal virtue, and was always hoping she would be able to practice it herself some day. So far, this had been impossible. Something always happened. The men she married changed. From gay and tender lovers, eager to please, they evolved, as husbands, into the most unreasonable and uncongenial bores. Sometimes this happened so slowly and insidiously that she was unaware of it until some little thing happened to open her eyes. With Alan, her first husband, the moment of revelation had come one April morning when they had been married a little over a year. He was "resting"—his definition of being jobless—and had gone down to the corner to buy milk. He was gone perhaps five minutes. When he returned he said. "What's new, hon?" and she suddenly realized that he had asked the same question on an average of five times a day for something like four hundred and fifty days. What was more, he expected an answer.

Eliot had never been gay, but he had been rather nice at first. The way he fussed over her. The trouble was, though, that if you were fussed over too much, it got to be a nuisance. And then Eliot fussed over everything he owned, including himself. He had to get a certain amount of sleep each night, and take certain pills at certain hours. He must do this this way, and that that way. He treated his body like the clock in the dining room, which must be wound, set, and oiled by himself

174

at stated intervals on the dot and never jarred lest its precious interior be thrown out of balance. His recent misfortune had not made much difference in their lives.

"Don't wait lunch for me," Isobel told Mrs. Pringle in the kitchen. There was no need, now, to buy the absurd gift, since the person for whom it was intended had gotten cold feet and decided that his career was too important to risk for love's sake, but she would drive into town, anyway. There was no point in sitting at home brooding, getting bags under the eyes.

"Lord, you gave me a start! I thought for a minute you were your mother standing there." Mrs. Pringle clasped her hands in front of her and admired Isobel. "You're the very image of her, with your hair like that."

"You were very fond of Mama, weren't you?"

"Fond? She was my best friend in all the world. My only friend." Mrs. Pringle's eyes grew moist. "The laughs we used to have, right in this kitchen. The day before I married Ernie she sat in that very chair and said, 'Daisy, I presume it's unnecessary for me to explain the facts of life to you?' Laugh, I thought we'd die! Me three months pregnant. That was the little one I lost," she added, wiping her eyes. "Your mother was a perfect angel. Everybody loved her."

"Not Mildred. She always hated her."

"Oh, Mildred," Mrs. Pringle sniffed. "She thought her precious Harry was in love with your mother. So what of it? Was that her fault? She was only trying to be nice to him."

"I was about fourteen when Harry started coming here. I remember him dancing with Mama, and Mildred pretending not to watch them . . . And then there was that gangling boy who used to come to see Fanny. I saw Mama kissing him out in the hall one night."

"Well, that's water under the bridge now. She was only trying to make him feel at home, most likely. Your mother was kind and good, and everybody loved her, except a few people who didn't matter."

"People talked about her," Isobel reminded. "They said she had no morals."

"What's morals got to do with being good? Of course she liked men. She might have had a bit of fun with the odd one, but it was only because she was too kind-hearted to refuse. She liked to make people happy. You only go this way once." Mrs. Pringle stared wistfully into space. "If I had my life to live over again . . ."

"Now, Pringle, you're not telling me you'd condone infidelity?" Isobel thought a negative answer might be comforting, under the circumstances, for she was so unhappy she was morbidly toying with the idea of repenting all past sins and turning over a new leaf, settling down to the dreary task of living out the rest of her life with Eliot.

Mrs. Pringle shrugged. "I take into account that we're all human," she said, glancing shrewdly at Isobel as if judging how much counsel she was prepared to accept. "Is there anything you'd like to tell me, dear?"

When Isobel smiled and shook her head, she went on, "You can always confide in me, dear, you know, if you've got anything on your mind. It'll never go beyond this room . . . I just happened to be thinking of those telephone calls you've been getting. No doubt the whole town's heard about them by now. Catch Mildred keeping quiet about a thing like that. To hear her talk, a person would think you'd been carrying on with the devil himself. It's nothing but jealousy, of course, plain jealousy. Nobody telephones *her*, not even her husband. You see a woman ranting on about how others are carrying on, all she's doing is complaining because she never got the chance herself. You remember what I said the other day, dear, and don't go worrying because your glands are in better shape than most women's. Just thank the Lord they are. Is he coming to see you?" She threw the question in as an afterthought, hoping to catch Isobel off guard.

"Eliot says he's coming up for the week end."

"Well, I suppose you can't keep him away. He's your husband." Mrs. Pringle sighed. "Some people never know when they're not wanted, do they?"

Half an hour later, Isobel was window-shopping along the main street of the little town when she came face to face with Theodore.

"What a pleasant surprise!" He took off his hat, smiling.

They were standing beside the steps of the Frontier Hotel. In the coffee shop adjoining it, lunch was being served. "I was just going in for a cup of coffee," Isobel said, though the idea had only that moment occurred to her. Seeing Theodore, she was reminded of her conversation with Fanny, and decided that this was as good an opportunity as any to find out something about him.

His hand crept into his pocket as if to make sure that he had enough money before he asked her to lunch with him. When she agreed, he took her elbow and guided her into the dim restaurant.

She rather enjoyed the sensation of appearing in public with someone so different, of being stared at by the other diners, who were mostly local tradesmen, with a smattering of tourists. Theodore seemed entirely oblivious of their curious glances, but when he touched his beard with a preening gesture, she wondered if he was really as unmindful as he pretended to be. He was extremely courteous, full of solicitous gestures, giving the impression that nothing in the world was more important to him than that she should enjoy this meal. But she felt rather than observed a shy uneasiness in his manner. Every once in a while he paused as if mentally reviewing a set of rules. She did not know why she felt sympathetic toward him. He was not a type she particularly admired. She knew too many professional charmers, dapper men of the world who tried to look as different from commonplace people as possible. But she had a feeling that, aside from the little dyed beard and affected manners, Theodore was quite ordinary and nice.

They chatted amiably. Remembering Mildred's tactless interrogation of him yesterday, Isobel hesitated about attempting to draw him out. When she did try, however, she found that he was quite willing to talk about himself.

"I can't believe you're a stodgy businessman," she said with her most engaging smile. "If I met you on the street, I'd take you for a Shakespearian actor, or a French count. I met a French count once," she improvised. "He was staying with some friends of mine in New York. He had the most beautiful manners. You remind me of him. You have that same air of distinction." She paused, wondering if she had laid it on a bit too thick. She need not have worried. His face lit up with pleasure.

"I'm not really much of a businessman," he admitted. "I have too great an appreciation of the worth-while things of life to waste my time chained to a desk. Fortunately, I'm in a position to do as I please."

Isobel nodded. "How wise you are. I do think it's silly of men, when they've got all the money they need, to keep on grubbing for more. I wish my husband were more like you."

"I wasn't always a philosopher," Theodore said. "Before I lost my wife . . ." He looked away. After a moment he was able to continue. "When I found myself alone, I had no heart for business any more. Life seemed drab, meaningless. I turned the management of my properties over to my lawyers, who do a much more efficient job than I. My only regret is that I didn't turn everything over to them years ago. I could have made my wife's last days so much happier. But of course I didn't know . . ." His voice trailed off sadly.

"I often think that if we could look into the future we would live our lives quite differently."

"How true that is!"

"What was your wife's name?"

He made a flurried movement with his hand, knocking over

178

the pepper-shaker. When he had righted it, he said, "Her name was Mary. Do you know Boston at all?"

"No."

"You wouldn't happen to know the Rolphs? I believe they're considered one of the leading Boston families."

Isobel shook her head. "I'm afraid I know nothing about Boston. And even if I did, I wouldn't be rubbing shoulders with the leading families."

He smiled. "I must confess that I wouldn't, either, if it hadn't been for my wife. She was Mary Rolph," he interposed, as if confirming a fact he had not been sure of before. "My father was a wealthy man, but a great many people disapproved of the way he made his money. They said he was unscrupulous. My mother was an actress. I'm afraid the good people of Boston rather looked down on her."

"I'm sure she didn't mind."

"No. She was a philosopher, too, in her way. She scandalized many people, but she had sense enough to realize that the opinion of others is not always important."

Isobel suspected that both the unscrupulous father and the actress mother were pure inventions, but she said, "Then you and I have a lot in common. You probably know that my family isn't considered entirely respectable."

He raised his hands protestingly. "I never allow gossip to interfere with my judgment of people. I've been very happy this past month," he added pensively. "I feel that I've begun to live again."

She risked a direct question. "Do you want to marry Lily?"

"It's not a question of what I want. The question is, am I worthy of her?"

"I'm sure you'd try to make her happy."

"I would do anything in my power," he answered with great sincerity.

"You haven't asked her yet?"

"Oh, no!" He appeared shocked at the suggestion. "It's

much too soon. Perhaps you think me stodgy, but the truth is, I've always been rather shy with women. And I would like to feel that I have the approval of all members of the family . . ." He looked away.

"If we seem to disapprove, it's only because we're so fond of Lily, and want her to be happy. She's had one unhappy experience, you know."

Theodore forgot himself, and put his elbows on the table, leaning forward. "She never speaks of her husband."

"He was an awful cad. He only married Lily for her money."

"No!" he cried, outraged.

"He hadn't a cent of his own, of course, and thought he'd found an easy way to avoid earning a living. Poor Lily—she's so gullible. I suppose she believed every word he told her."

Theodore wore a pained expression. He passed one hand across his forehead. "How any man could be so heartless as to treat her—to treat any woman—like that! Surely working for a living isn't so unpleasant."

"You know what men are. Some of them think of nothing but work, and others spend all their time trying to avoid it."

"I can't bear to think of it," Theodore said, closing his eyes as if he could not bear to see, either. "One doesn't realize how much wickedness there is in the world."

"You seem like an understanding sort of person," Isobel said, when he had opened his eyes. "The sort people go to for advice. I hope you don't mind if I ask you something."

His face became guarded.

"It's a personal problem. Nothing to do—directly, that is— with the rest of the family."

He relaxed, smiling. "There's nothing I like better than giving advice."

"It's my husband. I want to leave him, and I don't think I've got the courage."

He considered this. "Why not?" he asked.

"Well, you see, he's my third. And ever since I married him ten years ago people have been telling me how *lucky* I am, how thankful I should be to find such a gem of a husband after . . . well, it was rather a messy affair, getting rid of the last one. It really was noble of Eliot to marry me, especially since his family objected strongly. The trouble is, he *knows* it was noble of him."

"Is that why you want to divorce him?"

"Partly that." Isobel considered briefly and decided against telling the whole truth. "He's such a damned bore!"

"I see." Theodore fitted the tips of his fingers together and nodded over them. When the waitress came by, he beckoned to her and ordered more coffee.

"I liked Eliot well enough at first," Isobel went on, "though he was rather prim and proper, even then. Steady and dependable, I told myself, and I needed someone steady and dependable then, or thought I did. I had a nine-year-old daughter, too, you see. I suppose I was flattered because Eliot *begged* me to marry him. I didn't realize he'd be so damned dull."

"Perhaps you have more courage than you think," Theodore suggested.

Isobel shook her head. "Eliot loves me in his way. He's a bit older than I am—twenty years, to be exact—and proud of having a wife who's not too hard on the eyes. He likes showing me off to his friends. If I left him, his pride would be hurt. And there's his family . . . and mine. So many people disapprove of me already . . ."

They were silent while the waitress brought fresh coffee; then Theodore said, "I hate self-sacrifice. And nobody ever died of wounded pride."

Isobel stirred her coffee thoughtfully.

"Life is short," Theodore quoted.

"The thing that frightens me is the *boredom* of growing old with Eliot. He's beginning to get fussy and crotchety already,

181

wanting attention, describing his aches and pains. I try to sympathize, but all I feel is impatience."

"It might be unpleasant at first," Theodore said, as if Isobel had already made up her mind. "These things always are. But I do think it's a mistake for people to live together merely for the sake of appearance, when they're not compatible."

"You sound as if you'd had experience."

"Oh, no!"

"I was only teasing." Isobel laid her hand over his on the table. "You don't know how I've been wanting to talk to someone. It's wonderful of you to be so sympathetic. I think you've given me the courage I need." Later on, when she thought about this conversation, she realized that Theodore had not said very much, after all, but now she pressed his hand gratefully. "It was really Eliot's disapproval I was most afraid of. I can see his look now—wounded virtue, scarcely able to believe that anyone could treat him so, when he's so blameless himself!"

When they left the restaurant, Theodore declined Isobel's offer of a lift home. He swung off up the street, jauntily swinging his cane, and entered the tailor's shop on the corner.

Instead of taking her usual rest after luncheon, Mrs. Pringle pulled a chair neatly up to the kitchen table, sharpened a pencil, and attempted to figure out her earnings if Piccolo Pete won today's race—which he must do, she thought with a twinge of misgiving. Assuming that her own bet had lowered the odds somewhat, she still ought to make over two thousand dollars. An even two thousand, to be on the safe side. But— she glanced in sudden panic at the clock—suppose her system was wrong? Suppose this wasn't Piccolo Pete's day? She put her hands over her eyes for a moment, seeing as on a moving-picture screen the horses bunched for the home stretch, a bay gelding trailing the pack. She rose and poured herself a drink.

Ten minutes later, her optimism restored, she was spending

money recklessly. A nice trip to Bermuda. By herself. Why shouldn't I go on a trip by myself? she argued with her conscience. It's my money. I've worked and slaved for years, while Ernie flitted from one job to another. She would buy a nice lot of new clothes, have one last fling. On the boat she would meet an unattached man who, when they got to the islands, would take her sightseeing, buy dinners for her. Can I be blamed for wanting a little civilized companionship, she asked herself, after watching Ernie eat dinner in his undershirt for thirty years? Gargling and spitting, and taking his damned laxative every night, she went on in her thoughts, and leaving his teeth in the bathroom. She had now in imagination gone beyond the stage of dinners and sightseeing with her mythical cruise companion, and needed an excuse for her own behavior.

She was really consoling herself because she felt upset about her decision to leave, realizing that she felt more at home here than in the flat she shared with Ernie. She had been married in this house. Isobel, wearing pink organdy, had been her flower girl. What would she ever do if she left? *When* she left, for having given her notice, she could not take it back without losing face. Unless some miracle happened, which was unlikely.

I'll open a tea shop, she decided unhappily. Maybe I'll die rich.

For a change, a lovely peace had descended upon the house this afternoon. Isobel was lying down in her room, Fanny and Mildred had gone out somewhere. If it could always be like this, Mrs. Pringle thought, listening to the quiet: the clocks ticking, the refrigerator starting up, the lulling sounds of summer out of doors. She felt homesick about leaving it all. In the garden, Lily was lying in one of the canvas chairs under the birch trees. She was asleep, with her hands behind her head and her hair spread like a fan over the back of the chair. The garden looked asleep, too, shimmering in the heat. Yellow butterflies drifted over the flower beds, insects hummed.

Theodore walked through the beechwood and stepped over the low hedge. For a moment Mrs. Pringle did not recognize him in his new clothes; then she sat upright and opened her eyes wide. "My Lord, he's robbed a bank!" she said aloud.

Lily sat up, yawning and stretching; then she too opened her eyes wide and clasped her hands together in admiration. Oh, she'd tell him how handsome he looked. She was good at flattery. Theodore, wearing a light-gray flannel suit and a matching fedora, posed against the wall, trying to act as if he weren't posing. He looked pleased with himself.

Now I wonder why he's blossomed out like that all of a sudden, Mrs. Pringle asked herself. If he bought that outfit to impress *her*, why didn't he do it weeks ago? Her eyes fell on his new shoes, gray suede trimmed with navy-blue kid, and she looked away quickly.

Having been admired, Theodore sat down and flung one knee over the other, adjusting the crease of his trousers. The new suit made him look less like a foreign diplomat, more like a traveling showman. It was too light in color, a little too extreme in cut, and those shoes! I'd have given him credit for better taste than that, Mrs. Pringle thought. A nice subdued gray, now . . . She narrowed her eyes to stare at him.

Unconsciously, she had given her imaginary cruise companion a thin pointed face with a neat Vandyke. He would be extremely polite, too, forever lifting his hat to ladies, giving up his chair, running to open doors. But in her mind she now denied that she had been thinking of Theodore. I could never be comfortable with a man as thin as that, she told herself. I'd feel like a mountain.

Joe Nicholson had owned a suit much like the one Theodore was now wearing, and Lily's money had paid for it. Mrs. Pringle shook her head. Let's not go getting ideas, she scolded herself.

But the idea was already there, nagging at her mind. After a time she tucked away her bottle and went upstairs, tiptoeing down the hall so as not to disturb Isobel. Lily's room was never neat. No matter how often it was tidied up, in half an hour Lily could make it look as if a cyclone had struck. Gloves, scarfs, old lipsticks, even stockings, were jumbled together in a top drawer. Mrs. Pringle went through several handbags before she found Lily's bank book. The last entry, dated the previous day, showed a withdrawal of two hundred dollars.

"So that's it!" Mrs. Pringle whispered. She sat down heavily on the bed. "He's been taking money from her! And, poor thing, she doesn't know any better. We should never have given her all that money. She doesn't know the value of it. He's just a fortune-hunter, like Mildred said." She pushed herself up slowly and replaced the bank book.

Disenchantment saddened her. She felt old and weary. She would have staked her life on Mr. Fairfield's integrity, and here he'd turned out to be nothing but a gigolo. She would never be able to rely on her own judgment again. Her confidence had been destroyed along with her dream. I'll never trust another man as long as I live, she thought. They're all alike. Now what the hell am I to do? she asked her reflection in the mirror.

If she told the girls, they'd lose their heads, a thing you couldn't afford to do when dealing with Lily. Mildred would have the pleasure of saying, "I told you so!" She would lecture and denounce until there would be no living with her, and how would poor Lily take that?

I'll think about it, Mrs. Pringle decided, plodding heavily downstairs. I'm not sure I want Mildred to have the satisfaction of knowing she's right about him. And I *could* be mistaken, she reasoned, pausing halfway down the stairs. I may be accusing him unjustly. Lily could have spent that money on herself. "I wonder . . ." she mused aloud.

She wanted so desperately to believe her suspicions were unfounded that by the time she reached the lower hall she had almost convinced herself. Whatever made me go jumping to conclusions like that? she wondered. I haven't any *proof*. And what on earth would Mr. Fairfield want of Lily's money, when he's got so much of his own? Relief swept over her. "I don't know what I was thinking of!" she said aloud.

When she looked out the kitchen window again, the garden was empty, but Theodore had left his new gray hat on a chair.

Theodore hesitated at the top of the steps that zigzagged down the cliffside to the boathouse. Though there was no breeze at all in the garden, a current of cool air funneled up from the river and fanned his face. Far below, the steps were hidden in a tangle of vines. He could see one corner of the boathouse roof, with part of a dead tree lying across it. All down the rocks stunted bushes grew, and clumps of asters, and sumac candles turning red.

"Is it safe?" he asked.

"Of course!" Lily had started down the steps ahead of him. She leaned against the railing and waited.

The stairway was built in sections, short flights of steps going in opposite directions, with narrow landings between. He began the descent reluctantly, with the feeling—which he had experienced a number of times recently—of being drawn into childish games; but when he had gone part of the way down he gained confidence, and looked about him with interest, noting that the whole structure was hung on steel supports driven into the rock wall. He mentally applauded King Jameson's ingenuity in utilizing the cove. What a shame it's going to waste now, he thought. No doubt there was still a great volume of illegal trade between the United States and Canada. If you knew the right people . . .

"Did you say something about a boat?" he asked.

"The *Lilybell*. I suppose she's still in the boathouse. Nobody's been down for—oh—two years." Lily tore away a vine that had grown up between the timbers.

"What kind of a boat is she?"

"Just a boat. I don't know."

It would take a powerful engine to battle the current here, so close to the navigable limits of the river. Theodore knew nothing about boats, and shuddered at the mere idea of setting out across that menacing stretch of water in any craft. But there must be men in St. Charles who knew the river, who would be glad of a job. I could work up a nice little business, he mused.

In the cliff face opposite him, a little spring seeped from a cleft in the rock wall and trickled down over a moss-hung lip. There were sudden flurried movements in the underbrush as small animals were disturbed. Sunlight filtering through the screening leaves gave everything a diffused submarine appearance. The steps were strewn with the empty shells of last year's beechnuts and the caps of acorns.

Yes, there's an opportunity here, he thought. He had not before considered staying on at Hawkrest after he and Lily were married; but, why not? he asked himself now. It was as safe as anywhere. King Jameson had made one fortune on the river; why could not he, Theodore, make another, and wallow in riches for the rest of his life? Nobody would ever think to look for him in this little town. He began to imagine the country-squire sort of life he would lead—going in for stamp-collecting, perhaps, or some such gentlemanly pursuit. He would wear tweeds and drive a station wagon. Maybe even keep dogs—half a dozen of those black-and-white spotted ones.

Luncheon with Isobel had given him fresh confidence. In his experience, women asked advice only of men they liked, and, having asked it, were gratified when encouraged to go ahead and do what they had already made up their minds to do. He felt safe in assuming that he had scored a complete hit with Isobel. It had not seemed important, before, to curry favor with the entire family, but if he should decide to stay on at Hawkrest it would be most important to foster the good will of all. Mildred was now the only dissenter. Remembering that moment in the hall yesterday, he felt quite sure that he could win her over to his side if he cared to take the trouble.

He paused to look down into the sunlit gorge, feeling like a feudal lord surveying his domain. He would patch up the *Lilybell*, find a trustworthy man to run her. The Pringle woman's husband, perhaps, since he had worked with the old man and knew the ropes. The next problem was how to go about drumming up business. You couldn't very well advertise in the daily papers: "High-class smuggling. Reduced rates on bulk shipments." No, the thing to do would be to make discreet inquiries around the town, find out who might be interested in such a service. In his present optimistic state, the problem of soliciting customers did not appear difficult. King Jameson, whose mentality Theodore considered far inferior to his own, had certainly not found it so.

A Cadillac station wagon, he thought.

Dreaming, he had fallen behind Lily, and now hurried to catch up with her. "Wait!" he called.

Instead of waiting, she threw a teasing smile over her shoulder and began to run. At the turn, her skirt floated out and caught on some thorns. She jerked it away, leaving a triangle of red silk in the branches.

He caught up with her at the next landing. As they both grasped the railing, it began to give way. He flung himself backwards, pulling Lily with him. A section of the cliff itself, not the railing, was coming loose. Carried by its own weight, a great slab of rock dislodged, the steps below the landing on which they crouched tore away with a splintering sound, and the whole thing—rocks, steps, everything—went plunging downward and crashed on the roof of the boathouse.

Theodore lay back, pale and shaking, and clung to Lily's hand. He thought that the narrow platform on which they lay would fall at any moment, but he was too frightened to move. He closed his eyes. When he opened them again, Lily was kneeling on the splintered edge of the landing, looking down. She had not screamed, and she was not trembling now, as he still was.

"Are you all right, my darling?" he asked, his voice unsteady.

"I wanted to show you the boathouse!" Lily complained.

"We might have been killed!" He spoke more sharply than he intended to.

Lily looked back at him, faintly surprised. "Were you frightened?"

"I can think of more pleasant ways to die than falling off a cliff."

"Well, we didn't fall," Lily said cheerfully. When she sat back, the platform joggled alarmingly. "Look, you've torn your coat," she said. "You must have caught it on that branch."

He examined the jagged tear. His new suit was ruined.

"Well, we might as well go up." Lily rose and pulled at his hands, casting another petulant glance behind. "Now you'll never see the *Lilybell*."

Following her up the steps, he clung to the rail. Near the top he paused and forced himself to look back. The stairway down the cliff could be rebuilt, but he would never find the courage to make the descent again. He would never patch up the *Lilybell* and make a fortune on the river. His dream faded almost before it had taken shape.

When he closed the wooden gate at the top of the steps, it swung open again. He saw that the catch was broken. "We should put up a warning sign," he said, "or some sort of barrier."

"There's no need. Nobody ever uses the summerhouse."

"Still, if somebody did come, and saw the gate hanging open, they might be tempted to explore. A person could easily kill himself . . ." He looked around vaguely for something which could be used to point out the danger below, and at last

189

pried up a loose floor board and made a barrier across the gateway. "Not very effective," he said, "but if nobody ever comes into the summerhouse, it doesn't matter."

When Fanny went into the back garden after dinner, she walked first to the stone wall and looked at the river. It was a habit they all had, this staring into the gorge, as if they thought the river might have disappeared while their backs were turned. Strangers, too, were fascinated by the chasm, and peered timidly over the edge of it, making remarks like, "Heavens, doesn't it *frighten* you?" and "What a place to commit suicide."

After Hazel died, there had been many nights when Fanny was made fearfully aware of how easy it would be to end one's life here. Her father was the sort of person who suffered best when someone was watching, and he could not get into the proper sorrowing mood without getting drunk. He was drunk quite often after Hazel died. Then he moaned broken-heartedly that he had nothing left to live for, and threatened repeatedly to throw himself into the river. He chose the summerhouse as the logical place to jump, realizing that if he jumped from the garden he would fall into a tangle of vines, and that the trees would prevent him from reaching his objective. But from the summerhouse he could simply launch off into space. He explained all this in a drink-husky voice to Mrs. Pringle and Ernie, who stayed the night to keep an eye on him whenever he got into a sorrowing mood. Sometimes they were up all night trying to divert his attention from the summerhouse.

Later on Fanny wondered if he was really as grief-stricken as he pretended to be, or whether he was merely keeping up his reputation for never doing things by halves. If he was going to suffer at all, it must be the most inconsolable suffering ever witnessed. His desolation was short-lived, at any rate. Within a month he had forgotten all about throwing himself into the river. He was too busy chasing women.

The gorge was filled with deep shadow, the trees on the opposite bank were dark blue, the air oppressive. A storm was on the way. Fanny hoped it would hold off another day, for tomorrow morning was set aside for her weekly visit to the Orphan's Home. She had a bushel basket of apples, some nuts, candy, jars of preserves, oranges, and three dozen pairs of cotton stockings in the proper sizes stacked in the kitchen ready to be delivered. In the morning she would cut huge bouquets of flowers. Each time she visited the orphanage the matron insisted upon gathering the children in a group to recite their thanks. On fine days this was not so bad, for then Fanny was taken to the playground, where the children seemed less pathetic. But on stormy days, in the confined space of the schoolroom, they stood about like little sheep, wearing the meaningless smiles of unwanted children. Fanny never knew what to say to them or how to say it. When she tried to draw them out, she found herself employing an overbright old-maidish voice. The matron always hovered about, offering encouraging comments. She thinks me a perfect fool, Fanny often thought. If she would only leave me alone with them, I might find something to say. I might even take that little girl on my lap and fix her hair ribbons.

Nighthawks swooped past her in a downward flight over the river bank, and crickets sang monotonously. Inside the house, Mildred was shuffling the playing cards idly in her hands. Since late afternoon she had laid out hand after hand of solitaire, as if she were filling in time before some crisis, waiting, like Madame Lafarge, for something to happen. And as soon as dinner was over, she picked up the cards again, while Fanny went into the kitchen to see why Mrs. Pringle looked worried.

"It's nothing," Mrs. Pringle said impatiently, splashing around in the dishwater.

"I thought you seemed upset."

Mrs. Pringle shrugged.

"Don't you want to tell me about it?" Fanny picked up the dish towel and began to wipe the silver. "Did you lose today?" she asked, remembering the horse races.

Mrs. Pringle relaxed a bit. "I lost the whole bloody lot," she confessed, looking round, ready to accept sympathy. "A hundred and forty dollars."

"Oh, you didn't!"

"I did so. I ought to have my head examined. I could have bought a nice fur coat, one of those imitation mink—rabbit, but that's what they call them. Now I'll have to wear that moth-eaten muskrat for another forty years. I'm not worried about that, though. Easy come, easy go, as they say. No, it's something else."

"Can I help?"

Mrs. Pringle began to wipe her hands on her apron as if she might take time out to confide in Fanny. Then, changing her mind, she dropped her apron and plunged her hands into the dishwater again. "No sense getting you all upset, too. Besides, I can't be sure."

"Can't be sure of what? You upset me more when you hint that something is wrong."

"I shouldn't have mentioned it, then. There's enough fidgeting and stewing going on around here as it is."

"I wish you'd tell me, if it's something I should know."

"I'll worry along by myself for a while," Mrs. Pringle decided. "You've got enough on your mind."

This conversation had disturbed Fanny at the time, and now that she had had time to think it over, she became alarmed. As usual, her thoughts went first to Lily. But earlier in the day, when Isobel, having lunched downtown with Theodore, recounted part of her conversation with him, Fanny had grasped at the reassurance provided. "Then it may be months before he even asks Lily to marry him," she had said. "And he'll probably want a long engagement. He seems like the sort of man who would think a long engagement proper. By that time Lily will have grown tired of him."

She wandered over to the summerhouse. She had never liked this corner of the garden, had deliberately left it untended, and she brushed away imaginary cobwebs before she mounted the steps.

The side door of the house opened suddenly. Fanny retreated behind the butternut tree as Lily and Theodore walked across the lawn and stood for a moment gazing down at the river. She heard only two sentences of their conversation, but it was enough to leave her staring after them in dismay.

"I'll have to go shopping," Lily was saying.

"After we're married, I'll buy you a dozen dresses," Theodore answered placatingly. His voice faded off as they walked round to the front of the house.

After they were married! Fanny sat still. Was that what Pringle had been hinting at? Had she overheard a conversation, too?

It was almost dark now. Something was moving in the underbrush down the bank, and Fanny shivered, though the night was hot. She had never liked being alone at night. She had never liked being alone at any time, had always felt a great pity for poor women who worked and lived in rooms, who had nobody to go home to, no reason for existence. She, at least, had the house, and enough money. Nobody need ever pity her. But what would she do with herself, what would she live for if she were left alone? She couldn't stay on in that big house, with nothing to do except knit scarfs for the orphanage children and wait for Fridays, her day to visit them. She stood up, wanting to get quickly into the lamplit house, with other people.

The floor boards around the old butternut tree were loose, heaved up by the weather, and one was missing. She almost stepped into the hole before she noticed it. She looked around for the missing board. Someone had wedged it across the gate-way leading to the steps down the cliff. Now, who on earth could have done that? she wondered, and put it back on the floor where it belonged.

Much later that night, after tossing and turning for some time in his hot little room under the roof, Theodore rose and dressed, and went outside seeking a breath of cool air. The moon had come up, bright and full. He took several turns in the beechwood, and then, seeing the chairs grouped on the Jamesons' back lawn, stepped over the hedge and sat in one of them.

This was his last night in St. Charles. Tomorrow, after dinner, he and Lily would leave. They would have to wait until Saturday to be married, but the way Mildred had been watching him these past two days—several times during the evening he had caught her looking at him with a furtive watch-ful stare as if she knew something about him—had convinced him that it was time to move on. He had no trouble persuading Lily to leave a day earlier than planned. She agreed so readily to every suggestion he made regarding their marriage that he was sometimes puzzled. Either she had great faith in him, or she simply didn't care. He wanted her to have faith in him, and often lately he found himself daydreaming, inventing situations in which he proved his dependability. He knew that such dreams were impossible, that a day of reckoning was bound to come, but this would not bear thinking about. By refusing to dwell on the inevitable, he had in the past saved himself a good deal of worry.

It was after one o'clock. As he lay back with his face turned to catch the occasional puff of cool air from the river, his eyes closed, he suddenly felt watched. He opened his eyes. The windows of the house were all dark. The girls were probably asleep, but if one of them did happen to look out and see him there, she might think he was a prowler, and raise an alarm.

He was about to pull his chair farther back into the shadows under the trees when he caught sight of a face peering at him through the screen of the back porch.

It was Mildred. She called in a quavering voice, "Who's there?"

He didn't want her telephoning the police. "It's I—Theodore," he said reassuringly, and moved out into the open where he could be seen.

She retreated into the shadows of the porch, and her hands went up to her face. He thought she was about to scream. "Please don't be frightened," he begged, going up close to the screen door, speaking softly. She was only doing something to her hair, taking out pins and fluffing the curls over her ears. When she had finished this, she unlocked the door and stepped outside into the bright moonlight. She wore a long satin negligee with a frilled neckline.

"I thought you were a burglar," she faltered. "I was just going to call the girls." She lifted her face to his, and held out her hands like a sleepwalker.

"I'm awfully sorry," he apologized. "I couldn't sleep. I was taking a stroll in the woods."

She stood so close to him that he stepped back a pace, but still, when she raised her hands to her face, her arms brushed against him. Her hair, smelling of stale perfume and tobacco smoke, tickled his beard. "I couldn't sleep either," she said pathetically. "I was so frightened when I saw you."

"Don't cry!" He pulled her hands away from her face and held them. "There's nothing to be frightened of." She sagged against him and cried on his shoulder, while he patted her back and spoke soothingly, waiting patiently for her to finish. He expected any minute to see lights flash on in the house, hear voices calling down the stairs. When Mildred seemed about to stop crying, he led her inside. The couch gave a rasping groan as she lay back on it. He knelt beside her, all sympathy and attention. "Shall I make you a cup of tea?" he asked, wiping her eyes with his pocket handkerchief.

She shook her head and lifted her arms with a long sigh, clinging to him harder than ever, and he realized with a sudden jolt, as if he had run into something in the dark, that it was not tea she wanted.

He had found himself in a similar position many times before, and had long since given up trying to understand what women found so attractive about him. Middle-aged widows were forever luring him into shady corners, and hardened spinsters, who nobody would believe had a spark of passion in them, literally flung themselves into his arms when they got him alone in the dark. Because he was by nature obliging, and could not bear to see others disappointed, he had on numerous occasions found himself performing with false enthusiasm what he could only regard as an act of accommodation. But tonight he simply could not summon the energy. Hell hath no fury like a woman scorned, he reminded himself, gazing sadly down at Mildred's thin figure in its abandoned pose. He stroked her arms and murmured stock phrases while he racked his brains to find a way of escape without offending. Her wrath, if his refusal to cooperate made her look ridiculous, was something he did not care to contemplate. He sighed.

Mildred mistook his sigh for one of passion. He almost gave way to panic and bolted into the night. Then, with an effort, he got hold of himself. He enfolded her in his arms. After a moment he threw back his head in a listening attitude. "Someone's coming!" he whispered urgently.

Mildred jerked upright, her body tense.

As they both strained their ears toward the hall, an obliging creak sounded. It was only the normal settling of the timbers of the house, but Mildred whirled round guiltily, clutching the folds of her negligee together at the throat.

"They mustn't find us here!" Theodore groped for her hand and held it as if he could not bear to let go. "They mustn't guess that we . . ." He left the sentence dangling significantly. "I'll slip away quietly."

"Hurry!" Mildred was almost pushing him toward the door.

He hung back, still clinging to her hand. "May I come another time?"

"Yes, yes. Any time. Tomorrow. But please hurry now!"

As he walked home through the beechwood, he hoped she would not, if only to save herself disappointment, lie awake planning their next meeting.

# CHAPTER TWELVE

"WHO'S GOING TO KEEP AN EYE ON PAPA?" FANNY ASKED AFTER breakfast the next morning. She had cleared off one end of the kitchen table and was wrapping the stems of a great bunch of zinnias in damp newspaper. The children liked brightly colored flowers best, she had found—red and deep yellows. Mildred, in a pink negligee, her eyes still glazed with sleep, sat at the other end of the table peeling an orange.

Isobel said from the doorway, where she was shaking dusters, "Is this your morning at the orphanage?"

"I really should stay home and help Pringle with the laundry. She's not pleased about two washdays in one week. But I hate to disappoint the children. I thought I'd ask Lily to go along for the drive."

"I'd like to go, too." Isobel folded the dusters and stored them in the broom closet, pretending not to notice the bottle on the shelf. "I've finished all the downstairs rooms, so there isn't really much left for Pringle to do."

"Of course, come if you like," Fanny said, pleased, though

she did not look up as she gathered together the extra news-papers and folded them. "The only thing is, somebody's got to see that Papa gets his medicine. Do you know what dose he's supposed to have?" she asked, addressing Mildred.

Mildred started and looked round. "What?"

"Could you give Papa his medicine, and keep an eye on him while Pringle's busy with the laundry? Do you know how much he's supposed to have?"

"The directions are on the wall, aren't they?" Mildred said, taking offense at what she took to be a lack of confidence. "I would have seen to his medicine before, you know, if anybody had mentioned it. I've always tried to do my share."

Fanny gave her a second look. "Are you feeling all right?"

"Yes, of course."

"You look a little feverish. I hope you're not getting one of those summer colds."

"I'm all *right*!" Mildred said fretfully.

"I'll run up and change," Isobel said. "Be ready in five minutes. Here's the postman," she called back from the hall. "A letter for you, Mildred."

Mildred did not move. After a minute Fanny went into the hall and picked up the letter, a thick brown envelope with a return address but not the sender's name, and carried it back to the kitchen. Mildred looked at it frowning, began to lay it aside, then snatched it back and tore it open, fumbling in her pocket for her glasses.

Fanny went upstairs. The door of Lily's room was open, and Lily sat before the mirror brushing her hair. She took no notice when Fanny entered the room, but continued to gaze at her own reflection, drawing the brush lazily down the length of her pale hair. She was idling away the time, as she often did, and nothing about her actions suggested that she had any special plans for that day.

Lying awake in the night, Fanny had gone over and over that moment in the garden when she had overheard the snatch of conversation between Lily and Theodore. It seemed strange, to say the least, that less than ten hours after he had assured Isobel he had not asked Lily to marry him, he should be overheard discussing marriage with her as if it were something they had talked about and decided upon long ago. It seemed so strange, in fact, that Fanny found it unbelievable, and it was because she found it unbelievable that she had not mentioned the incident to anyone else. She felt sure that she must have missed something said just before or just after the two sentences that had reached her ears, something that would explain what they were talking about, that would reassure her. All night long suspicions hovered like ghosts on the edge of her mind, trying to creep in, but she drove them away. She was afraid to let even the smallest suspicion enter, for if she lost faith in *him*, how would she console herself?

She looked around the room. All Lily's things were in their usual place on her dressing table—except, Fanny noted suddenly, the blue enameled box where Lily kept her jewelry. There was nothing much of value in the box: a turquoise pin, a string of cultured pearls, the green-glass necklace and earrings, and a great many cheap bracelets and other ornaments. The door of the closet was ajar, showing a row of dresses hanging on the rod and a jumble of shoes on the floor.

"Are you doing anything special today?" It was a question Fanny asked habitually, often only half listening for an answer. She waited a moment and added, "Isobel and I are going to the orphanage. Would you like to come too?"

"No, thanks," Lily said, still looking at herself in the glass.

"We won't be gone long. Was that thunder?" Fanny listened. The storm which had been threatening since last night was still far off, a faint growl in the distance. "You're sure you don't want to come with us?"

Lily shook her head. "I'm going to do my nails."

"You'll be here when we get back? I mean, you're not going

anywhere? Well, good-by, dear." Fanny bent down and kissed Lily. "Your hair looks so pretty that way."

Lily smiled at her reflection.

"Remember to close your window if it rains," Fanny cautioned, and then did this herself. The window of Lily's room, which overlooked the summerhouse and the back garden, opened outwards and led to a balcony formed by the flat roof of the porch.

"Well, good-by then, honey," Fanny said again. At the head of the stairs she paused and looked back, then slowly began to descend.

Mrs. Pringle walked down the hall with a martyr's tread, carrying a bag of laundry, which she heaved over the banister. It hit the floor below with a heavy thud and a great rush of air. Mildred, at the telephone, jumped, and looked up with a murderous expression.

"Pardon *me*, dear!" Mrs. Pringle leaned over the banister with a false air of apology.

"Operator," Mildred said into the telephone, "I want New York . . ." She consulted the letter she had received that morning and gave a number.

"What's *she* so excited about?" Mrs. Pringle said aloud to herself, jerking her head in the direction of the telephone as she lumbered downstairs.

In the laundry room, Mrs. Pringle sorted the dirty clothes and arranged them in piles: towels in one, bedding and linen in another, colored things in a third. The hardest part of her washday was now over. When she had filled the washer and adjusted the controls, she lay down on an old-fashioned couch she had salvaged from upstairs. The laundry room was the coolest spot in the house. There was even a suggestion of breeze rippling across the grass in the back garden, and a summer perfume drifted through the open windows that were set high up, giving her a worm's-eye view of the lawn and a patch of darkening sky.

It was going to be a typical September washday—sudden drenching thunder showers, then sunshine. They could expect a good many such days during the next month. Tricky weather, if you had to depend on it for drying clothes, but thank God for modern conveniences, she thought. She would never tell the girls—in fact, she made a point of letting them know that doing the laundry used up every ounce of strength she possessed—but she enjoyed washday almost more than any other day. It served as a good excuse for not doing anything else. She could lie down here with nothing to do but keep an eye on things—except, of course, for putting in the clothes and taking them out, which was no effort—and listen to Fanny upstairs dusting, mopping, with pity in her heart for the poor overworked washerwoman, cooking up little treats for lunch. And every time she staggered upstairs with a pile of dry sheets, Mrs. Pringle sank into a chair and let Fanny fuss over her.

She kicked off her shoes. The hum of the washer going through its cycle had a soothing effect. She wished she had something to drink. Beer, perhaps, for a day like this. There was never any beer in the house, for the old man would never touch anything so mild. Just as well, she thought philosophically. She needed a clear head this morning. She had some thinking to do, must decide whether or not to tell Fanny that Lily was drawing all that money out of the bank.

Above her, she could hear Mildred at the telephone, still trying to place a long-distance call to New York. She was making a great fuss about it, acting as if her life depended upon talking with whomever she was trying to get. It wasn't Harry. Mrs. Pringle knew Harry's number.

Listening, she heard Mildred tell the operator in a hysterical voice that the call was *important*, it *must* be put through, no matter how many lines were down. Then, a little later, Mildred's chair scraped back and she went upstairs, her mules slapping.

*She's* in an awful stew this morning, Mrs. Pringle mused. But, my Lord, is she ever in anything else? I wish to God she'd go back where she belongs. We'd be a happier family without her.

In the empty schoolroom at the orphanage, Fanny arranged her flowers in small bunches, which she placed in cheap pottery vases. She had donated the vases herself—three dozen of them, fifteen cents apiece at the five-and-ten—so that each child might have a little flower arrangement for his own desk, something that he need not share with another. One of the most depressing things about the orphanage, to Fanny, was that nothing belonged to an individual. Everything was shared. "But we mustn't encourage them to be selfish," the matron warned. How could they be selfish? Fanny wondered. What have they got to be selfish about?

The schoolroom smelled of disinfectant. It was a large drab room with blackboards along each wall, and paper tulips pasted on the windows. The desk stood on a raised platform, and behind it was a scarred upright piano. There were no pictures on the wall, no curtains at the windows.

Ruth, one of the older girls, came in. "I've been sent to help you with the flowers, Miss Jameson," she simpered, shifting from one foot to the other. "Shall I bring some water?"

"Oh, thank you, dear," Fanny said. Ruth was overweight, with a heavy, unattractive face. I don't suppose she gets the right food, Fanny thought. Macaroni and cheese one day, baked beans the next . . . "How old are you?" she asked when Ruth returned with a pitcher of water.

"Eleven."

"What do you plan to be when you grow up?"

"I don't know."

I was like that when I was her age, Fanny thought. Heavy, clumsy, but surely not that unattractive, for I had nice clothes. Next time, I'll bring some old things of Lily's. They could be made over to fit.

Ruth was eager to be helpful. She plodded back and forth, placing a vase of flowers on each desk, then went round with the pitcher and filled each one with water. The last vase was for her own desk at the back of the room. Before she carried it down, she picked up a blossom that had fallen to the floor. "Is it all right if I take this one, Miss Jameson?"

"But it's crushed, dear!"

"It's a pretty color," Ruth said wistfully.

Fanny had saved the largest bouquet for the dining room. She took three of the brightest flowers from it and handed them to Ruth.

The girl looked around doubtfully. "Now I've got more than the others."

"That's a bonus for helping me," Fanny said briskly, and turned away, appalled by the sudden rush of tears behind her eyes. A little bunch of flowers, she thought, and you'd think I'd given her the world.

The children, driven inside by a sudden spattering of rain, were now being herded along the hall. Isobel, who had been taken on a tour of the kitchen, entered the schoolroom with them, followed by the matron, Mrs. Smith. Each child clutched an apple, but not one of them had dared to take a bite. An apple was a thing to be treasured, to be looked at and admired. Later on, when they had been told to do so, they would begin to eat, but reluctantly, because when they had eaten the apple they would have no treasure left. Little peaky faces stared at Fanny, or turned away self-consciously. A few children, fascinated by Isobel's smile, stole glances at her, then at each other.

"Now, then," Mrs. Smith announced in a bright, affected voice, "Miss Jameson has brought her sister to visit us today, children. Her name is Mrs. Whitmore." She repeated the name, enunciating each syllable distinctly. "They have brought us some lovely gifts: an apple for each of you, the flowers on your desks, nice new stockings for everyone, and a lot of lovely things besides. Now, what do we all say?" Raising her hands as if directing an orchestra, she led the chorus: "Good morning, Miss Jameson. Good morning, Mrs. Whitmore. Thank you for your gifts."

What the matron called "the social half hour" followed. This was the time Fanny always dreaded, when she was expected to make friends with the children, and they were expected to show their appreciation of her generosity by enjoying themselves. She felt that the children dreaded this time as much as she did. When exhorted, without specific direction, to enjoy themselves for half an hour, they did not know what to do or where to begin.

Isobel sat down beside Fanny. "Are we supposed to entertain them, or they us?"

"Usually they show me things—pictures they've drawn, handkerchiefs they've hemmed. I'm afraid they don't get much pleasure out of it."

In a minute the matron would say coaxingly, "Cynthia, dear, why don't you show the ladies your lovely picture? Now, Robert, tell the ladies about the bird you saw yesterday."

"Wouldn't it be more fun to play a game, or sing songs?" Isobel asked. "Poor things, they look so doleful."

"By all means, if you'd like to play a little game," Mrs. Smith said. "Some of them recite very nicely, too."

Isobel looked doubtfully at her.

"Now, children, we're going to have a lovely visit with the ladies." Mrs. Smith tried to get things started. "John, don't you want to show Miss Jameson the nice little animal you made yesterday?"

John, a small red-headed boy, looked at the floor and mumbled that he had lost it.

Isobel rose and went to the piano. She glanced over the stack of music on the rack and swept it aside. "Does anyone know this song?" She struck a chord and began to sing an old French-Canadian *chanson* that she had picked up when on tour with Alan, her first husband. The children's faces brightened a little. One or two let out timid giggles.

"Or this?" Isobel switched to a more familiar tune. Mrs. Smith raised her hands encouragingly, keeping time, and a number of voices joined Isobel's. Smiles appeared on the children's faces. Their self-consciousness dropped away, since now they knew what was expected of them. They gravitated toward the front of the room and clustered around the piano. The matron, still keeping time, even singing snatches of the song in a quavering soprano, gave Fanny an approving nod. "Your sister's got a nice way with children, Miss Jameson."

Yes, Isobel was good with people. Even Mrs. Smith seemed more human today. Her eyes behind her steel-rimmed glasses were less anxious. Perhaps she worries about *me*, Fanny thought. Perhaps she's afraid I'll become bored and not bother coming back next week. I suppose she has to send in reports, lists of donations, and if I stopped coming, whoever she sends the reports to would want to know why. She felt suddenly at ease with Mrs. Smith, who seemed no longer a fussy and affected orphanage employee, but a woman with problems, who needed sympathy.

"I hope Mrs. Whitmore will visit us next week as well."

"Her husband's coming up this week end," Fanny said. "I expect she'll go back to New York with him, now that Papa's out of danger." No hope of Isobel staying. No hope, even, of repairing the gap that Fanny had so foolishly created between them. But what on earth do you *say* when your sister announces that she's having an affair with a stranger? Offer congratulations and invite him up for dinner? If I only knew how to deal with people, Fanny thought despairingly.

"Now, who wants to play a game?" Isobel asked gaily. She came down from the platform, and the children crowded after her. One little girl, still clutching a red apple, stumbled against the desk and fell. Her apple went rolling away. Isobel bent down swiftly and picked her up. "Does it hurt?" she asked, examining the bruised forehead. The child, a thin little girl whose pigtails were tied with unmatched ribbons, shook her head, but could not keep from crying.

"Let *me*!" Fanny astonished herself by saying as she took the child from Isobel's arms. "You go on with the game."

Then a surprising thing happened. The little girl turned, and seeing whose arms now held her, put her own arms trustingly round Fanny's neck and buried her face in her shoulder.

This time the tears rushed up so fast that Fanny could not stop them. I hope I'm not going to make a damned fool of myself, she thought, and bent her head so that her eyes were hidden beneath the brim of her hat.

Mildred was in a great state of agitation. "Oh, what's *wrong* with that stupid operator?" she fretted aloud. For a solid hour she had been trying to telephone the Peerless Detective Agency in New York, to confirm their written report. Some lines were down on account of the storm, the operator said. Mildred could hear cracklings along the wire. Ordinarily she would not use the telephone during a storm, but today she scarcely noticed the faint mutterings of thunder, the occasional flashes of lightning. The brown envelope containing the report, which she had received that morning, was in her pocket. It was not that she doubted what the report said. She simply wanted to confirm it, to be furnished with details.

She paced back and forth between the living room and the hall, waiting for the operator to call back. Since the letter had come, she had been unable to sit still. From time to time she took it from her pocket and read it with mounting triumph, and a breathless, half-frightened feeling, too, as she imagined facing Theodore with the truth about himself.

How would he take it? Would he try bluff—assume an air

of hurt bewilderment and deny everything? Or would he beg for mercy? Most often, during the past hour, Mildred had pictured him doing the latter. She saw herself standing over him —for in her imagination he had now shrunk until he was shorter than she was—and he was looking up at her imploringly, the boldness gone from his eyes, the smile from his face. "Yes, and wait until I tell the girls about you forcing your way into the house last night!" she said as if he were standing in the room with her. Last night's encounter was now taking a different shape in her mind. "I simply went downstairs for a breath of air," she would tell the girls, "and there he was, prowling about the garden. He simply forced his way in."

She had smoked one cigarette after another during the morning. She lit a fresh one now, with trembling hands, and put on her glasses to read the letter over again.

"In answer to your inquiry regarding the man known to you as Theodore Fairfield," the letter began, and went on to say that from Mildred's description and the picture enclosed, Theodore had been positively identified as one George Morton, alias several other names, who had recently been released from prison after serving a one-year sentence. The charge was obtaining money under false pretenses. He should have served time for bigamy as well, but none of the women involved cared to make the charge, and since he had married each one under a different name, and later denied even knowing them, he had gone scot-free on that count. His mistake had been in not marrying his latest victim—she knew him as Gregory Entwistle—before he spent her money. His method was to go to some quiet resort, posing as a retired banker, a writer, or whatever profession he happened to fancy at the moment. There he soon struck up an acquaintance with some respectable woman, a widow or a spinster with means, married her under whatever name he was using at the time, and disappeared as soon as her money was gone. There were believed to be three, possibly four, of these forsaken ladies scattered across the country, waiting for him to come back. Being respectable, they mourned in silence, and concocted various stories to tell their friends regarding his disappearance.

Besides the ladies he had wronged, he had a wife—a woman he had married legally, using his real name, George Morton—and three children. He was not from Boston at all. His permanent home, the place where his wife lived, was a small suburb in New Jersey. He did not own any factories. He owned nothing except a wife and three children. Off and on, between seasons, so to speak, he returned to them and worked at an insignificant clerking job to support them. His wife apparently knew about the other women in his life, and wasted no pity on them. On several occasions when he had disappeared from home, she had tracked him down to whatever resort he was visiting, and whisked him off like a naughty child.

"I *knew* he wasn't what he pretended to be!" Mildred whispered vehemently. "From the beginning, I thought there was something funny about him. Prowling around other people's houses in the dead of night, forcing his attentions on innocent women . . ."

The telephone at last. She was out of her chair before it stopped ringing.

The man from the detective agency seemed amused. "Oh, Morton's not a bad little guy. He's just like a lot of us—gets tired of the humdrum life once in a while."

"He's a bigamist."

"We can't prove that. Actually, we haven't got anything on him right now."

"You mean you're not going to report him to the police, and have them send someone up to arrest him?"

"Not unless you've got something specific on him. What's he been up to this time, anyway?"

"He's a criminal. He's been in jail."

"And served his sentence. Don't forget that. If you want him arrested, I'm afraid you'll have to make your complaint to the local police, and let them handle it."

"No. No, of course I won't go to them," Mildred said angrily.

"I'm afraid we can't do anything from here."

"But something *must* be done!" Mildred protested.

The man at the other end of the line chuckled. "As a matter of fact, I have an idea something might be done soon. His wife's been looking for him, you know."

"Oh . . ." Mildred said faintly. "What sort of a woman is she?"

"Pardon? I can't hear you."

"What is she like?"

"The wife? She's not a bad sort, really. Stout, rather red-faced. Looks like a charwoman. That's what she is, as a matter of fact. Really not a bad soul."

"Did you say she knows where he is?"

The man laughed. "It wouldn't surprise me if some little bird told her where to find him. Say, by the way, what's he posing as this time? A member of the royal family?"

Mildred was not listening to him any more. She said good-by and replaced the receiver in its cradle. He had no *right* to tell that woman, she thought unreasonably. He has no right being in business if he's going to give confidential information to every person who asks for it.

She went upstairs and changed her dress, creamed her face, and smoothed on fresh make-up. She combed her hair carefully, coaxing the curls into place. Then she went back downstairs and telephoned the Willows. Mrs. Kinch informed her that Theodore was out, and she had no idea when he would return.

"Would you like to leave a message?" she asked.

"No, I'll call again." Mildred slammed down the receiver and sat drumming her fingers impatiently. Unable to sit still, she wandered upstairs again, and out onto the balcony over the front door. The rain came in quick showers, soon over, with a flash of sunshine through the clouds. A summer storm, with thunder growling overhead, then moving away. Cars went by on the highway, their tires licking the wet asphalt. A gust of wind shook the trees, drenching the lawn.

"Papa—my God!" Mildred exclaimed suddenly. She had forgotten all about him. She squinted nearsightedly at her watch. He should have had his medicine an hour ago.

He was lying on his back with his eyes closed, breathing heavily. He was not dead, then. Her negligence had not killed him. What medicine had Fanny said? Mildred looked over the bottles on the table and picked one up, peering at the label. This was it: the brown bottle. Oh, and there were directions on a printed sheet stuck to the wall over the table with bits of adhesive tape. She could not read the directions without her glasses, but she remembered now: a teaspoonful every hour. She had allowed almost two hours to go by without giving him a dose. Why had they left her alone like this, anyway? They leave me alone with him so that they can blame me if anything happens, Mildred thought.

She poured medicine into a spoon and held it to her father's mouth. He choked, spilling some over his chin, but most of it went down his throat. She stood watching him. His breathing grew more labored. In a panic, she pulled at his shoulders to make him sit up, and tucked another pillow behind his head. Gradually, his breathing grew quieter. He was all right, then. Her hands stopped shaking. She left him as he was, half sitting, half lying against the pillows.

The clouds had piled up again, the thunder moved closer. She closed the window and stood watching the storm sweep up the gorge. It came like a gray wall, hiding the river and the houses on the opposite bank. Rain was flung suddenly against the windows, and the trees in the garden bent down, shedding leaves.

Halfway home, Fanny and Isobel were caught in the heaviest shower of the day. The windshield-wipers kept time frantically, but the water sluiced over them, distorting vision. Approaching cars seemed to plow along, sending up twin sprays. "I think we should stop until it lets up," Fanny said.

"Not under these trees. That's the worst place in a thunder storm."

"There's a clear spot up ahead." Fanny glanced nervously at the sky. All the elm boughs bent down under the weight of the rain, and brushed the top of the car. Thunder cracked overhead and went rolling away toward the horizon. Flashes of lightning turned the landscape blue. Storms like this were common in the Niagara Peninsula at the end of summer, and she had read somewhere that an automobile was the safest place to be; but she was apprehensive just the same, and would much rather have been at home.

Several other motorists had decided to wait out the downpour on the treeless stretch at the top of the rise. Fanny pulled up behind a green sedan. On one side of the road a plowed field went up a hill. Brown water gushed along every furrow and into the ditch beside the road, where asters lay in flattened heaps. She wiped off the windshield with her sleeve, then remembered the air-conditioner. "I keep forgetting we have all these new inventions," she said. "I don't know what half these buttons are for."

They stared out at the drenched landscape. This forced stop, with the rain beating down, the lightning and the swaying trees to look at, seemed made to order for a good talk, and Fanny began testing phrases in her mind.

Before she could find a suitable one, Isobel said abruptly, "I'm going to divorce Eliot."

Fanny fumbled in her handbag for cigarettes. Perhaps it was her success with the little girl at the orphanage that gave her confidence; perhaps it was Isobel's voice, in which she fancied she detected a shade of uncertainty. "I never liked him," she said, lighting up, handing the package to Isobel. "I can't think why you ever married him in the first place."

Isobel shrugged. "Because I'm afraid to be alone. Because I hate not having attention. I need someone—preferably a man —to make decisions for me. I've always depended on other people."

"I shouldn't have thought *you'd* ever need anyone," Fanny was surprised into saying. She had read enough articles on how to live to know that many people have secret fears, private miseries that never show. The only thing was that she had never thought of Isobel as being one of this majority. The discovery that she was gave Fanny a feeling of power, as if she had been told that what she had for years considered a flaw in herself was in reality an asset. She knew suddenly how to behave toward Isobel.

"But I wonder," she said severely, "if you aren't being a little rash. I don't mind about Eliot . . . but this other man who's been telephoning you, the one you said you'd asked up for the week end—don't you realize you're *inviting* people to talk about you? What sort of an example is this to your child? How do you suppose *we* feel?" She was puffing so hard on her cigarette that her head was wreathed in smoke. "I do think you might have waited until you're free to start running around with someone else, if only to spare our feelings."

"It looks as though I'll *have* to wait. That letter I got yesterday was from him—the man who's been telephoning. It was beautifully written; I'm sure he must have spent hours composing it. The gist of it was that he's thought it over and decided it will be best for all concerned if we don't see each other again. Which is another way of saying that he doesn't care as much as he once thought he did."

"I'm sorry."

"Probably all for the best."

"I wouldn't have scolded if I'd known about the letter."

"I'm glad you did. That's what I meant about depending on

other people—even to the point of wanting to be told when I'm wrong. I don't mean criticized; I mean *told*, by someone who cares. I suppose a psychiatrist would say I've never grown up."

"Pringle told me about Eliot," Fanny said bravely, and felt a great relief when the words were out.

"Poor Eliot. Not that it's made much difference in his life."

The rain had begun to slacken, the thunder clouds rolled away to the east. Mist rose up from the plowed furrows, and beyond them in a field of late clover the purple blossoms lay down as if exhausted. Yellow leaves were stuck all over the flattened grass. Fanny started the car. She felt wonderfully at ease with Isobel. The air about them seemed to have cleared, as the landscape was clearing up now after the rain.

"I suppose it's all right if I stay at home for a while?" Isobel asked as they drove along under the still-dripping trees.

Fanny tramped on the brake so suddenly that a motorist behind her swerved aside with an angry blare of his horn, missing a collision by a hair's breadth. "All *right*?" she demanded. "I can't believe you'd ask such a foolish question, Isobel. Where else would you stay, but home with us where you belong?"

## CHAPTER THIRTEEN

MILDRED WATCHED THE CLOCK. SHE HAD PROMISED HERSELF THAT she would not go near the telephone for another half hour, but as soon as the thunder died away and the rain stopped, she called the Willows again. Mrs. Kinch sounded ready to burst with curiosity as she informed her that Theodore had not yet returned.

"Could you tell me where to find him?"

"I'm sure I couldn't say where he is, Mrs. McKinley. He left the house around nine o'clock this morning. I haven't seen him since. Is it something important? Perhaps if you'd leave a message . . ."

"I'll call again." Mildred cut her off and sat beside the telephone, trembling with exasperation. Nosy old woman.

She went upstairs again. Lily's door was closed, as it had been ever since the girls left for the orphanage. Mildred believed that Lily had gone with them. All the other doors along the passage were ajar. Isobel had left some bills on her dresser, four tens and a five. There were two letters in her top drawer, both from Eliot: "My dear Isobel, I had hoped to find at least a postcard from you in this morning's mail . . ." No trace of the letter from that other man. In Fanny's room the windows had been left open. The curtains were soaked. It was unlike Fanny to be careless, to forget things. She had seemed fidgety this morning, too. Was it because she had guessed Theodore's secret? Mildred wondered, instantly suspicious because she wanted no one else to share her triumph. It's *my* discovery, she thought. Fanny has no business meddling.

Pausing on the threshold of her father's room, she saw that he was asleep. He had slipped off the pillows and lay in an awkward position, his arms flung out, but she did not go near him, for with the window closed the room smelled more than ever of medicine and sickness, a heavy disagreeable odor that made her hold her breath.

When she opened Lily's door, she stopped short. "I thought you'd gone with the others," she said, beginning to back out. Then she saw the suitcase on the bed. "What are you doing?" she asked sharply.

Lily did not even glance up. She placed her brush and comb in the suitcase, which already contained her jewel box and some gloves, and patted them daintily into place with her fingertips.

"Lily, I want you to tell me why you're packing that bag." Mildred closed the door and stood with her back to it. So I was right! she was thinking. They *were* planning to run away together, as I tried to tell Fanny. "Are you going somewhere?" she demanded.

Lily frowned. "It's none of your business what I do."

"I think it's very much my business." Mildred knew she should try to distract Lily in some way, subtly turn her mind from her purpose and keep her occupied until the girls came home, but she said, "If you have any intention of going anywhere with that man . . ."

Lily looked sideways at her. "What man?"

"You know who I mean. That man who calls himself Theodore Fairfield, which doesn't happen to be his name."

"What makes you blush when you talk about him?"

Mildred had not been blushing at all, but immediately she felt a rush of blood to her face.

"You always look funny when anyone mentions him." Lily took a dress from the closet, folded it, and arranged it in the suitcase, a battered imitation leather bag lined with flowered cotton that she must have found in the attic. "Your eyes go funny."

Mildred kept her temper. "You haven't answered my question. I've asked you why you're packing that bag."

The familiar blank, distant expression came down over Lily's face. She walked to the window and threw it open, letting in the wet leafy smell of the garden and the sound of dripping trees.

"I think I know. You were planning to run away with that man, weren't you? I believe you'll change your mind when you've read this." Mildred thrust one hand down the front of her dress and pulled out the letter. "I've suspected him all along, you know, so I had him investigated. He's just a common little clerk, with a wife and three children. He's been in jail."

Lily gazed dreamily into the garden.

"If you don't believe me, here's what the detective agency

says about him." Mildred read the letter aloud, then folded it back into its envelope. "So we've been entertaining a convict in our home," she continued, infuriated by Lily's silence. "A bigamist. A man who preys upon women and robs them."

Lily was looking at the summerhouse. She leaned forward, her cheek against the curtain as if lost in reverie.

"A man who's spent a year in jail. And you were fool enough to be taken in by him!"

"Theodore said you'd try to stop us," Lily said musingly.

"I'm only telling you the truth about him. Read the letter yourself if you don't believe me. Here." Mildred placed the envelope temptingly on the dresser. "Why don't you read it?"

Lily did not glance at it, but continued to lean against the curtain. She wound a strand of hair round her little finger and chewed it.

"I've talked to the detective agency on the phone. The New York police are sending a man up to arrest him."

Lily turned, staring meditatively. Her silence was full of meaning, as if she knew this to be a lie and was waiting for a retraction. Mildred had a sudden suspicion that Lily knew her thoughts, that her abstracted expression covered secret amusement. Lily glanced into the garden again, then sat on the window sill and folded her hands in her lap. "I bet you don't know where Theodore is," she said with a sly upward glance.

"Where is he?"

"*I* know." Lily clasped her hands round one knee and swung her foot, smiling down at it.

"He's not at home. I've been trying all morning—" Mildred checked herself.

"You'd never guess where he is, by yourself," Lily mused.

"Where *is* he?" Mildred demanded. "You might as well tell me. I'll find out, sooner or later."

"He's in the boathouse," Lily said, and then put her hands over her mouth as if she had not meant to tell.

"The boathouse? What's he doing down there?"

216

"He's taking out the *Lilybell*."

"That old boat? It must be falling to pieces by now. Nobody's been down to the boathouse for years."

"Theodore and I go down almost every day. He's down there now, waiting for me."

"I don't believe it!" Mildred said, backing toward the door. "I think you're lying, Lily."

Lily shrugged. "All you have to do is *look*."

Mildred ran along the hall and down the stairs, her heart pounding. A scattering of raindrops was flung in her face as she opened the side door. In her high heels, she sprinted across the lawn and into the summerhouse, slipping on wet leaves, shaking water out of her eyes, and ran down the steps to the boathouse.

Mrs. Pringle was taking the last load out of the dryer when she heard Mildred run down the stairs and into the back garden. "Now, where in heaven's name is that one going?" she wondered aloud. "The way she's been stewing around all morning, it wouldn't surprise me if she's out there commanding God to make it stop raining." This observation struck her as extremely humorous, and she was sorry no one was there to hear it. Sometimes she wondered if she had missed her calling, and ought to be writing books instead of housekeeping. She was certainly more observant than the average. She was the only one, for instance, who suspected that Mildred had a hankering for Mr. Fairfield. Of course, I'm more experienced, she told herself complacently. One of the little delusions she comforted herself with was that she was more worldly than any of her friends, and by this she meant that she could, if she wished, reveal details of her private life which would make them feel as if they had never lived. Actually—though from the innuendoes she exchanged with men at parties it would be difficult to guess this—her behavior had been fairly decorous. Lack of opportunity had prevented her from taking more than a good look up the primrose path and thinking how nice it would be to try it. She did not count as contributing particularly to her knowledge of the world those rumpled evenings in the park before she married Ernie. She regretted those evenings now. If she had been more particular, Ernie might have more respect for her. He might think twice before he sat around belching after every meal, or letting off wind in bed without so much as saying, "Pardon me."

She went up to the kitchen, carrying a pile of folded sheets. No lunch in sight. Not even a pot of coffee brewing for a poor exhausted woman who'd spent two hours slaving over the laundry. That's gratitude, she thought. And I suppose *she'll* be coming in any minute, wanting something to eat. "What's for lunch, Pringle?" Her mouth curled disdainfully as she imitated Mildred. "How do I know what's for lunch?" she asked of the empty kitchen. "I'm not a magician. I can only be one place at a time." She pulled back the curtain and looked toward the summerhouse, but saw no sign of Mildred.

She went upstairs.

Lily, standing beside the open window, turned as Mrs. Pringle entered her room. She looked as if she had just wakened from sleep, was still half in a dream. Her eyes were dazed.

Mrs. Pringle was instantly alert. She had seen that look on Lily's face before. She glanced around the room, which looked tidier than usual. There was a brown envelope on the dresser. Addressed to Mildred, she found, when she picked it up and examined it. Now, that was funny. What was it doing here? Then her eyes fell on the suitcase, and the letter dropped from her hand, forgotten. Oh, Lordy! she thought. So that's what she's been up to!

She composed herself with an effort, trying to look as if she had noticed nothing. "Well, dear," she said in the persuasive rallying tone they all used when trying to divert Lily without arousing her suspicions. "You've tidied up your room, I see.

That's my good girl!" She dropped a playful kiss on Lily's forehead. "My, doesn't it look lovely—just as neat as a new pin. You deserve a nice little treat for lunch." She cocked her head on one side, smiling. "Now, ducky, what shall we have—a lovely omelet, or a nice little minced-steak patty on a bun? I'll just close this window," she added, "though I do believe the rain's over." She bustled about the room. "Oh, and look what somebody's gone and put on your bed!" she exclaimed. "That old suitcase! Well, we don't want *that* cluttering up our nice room, do we, dear? Such a battered old thing." While she was talking, she was removing articles from the suitcase. I came in the nick of time, she was thinking. What would the girls say if they'd come home and found Lily gone? And where's Mildred? Why isn't she here? Always Johnny on the spot when she's not wanted . . .

"There now, I'll hang your pretty dress in the closet. We don't want it to get all wrinkled, do we? Have you seen Mildred?" she asked in a normal voice.

"*She* put that suitcase there," Lily said.

Mrs. Pringle pretended to believe this. "Now, wasn't that silly of her? Well, we'll just fool her, won't we, dear? We'll put this old suitcase back in the attic and not tell a soul. And your little brush and comb where they belong, too. Oh, my, some people get funny ideas, don't they?" She laughed gaily, and breathed a sigh of relief. Experience told her that she was not alone responsible for deflecting Lily's mind from her purpose in packing the bag. Something had already happened to make her forget why she was doing it. Just so long as something took her mind off it, Mrs. Pringle thought. She whisked the bag out of sight under the bed.

"It's past time for your poor father's medicine. Mildred was *supposed* to be keeping an eye on him."

"Mildred's gone," Lily said in a faraway voice.

"Gone? Gone where, dear?"

"I don't know. She went out." Lily looked around the room, perplexed. "Why isn't Fanny here?"

"She'll be along directly, dear. I expect they got held up by the rain. Now then, why don't you come downstairs with me while I fix a nice lunch? We'll take a look at the old gentleman on the way."

"Lord, it's stuffy in here," Mrs. Pringle said as they entered the sickroom. "And look at your poor father—all at sixes and sevens. You throw open the window, dear, while I see if I can straighten him out."

She grasped the old man's shoulders, and pulled her hands away as if she had touched something hot.

"He's dead!" she said in a high voice, staring at Lily. "My God, here he is dead as a doornail!"

Theodore spent the morning shopping for a used car. He decided at last on a low-priced model, two years old. It was a conservative, dark-gray color, and looked like hundreds of other cars seen on the highway every day. He would have preferred something more sporty, but could not run the risk of appearing conspicuous. He told the salesman he was buying it for a friend, and that they would come around after lunch with a check.

It was raining, and he sat in a café drinking coffee, looking out on the wet street. Around noon, when the last shower seemed to have cleared away, he thought he could risk walking home without getting wet.

He was well pleased with himself. No hitch had occurred in his plans so far, though he would not feel entirely free of anxiety until he got Lily away from her family. This afternoon, he and Lily would go to the bank, after which they would pick up the new car. And later, in the early evening, they would start out on their adventure. He pictured them driving through a sunny landscape with green trees, and flowers spread on the grass, in the distance the pink towers of a city. He did not look much beyond this point.

Humming a tune, he strode along between the scented hedges breathing the resinous smell of wet cedar. The flowers in the garden were broken, the striped grass along the border lying flat. The two Miss Baxters were venturing out again, tentatively, to stroll on the wet lawn and sniff the air. They wore white plastic boots over their sandals, and sweaters thrown about their shoulders. He gave them a cordial smile, and stopped for a moment to chat about the weather. Their shrill genteel voices no longer irritated him, since after tonight he would never have to listen to them again.

Still humming, he opened the front door and started up the stairs. A stout woman with a weathered face and untidy gray hair rose up from the green-plush sofa in the reception room. She wore a sailor hat with a bunch of pink roses tacked to the brim. Her hands clutched a limp black purse with a broken strap.

"Well, George!" she said pleasantly.

He backed slowly down the stairs.

"You *have* been gone a long time, George."

"How . . . how did you get here?" he faltered.

"I came on the morning train. I've been here two hours, waiting for you. But it's all right," she added in a bustling cheerful way, gathering up her umbrella and a pair of pink lace gloves. "Mrs. Kinch gave me a nice cup of tea. And I've got your bag all packed . . . Oh, George, that *beard*!" she exclaimed suddenly. "I *thought* I noticed something different. It's just dawned on me what it is. Whatever made you grow a beard?" She stepped back for a better view and pursed her lips doubtfully. "I'm not at all sure it suits you. I think when we get home we'll shave it off, or the children will never know their Daddy—and let your hair grow back to its natural color, too. I always thought you had nice hair . . . Well, then," she concluded, smiling at him, "are we ready? There's a bus in half an hour. I think we've just got time to make it."

# CHAPTER FOURTEEN

"THERE HE WAS, SPRAWLED ALL OVER THE PILLOW," MRS. PRINGLE told Fanny and Isobel, "and when I took hold of him to straighten him up—" She threw out her hands. "Stiff as a board! Oh, Lord, it gave me a turn. 'He's done for,' I said to Lily. He must have popped off in his sleep."

"Have you called Dr. Randolph?"

Mrs. Pringle nodded. "He's on the way, though it seems like locking the stable door. He can't *do* anything. I called the undertaker, too, while I was on the phone . . . Well, girls," she went on cheerfully, "if someone will give me a hand in the kitchen, I'll see what's for lunch. No sense starving ourselves," she added when Fanny glanced up the stairs. Poor Fanny—she hated to go up, but felt she ought to.

The *relief*! Mrs. Pringle said to herself. She had just about given up hope. In moments of despair she had pictured the old B. living on for ten, twenty years, until they were all too old, too worn out to benefit from his dying. Funny, she'd have thought a corpse in the house would give the whole place a creepy feeling, but after the first shock of finding him dead, she had felt as if all the rooms had been given a good airing. The sun had come out, which may have had something to do with it, though she doubted that. Squares of sunlight lay on the rug, the clocks ticked, the refrigerator started up. So peaceful and lovely. The girls were behaving well, too. No pretense of grief they did not feel.

"Where is Mildred?" Fanny asked.

"I don't know *where* Mildred is. I've looked everywhere. She went into the garden—I saw her as I was coming up from the laundry room—but where she's gone from there I couldn't say. She wouldn't go visiting the neighbors, not when she was supposed to be keeping an eye on him. I can't think . . ." Mrs.

Pringle screwed up her forehead. "She didn't tell you where she was going, did she, love?" she asked Lily.

Lily looked up with a blank stare. She turned to Fanny as if seeking help in remembering something that eluded her.

Oh, the poor thing! Mrs. Pringle thought. She's having one of her queer spells. It's all gone from her poor mind. Now, why? I wonder. She never cared that much about her father.

Fanny saw the bewilderment in Lily's eyes, too. She moved close to her and stroked her hair, smiling reassuringly.

Mrs. Pringle suddenly remembered the suitcase, and motioned Fanny upstairs. "I don't know what to make of it, dear," she said, opening the door of Lily's room. "But look—" She fished under the bed. "She was packing this bag. I just happened to come upstairs and catch her at it. I had no trouble taking her mind off it; it almost seemed as if she'd already given up the idea—as if something made her change her mind before I came along. Now, what do you make of it? There was a letter, too," she remembered. "Oh, I see you've found it. Addressed to Mildred, isn't it?"

"Yes." Fanny was examining the brown envelope that had lain on the dresser. To Mrs. Pringle's disappointment, she tucked it into her pocket without opening it. A moment later they heard Dr. Randolph on the stairs. Fanny went into the bedroom with him.

Mrs. Pringle was eating a sandwich in the kitchen by herself when the doctor came downstairs. The girls had decided to go without lunch for the time being, which was foolish of them. Now was the time they needed to keep up their strength, with all the pother of a funeral to go through before they could enjoy their freedom.

Dr. Randolph came into the kitchen and closed the door. "They tell me you found him." He sat down, laced his knobby fingers together, and rested his chin on them, peering nearsightedly across the table.

"Lord, yes. It was about ten minutes to twelve." Mrs. Pringle glanced at the clock. "I'd been downstairs all morning doing the laundry, and when I finished that I went upstairs to see where everybody was. Here, let me give you a cup of tea—no, you don't drink tea, do you?" she interrupted herself. "Well, I think we can find something more to your liking." She bustled into the dining room to fetch the decanter from the sideboard. "I'll have a spot, too, I believe. After what I've been through . . ." She set out two glasses and filled them.

Dr. Randolph held his up to the light, squinting. "He was dead when you found him?"

"Stone-cold. I went to his room, and there he was, dead as a doornail. You could have knocked me over with a feather. Died in his sleep, by the look of things." She raised her glass and drank. "Poor old man," she added piously. "Though it's a blessing, in a way. He was no earthly use to anyone, the way he was."

Dr. Randolph smacked his lips thoughtfully, as if considering this. His eyes avoided Mrs. Pringle's. "When did he have his last dose of medicine?" he asked.

"I gave him his nine o'clock myself. Fanny was there, too, fixing up his room. We changed the sheets on his bed. Mildred was *supposed* to give it to him after that. She was keeping an eye on him this morning. The first time, too. She makes such a to-do about her father being sick, crying and carrying on, but never offers to help. She didn't go and forget about his medicine, did she?"

"She was with him all morning?"

"Well, she wouldn't be with him every minute, naturally." Mrs. Pringle glanced sharply at the doctor. What was he getting at? "The other girls were at the orphanage. They got back half an hour ago."

Dr. Randolph pulled at his long upper lip. "Where is Mildred now?"

"That's just it; we don't know where she is."

His eyebrows came together. After a moment he pushed

aside his empty glass and scraped back his chair. "Come upstairs for a minute." His brisk manner alarmed her. The worst
she could think of was that the old man was not dead, after
all, or by some monstrous freak of nature had come back to
life.

He was dead, all right. She saw that as soon as they entered
the bedroom. Fanny was standing beside the window, waiting.
She had partly drawn the curtains, so that the room seemed
filled with green twilight. One narrow band of sunlight cut
across the carpet.

"Now, this . . ." Dr. Randolph picked up the two-ounce
bottle that had contained the dead man's medicine. He held
it in a deceptively casual way, rubbing his chin with his free
hand. "How much would you say was in it this morning?"

"Why—" Mrs. Pringle's hands flew to her face. She looked
wildly at Fanny, who stared back at her. The bottle had gone
down a good inch since nine o'clock. Mildred must have killed
the old man with an overdose. Oh, what a mess! she thought.
It would be in all the papers. Headlines. "Woman Kills Aged
Father." There would be an inquest, with the coroner asking
questions. "Now, Mrs. Pringle, where were you when the
crime took place?" Mildred would go into a decline. They'd
have her on their hands for months. And while all this was
going on, nobody would think of reading the will.

Dr. Randolph and Fanny were both looking at her with the
queerest expressions—as if they were afraid she might say the
wrong thing. The doctor's turtle neck was thrust out. His coat
hung open. His stethoscope still hung round his neck, over the
gravy stains on his vest.

"Why—" Mrs. Pringle held out her hand and took the bottle
from him. She examined it with her head on one side. "I don't
know what you mean," she said at last, innocently. "It looks
the same to me as it did this morning."

Dr. Randolph and Fanny relaxed. The anxiety faded from
their eyes.

15—J.G.                    225

"Did you think there was something wrong with his medicine?" Mrs. Pringle inquired.

Dr. Randolph shook his head. "Just wanted to check, that's all. As long as you say . . ." He hung his thumbs in his suspenders and looked down at the corpse. "Have to make out a death certificate, you know." He glanced from Fanny to Mrs. Pringle, then quickly away, and felt in his pocket for a pen.

"I'd say he died of stroke, wouldn't you?" Mrs. Pringle suggested. Pretending to hunt for a handkerchief, she thrust the bottle into the warm pocket between her breasts. "Or heart failure. Maybe plain old age. Is that the form you have to fill out?"

"That's it." He spread the form on the table. "Let's see, what's the date? Left my glasses around somewhere . . ." He slapped his pockets and found a pair of steel-rimmed spectacles, which he put on. Mrs. Pringle stood over him while he puttered and fumbled. His writing was completely illegible.

He oughtn't to be practicing, she thought spitefully, wanting to blame someone for the fright she'd had. At his age. A doddering old man in his second childhood. Smelling of liquor.

Mildred! she thought suddenly, stopping short in the hall. Oh, Lord, what's happened to her? When Fanny came up behind her, she jumped guiltily.

"How long has she been gone?" Fanny asked, and Mrs. Pringle could tell by her voice that the same thought had occurred to both of them.

"She was on the phone half the morning. I was down cellar, but I could hear her. Calling some number in New York. Not Harry—she had to give the operator the address. She sounded sort of worked up—you know how she gets. Then, when I was coming up—it wasn't ten minutes before I found the old gentleman—she went pelting downstairs and out into the garden, toward the summerhouse . . ." Mrs. Pringle put her hand to her mouth and stared at Fanny. "The summerhouse! Oh, Lord, you don't suppose—"

"No!" Fanny said sharply.

But Mrs. Pringle was running down the stairs, pounding along the hall to the side door. In her mind was a picture of what had happened: Mildred in her father's room, looking down at him with terrified eyes, realizing in a flash what she'd done, then running wildly down the stairs and through the garden, hair flying, pursued by her guilt, to throw herself into the river.

As she sprinted across the lawn, she could hear Fanny behind her saying, "Wait! Wait!" in an urgent voice, but she couldn't stop. Sodden blossoms hit her ankles like wet sponges. A breeze shook the trees and flung down a shower of bright raindrops. She reached the summerhouse and paused, panting, waiting for Fanny to catch up with her. In that moment she regained her senses a little.

"But she wouldn't do that!" she exclaimed. "She wouldn't *care* that much."

Fanny took her arm to steady her. They sat down together.

"She wouldn't care *that* much!" Mrs. Pringle repeated. "Whatever are we thinking?" She was unwilling to take all the blame for believing Mildred would do away with herself. "Getting all steamed up!" she scolded, as if the whole thing had been Fanny's idea. "She might be upset, but she'd never go and—she'd never do anything desperate."

Fanny shook her head weakly.

"We're all worked up over nothing." Mrs. Pringle could not control her voice. It came out high and querulous. "Going all to pieces like this when we know very well she wouldn't care *how* the old man went, just so long—!" She checked herself. "My God, we must be crazy!"

Fanny drew her hand across her forehead and pushed back

her hair. It was warm and steamy in the summerhouse, smelling of dying autumn flowers. A trail of mist hung in the gorge, and sunlight slanting through it made a scrap of rainbow, which disappeared when the mist shifted. In the garden, the canvas chairs were all overturned.

"But where *is* she?"

"God knows." The seat was damp, but Mrs. Pringle continued to sit. "Did we look in her room? She could be taking a nap or something—lying down with one of her headaches." She lifted her apron and wiped her face. "We've got to get hold of ourselves, dear," she said after a minute. "We've got to use our heads. What would we say if anyone asked what we're doing out here now—why we came running out the way we did? Look, what we ought to do is go inside and have a nice drink to quiet our nerves. And stop acting as if we knew something we shouldn't." She stood up, testing her knees, which had gone weak and rubbery after her dash through the garden.

"We ought to tear this old place down before it falls down by itself," she went on. Talking steadied her. "That tree's a thousand years old, full of grubs." She went round the butternut tree and with her back to Fanny fished the medicine bottle out from between her breasts. It was warm, oily with perspiration. She threw it over the wall. It went in a long arc, then dropped straight down until it was lost from sight. "Look at those old steps down the cliff," she rattled on to cover her action. "Still there. Lord, I'd almost forgotten them."

Just before she turned back, she leaned over the rail for a timid look down. Even looking over the garden wall sometimes made her dizzy, and she had never in her life found the courage to go down the cliff steps. Afterwards, she was sure that something *made* her look down, that some supernatural power drew her eyes past the broken steps to the pile of rubble where the boathouse had once been—and where something else now lay among the dying vines.

She opened her mouth and no sound came, but far away she could hear her own voice screaming.

"Don't look! Don't look!" she babbled, clinging to Fanny. Then her legs gave way, and she slumped to the floor.


## CHAPTER FIFTEEN


MRS. PRINGLE SAT IN THE KITCHEN A WEEK LATER TAKING HER customary rest. The double funeral was over; everything was back to normal again. It was surprising *how* normal everything was, considering. The hubbub and commotion of that afternoon they'd found Mildred! The people coming and going. Dr. Randolph was still upstairs when Fanny staggered into the house with the awful news, and he had called the police. They came, and sent for other men who brought ladders and ropes, and trampled over the flower beds explaining to one another what had happened. They had quite a time getting Mildred up. Mrs. Pringle had tried to escape it all by taking a sedative and lying down in her room with a wet cloth over her eyes, but the police insisted upon questioning her. Just routine, they assured her, poker-faced as characters in a television play. Mildred's death was unquestionably accidental. The broken steps confirmed that.

The news was on the radio that night, and in the local papers. The death of any member of the Jameson family, by itself, would not have attracted much attention outside the limits of St. Charles, but two deaths within the hour—one of them a tragic accident—rated space in the newspapers of nearby cities. Reporters and photographers came, and though they didn't get inside the house—Ernie saw to that; he came the minute he heard the news, and took charge—they questioned various people around town and collected some interesting data on the Jameson family. Mrs. Pringle had saved all the papers. She picked one up now and read it.

"Famous Rum-runner Dies Following Daughter's Death," the headline said. "King Jameson, who served a sentence for rum-running in the thirties, died yesterday of a heart attack after learning that his oldest daughter had plunged to her death from the garden of their home overlooking the Niagara River gorge."

For some reason, the reporters had jumped to the conclusion that it was the shock of hearing about Mildred that killed the old man. Or perhaps they had been *told* it happened that way. Mrs. Pringle had a strong suspicion that Dr. Randolph had given out this information to salve his own conscience. For no matter what the police said, he knew, and so did Fanny and Isobel, that Mildred's death was no accident, nor had the old man died of a heart attack. Mildred had killed him; then, unable to bear her guilt, had flung herself into the gorge.

Mrs. Pringle had not been home to her own little flat for a week. A good thing Ernie happened to be out of work. She didn't know what they'd have done without him, especially that first night, before Harry and Eliot arrived. Harry and Eliot were not much good, at that. Harry sat around looking dazed. Eliot was officious, but offered very little comfort. After the funeral he went back to New York by himself, moping and moaning because Isobel had told him she wanted a divorce.

Serve him right, Mrs. Pringle thought. And serve that mother of his right, too. They're birds of a feather. "If you'd taken my advice, you never would have married him," she remarked when Isobel told her. "He's got brains and money," she admitted, "but what good are they in the long run? Money's nice, but can you take it to bed with you? Can you talk to it? No, dear, you're better off without him."

It would be lovely to have Isobel home again. We'll be a

happy family, Mrs. Pringle thought. Already she was picturing the pleasant companionship of the days ahead—just the three girls and herself. Nobody yelling down the stairs, nobody finding fault. But she knew better than to expect Isobel to stay at home for long—even though, when she mentioned this, Isobel had protested, "I'm sick and tired of men, Pringle." Mrs. Pringle raised her eyebrows tolerantly. "That's what you think now, dear. Give yourself time." If they were lucky, Isobel might be around—oh, say two years. By that time she would have found someone else, because that was the way she was made. She was one of those women who feel lost, incomplete, without a man, and that kind always attracts them as a flypaper does flies. She didn't have her mother's smile, her mother's way of flashing those dark eyes, for nothing. When she was seventy, men would still be chasing her, no doubt. Well, she'll be here for a time, at least, Mrs. Pringle told herself philosophically. We don't expect miracles. And perhaps the next one she gets won't make such a to-do every time she comes home and leaves him for a few days.

Fanny was in the garden tying up zinnias. Ernie, making himself useful for a change, was mowing the lawn. Lily and Isobel were sitting under the birch trees, with magazines scattered on the grass at their feet. Poor Lily hadn't been quite the same since that day. Nothing that a stranger would notice, perhaps. She was very quiet, with a faraway expression in her eyes—not the least bit unhappy, only withdrawn, off in another world, but a world which apparently puzzled her. She had had spells like that in the past. This time, however, nobody could put a finger on the exact cause, or, more specifically, figure out which of the happenings of last week to assign as the cause. Fanny and Mrs. Pringle, talking it over, wondered if Theodore's disappearance had anything to do with it. They finally concluded that it had not, though they could not understand why Lily was packing that day. They knew better than to question her, since she appeared to have forgotten that she *was* packing. She even seemed to have forgotten Theodore's existence. And for all the emotion she displayed, her father and Mildred might have died years ago.

It was not until the day after the funeral that they heard Theodore had left town. Mrs. Kinch told them; or rather she told Mrs. Pringle in the kitchen following a visit of condolence with the girls during which his name was not mentioned.

"I haven't let on to a soul," Mrs. Kinch confided. "It might give the Willows a bad name if it got out. But I tell you it's got me stumped. I wish I'd asked her a few questions, that woman. She was so *common*-looking, is what gets me. Badly dressed—I don't suppose she's ever owned a corset—with big dishpan hands . . . You'd never think to connect her with Mr. Fairfield."

"What did she *say*?" Mrs. Pringle, who had already been given a preliminary account of what happened, now pressed for details.

"She just asked if he was in. 'Is Mr. Fairfield in?' she said, and when I said he wasn't, she plunked herself down and said she'd wait."

"So, then?"

"I tried to make conversation, naturally. I like people to feel at home. She'd come up on the morning train. She admitted that much, but didn't say where from. I gave her a cup of tea. She kept looking at the clock, and when she'd finished the tea, she asked if I had any idea when he'd be back. I said I *thought* he'd be back for lunch, though I couldn't guarantee. So then she looked straight at me—cool as a cucumber, mind! —and said, 'Perhaps I ought to pack his things, if we're to catch the twelve-thirty bus.' I just looked at her."

"What did you say?"

"Well, naturally, I told her I couldn't go letting strangers into the guests' rooms. And she said, 'I'm not a stranger; I'm his wife.' I nearly dropped dead."

"Lord, I should *think*—!" Mrs. Pringle exclaimed.

"I was so flabbergasted I didn't think to ask her to prove it. She stood up and said, 'If you'll be kind enough to show me his room . . .' and I was in such a state I walked upstairs like a lamb to the slaughter. Before I told her which was his room —his door was open—she said, 'There's his suitcase on the bed,' and sure enough! Which makes it look as if she *was* his wife, don't you think?—the way she knew all his things. His bag was half packed. He'd told me he was leaving after dinner, you know."

Mrs. Pringle started, then composed herself quickly.

Mrs. Kinch continued, "So then, while she was folding up his old one, she said, 'He must have bought a new suit.' And do you know, when he came, he only had that one suit—that dark blue. I thought it was funny, him having so little, though I never said anything."

"I thought so, too," Mrs. Pringle agreed. "I said to Fanny . . ."

"I was getting my bearings by this time, so I said to her, 'Mr. Fairfield didn't mention he was married.' She gave me the funniest look. 'I don't suppose he did,' she said. I couldn't tell whether she was being sarcastic or not."

"He told us his wife was dead. It just shows you can't trust anybody these days, doesn't it?"

"We all thought he'd marry Lily. Does she know anything? I didn't like to mention it to the girls in their time of sorrow."

"Lily?" Mrs. Pringle was on guard instantly. "Lordy, dear!" She attempted a light laugh. "Lily wasn't interested in him."

Mrs. Kinch took that with a grain of salt. She glanced sharply over her glasses. "He spent enough time here."

"Didn't he, though?" Mrs. Pringle smiled innocently. "We used to laugh." She gave an amused chuckle, to illustrate. "No doubt about it, he had a case on Lily, but she didn't care two pins about him."

"Perhaps he was more a family friend." Mrs. Kinch compromised. "Mildred telephoned a dozen times that morning, looking for him."

"Mildred?"

"She *was* in a state. I kept wondering afterwards what she wanted him for."

"It probably wasn't anything," Mrs. Pringle said as calmly as she could, though her mind was in a turmoil of speculation. "What happened then?" she asked, luring Mrs. Kinch back to Theodore's wife.

"She packed up his things and went downstairs. I had to start lunch, so I left her in the reception room. And when he came in, do you know what she said to him?" Mrs. Kinch paused, staring solemnly. "She called him George."

"George?"

"She said, 'Well, George,' or something like that, as if he'd only been gone five minutes."

"So he was using a trumped-up name as well."

"It looks that way, doesn't it? Funny . . ." Mrs. Kinch mused. "The way she spoke to him, quite pleasantly. If it'd been me, I'd have broken his neck."

"Hanging's too good for a man like that," Mrs. Pringle announced implacably. She was thoroughly disillusioned, angry now rather than sad. It was the dowdy wife who added the finishing touches to her disenchantment. She might in time have forgiven Theodore almost anything except a wife who wore no corsets, who looked like a washerwoman. I knew there was something funny about him all the time, she told herself. He didn't fool me for one minute, not after I caught him taking money from poor Lily.

"She really seemed quite a nice woman, his wife," Mrs. Kinch went on. "Such a kind face, though nothing much to look at. Oh, it turns my stomach to think of it—him carrying on like that. Pretending to be a heartbroken widower when he

234

had a wife all the time. I don't know what people would say if they knew I'd been harboring a creature like that."

"There's no need for people to know," Mrs. Pringle assured her. "You can depend on me to keep your secret. I know you've got your reputation to think of. Tell me, now—what else happened? What did *he* say?"

"That was all I heard. She said something about catching a bus, and the next thing I knew they were gone, walking off down the road. That was the last I saw of them."

When her visitor had gone, Mrs. Pringle sat thinking for some time. Would this have anything to do with Lily's queer behavior? But Lily wouldn't *know* about Theodore's wife, for when the events that Mrs. Kinch had just described were taking place, Lily was at home, and she had not been out or talked to anyone outside the family since then. I give up, Mrs. Pringle thought. I can't make head nor tail of it.

That evening she repeated everything she had learned, including her suspicions regarding the withdrawal from Lily's bank account, to Fanny. "Now, what do you make of it all, dear?" she asked.

It struck her that Fanny was rather evasive, her expression of surprise overdone, as if she knew the whole story already but thought it best to pretend it was all news to her. Having anticipated a good long session of conjecture and deduction, Mrs. Pringle felt deflated when, after a brief discussion, Fanny changed the subject.

"I'm glad you've decided to stay with us, Daisy. I don't know what we'd ever do without you."

"Oh, pooh!"

"I've spoken to Ernie about staying on, too. We really need a man around to keep an eye on the garden, and to look after repairs. To see to things. . . . Would you and Ernie consider giving up your flat and living here, now we've got those extra rooms?"

Fanny did not say, as she might have, that Ernie had given

her a great song and dance that very morning about the difficulty of finding employment, practically begged her for a job. Mrs. Pringle had heard him. She was grateful to Fanny for offering to help, but could not say so without feeling embarrassed.

"We'd want our own sitting room, mind," she warned.

"We could fix up the room you have now, put a nice rug down, and hang new curtains. You could sleep in the back bedroom upstairs."

"And my usual time off."

"Of course."

"Well, I suppose we could manage it, then." Mrs. Pringle inclined her head graciously. "Though, mind, if you expect to get a day's work out of Ernie, you're in for a let-down."

After a long silence Fanny said, "About Mr. Fairfield, or whatever his name is . . . I wonder if we should keep what you've just told me to ourselves. I mean, not speak of him to—well, anyone. Lily hasn't mentioned his name since that day, have you noticed?"

"Yes, I wondered . . ." Mrs. Pringle drew her brows together. "There's something funny about all this. Some part we don't know about. I keep going over it in my mind, and I can't help feeling there's a part missing somewhere. *Why* was Mildred telephoning him that morning, for instance? What would she want of him? And doesn't it seem funny to you, Lily packing her bag on the very day he told Mrs. Kinch he was leaving? If they'd planned something, why hasn't she spoken of him since? She couldn't know about his wife. It all seems as if it's going to add up to something any minute. But what? If we could only put our fingers on that missing piece . . ." She looked up, sensing suddenly that Fanny had drawn into herself, grown stealthy with apprehension; and she began to wonder if searching for the missing part might result in unhappiness for all of them. "But maybe it's best not to go delving," she added, cautioning herself as well. After thinking this over, she asserted firmly, "You're quite right, dear: let sleeping dogs lie, as they say. It's a good thing Lily does forget, perhaps." She eased off her shoes and stuck her feet up. "Well, we've got that worry off our hands, at any rate. Lily's still with us—she's still our little girl. What we ought to do now is plan how to keep her happy. If she's contented enough here, she won't be so likely to listen to every wolf in sheep's clothing that comes along trying to turn her poor head. It should be easier now, with no one to interfere—I mean," she corrected herself hastily, "with Isobel to help out. We ought to plan some nice little surprises."

"Yes." Fanny turned to the window and pulled the curtains across, shutting out the blue evening light—and seeming to shut out something else, too, or to capture within the room the safety of familiar things.

Now, sitting in her own kitchen, basking in the dreamy monotony of early afternoon, Mrs. Pringle sighed and nodded to herself. In the end, the only thing that really mattered was to keep Lily happy. We're a perfect family just as we are, she thought, not consciously rejoicing because fate had removed the two least compatible members, but simply thankful that for the time being, at least, her contentment was not threatened.

After dinner Fanny went to her room and felt behind a stack of handkerchiefs for the letter she had found in Lily's room that day. It was such an innocent-looking thing to have caused her so much concern: a plain brown envelope with a return address printed on the flap—nothing to give away the sender's occupation—and Mildred's name and address on the face. She removed the letter and read it, though she almost knew it by heart, then sat with it in her hand, frowning and biting her lips while she stared at the picture of her mother on the wall.

When she had first read the letter, she had waited for what she knew she *should* feel: indignation because Theodore had deceived them, because he had deceived poor Lily. It surprised her when she could find no resentment in her thoughts of him, only great pity as she imagined the life he must return to, the hopelessness he must feel, submerged in the monotony of his dreary job, a man who loved flowers. His smile—if he could smile at all—would be more wistful than ever. His wife and children were in Fanny's mind shadowy figures, allotted a place in his life by uncharitable fate. So were those other women. She could not feel that any one of them was quite real.

All week she had been apprehensive lest the detective agency should send another report, a follow-up, which somebody else might take from the postman and read. Another letter had come yesterday, but was only a bill "for services rendered." She wrote out a check and sent it off at once, driving all the way down to the station with it and dropping it into the box there.

She could not have put into words her reasons for wanting to keep the report a secret from Mrs. Pringle and Isobel, for she shrank from acknowledging that they, too, might see something inconsistent in the letter's being found in Lily's room at that particular time. Would they wonder *why* Mildred had left it there, and perhaps after a time realize that Mildred was likely to be too upset by the contents of the letter to notice any mistake she might have made in the sickroom? Or would they go on believing that Mildred had deliberately jumped into the gorge when she discovered that her carelessness had killed her father? Poor old Dr. Randolph believed this. At the funeral his haunted eyes looked into corners, at the ceiling, anywhere but at the bereaved family. "We must never breathe a word," his actions said. "We must never give Mildred away."

She spread the letter out on the little cluttered desk in the corner of her room and turned on the lamp there. All week she had been wasting electricity, drawing the curtains and turning on all the lamps as soon as the light began to fail, hating any pool of darkness caught in a corner, any shadow. She could hear Lily and Isobel across the hall in Isobel's room, playing some card game, and she knew that Lily was dealing the cards out slowly, inattentively, being prompted now and then. Isobel believed that Lily was dazed by the shock of losing two members of the family in one day; but Fanny knew that Lily had no horror of death.

There had been other times, in the past, when Lily's poor brain had played tricks on her; when, having been prompted by some perverse reasoning to unnatural behavior, her conscious mind immediately rejected all memory of it, and she wandered about for a time in a sort of trance. But there had always been a *reason* for this: some action that could not bear remembering, like the time she threw the little dog over the cliff. In a way, it was a mercy she did forget; it saved her from self-reproach. Her conscience could never bother her about an action she had no recollection of performing. And no one could possibly *blame* her.

No idle curiosity would make Mildred run down those steps so fast she could not stop when she came to the broken part— they knew the steps were broken before she fell; the rain-soaked timbers showed that—so perhaps she thought something was down there at the foot of the cliff, something important, that should be investigated. Perhaps she had been *told* there was something at the foot of the steps.

What is the truth? Fanny asked herself, knowing that later on she would want to look back and assure herself that she had asked this question before she allowed herself to arrive at her foregone conclusion. What she really meant was, how can I accept what all of us believe to be the truth without sacrificing Mildred? Which was better—to allow four people to go on believing that Mildred had killed her father in a moment of carelessness and then, to escape exposure, had destroyed herself; or to search for a bit here, a bit there, of a puzzle which if finally pieced together might destroy their peace of mind forever?

When she had thought about this for a long time, Fanny

239

made her decision. If she refused to put the parts of the puzzle together, if she refused even to acknowledge that there was a puzzle, she could look forward again to the days ahead, as she had before Theodore came—days as tranquil as the late-summer garden, filled with the pleasant monotony she loved, the three people she loved safe at home with her, bound to the familiar routine and her devotion.

We must never allow anyone to guess what happened, she thought, as she tore up the letter. The four of us, Dr. Randolph, Pringle, Isobel, and myself, must protect Mildred. We must never speak of what she did, even among ourselves.

She carried the scraps of the letter down to the kitchen and burned them in an ashtray, tending the flames until nothing was left but a mound of ashes.

She walked back through the lamplit rooms where everything was in place—tables gleaming, flowers massed in low bowls—and up the stairs. She stood behind Lily's chair and stroked her hair.

"Here I am, dear," she said in a reassuring voice, as if answering a call long after it was given.